THE LIGHTS BEGAN TO FLICKER . . .

Shetland heard something in the empty study. Books were being knocked off the shelves, spilling onto the floor. Mrs. Peel froze in her tracks. She was stammering, on the verge of hysteria. A bar of light shone beneath the study door.

He couldn't stop his hand as it reached for the doorknob. His guts were burning. He twisted around, then hesitated. "Go back, Mrs. Peel!" She stood frozen. He started to back off, his courage faltering. The lights went out and the door, its handle firmly in his grasp, flew open . . .

You will learn the secret of THE SUMMONING in a climax of apocalyptic horror that is unprecedented in modern fiction.

THE SUMMONING

JOHN PINTORO

AVON
PUBLISHERS OF BARD, CAMELOT AND DISCUS BOOKS

THE SUMMONING is an original publication of Avon
Books. This work has never before appeared in book form.

AVON BOOKS
A division of
The Hearst Corporation
959 Eighth Avenue
New York, New York 10019

Copyright © 1979 by John Pintoro
Published by arrangement with the author
Library of Congress Catalog Card Number: 79-88559
ISBN: 0-380-47639-8

First Avon Printing, November, 1979

AVON TRADEMARK REG. U.S. PAT. OFF. AND IN
OTHER COUNTRIES, MARCA REGISTRADA, HECHO EN
U.S.A.

Printed in the U.S.A.

To my loving wife, Barbara

CHAPTER ONE

SHETLAND SPED PAST the summer cottages pressed together on both sides of the road and hit the flat one-mile stretch of Crane's Neck Road just as the sun came up over the Sound. Glancing out the driver's side window he could see the town of Oysterville just across the bay, bent like a horseshoe around the harbor. Jarred awake by the firehouse sirens during the night, the town had gone back to sleep. His car radio was tuned to a news station. "Extensive high-wind damage and lowland flooding along Long Island's North Shore resulted from last night's storm; heaviest hit were the Oysterville and Crane's Neck area." The radio went on to report power losses in many communities and warned that the downed electrical wires were dangerous and should be reported to the Long Island Lighting Company. It also advised that secondary roads were blocked by fallen tree limbs and caution should be exercised when traveling. Shetland turned off the radio, lit a cigarette and depressed the accelerator.

At the Crane's Neck hook the road bent treacherously toward the head of the harbor. Suddenly, Shetland was negotiating a ninety-degree left turn. With a jolt he felt himself pressed back in the seat as the road climbed steeply and then leveled out in a precarious run along the edge of the bluff. Below was the entrance to the bay and Long Island Sound. The view was breathtaking but Shetland sighed with relief when the road swung away into the woods.

Dobb's Lane was blocked by a power company crew working on downed wires. Shetland had to park his car on the next street over, pulling it halfway into the brush on the shoulder of the road to avoid blocking the fire trucks working to put out the last smoldering remnants of a blaze. There was a lot of smoke mingled with the natural haze and it was difficult to see what was going on. He came to where one of the firemen said there would be a path through the woods and turned up it. Shetland emerged onto an open expanse of lawn dominated by an ancient, long-untended apple tree. The house was a big two-story clapboard with large bay windows on the ground floor. Even from this distance he could see the rust on the gutters and the peeling paint.

The patrolman guarding the back door of the large house observed the familiar figure ambling nonchalantly out of the woods toward him; in bell-bottom jeans, foul-weather parka and a Greek sailor's cap, the man looked more like a prematurely aging sea captain than a homicide detective. "Hi, Lieutenant, when did you get back?"

"Last night," Shetland said, lighting another cigarette. "Two weeks without a smoke and five minutes on the job and I'm an addict again."

"Occupational hazard," the officer smiled. "How did you happen to come up that way?"

"Got turned around on that rabbit path they call a quaint rural road." Shetland glanced over his shoulder; "Fireman headed me in the right direction."

The officer cocked his jaw, pointing with it. "They've been at it all night," he said. "How's it going?"

"The last I saw they were still at it, watering down a pile of ashes."

"It was some fire. At one point the flames were above the treetops."

Shetland nodded in acknowledgment.

The officer doffed his cap to wipe the sweat from his brow. "Every dog in the neighborhood was putting up a hell of a fuss over it; gave me the shivers."

"Where are they?" Shetland asked, flicking his cigarette into the grass with disdain.

"Front of the house, straight through." The officer opened the door. "By the way, Lieutenant, how was your vacation?"

"Good, though it got a little hairy toward the end," he answered, noting the splintered wood molding as he stepped through the doorway. Two weeks was a long time off the job. Part of him was still skippering his twenty-two-foot sailboat through the Great South Bay, skirting Gardner's Island and tacking into the wind off Mystic Seaport; just bumming a ride with the breeze and not caring where to. Being back was like starting a cold engine; as he made his way through the house he forced himself to observe. Most obvious was the lack of personal taste, personal mementos, photographs of family or friends, the inconsequential collectivities, the debris left in the wake of a passing life for others to speculate about.

Sergeant Tedeschevich met Shetland in the hallway. They traded cool, noncommittal looks. "This way, Lieutenant," he said.

He followed his colleague into the midst of activity and death. Blake, the assistant medical examiner, was bent over the body, engrossed in his work. A police photographer standing behind the door touched off a blinding flash with his camera, nuzzled past Shetland, took another photo from a different angle, announced, "That should do it," and then side-stepped out of the room. There were men out in the hall, men clomping up and down the stairs and above them on the second floor. Detective Casey came into the study, went to the desk, picked up a bloody letter opener, deftly slipped it into a clear plastic bag and charged out again. Through the window Shetland could see Forensic working industriously over the Porsche in the driveway. "Murder or suicide," he said, announcing his presence.

Blake was pleased to see him. He stopped what he was

doing and came over to shake his hand. "Harry said you were back—your case?"

"I talked with Harry on the phone yesterday morning; said I'd be back some time after three A.M. When I walked into the apartment around four-thirty the phone was ringing itself off the hook. It was the captain telling me to come straight over here. As you can see I didn't have time to change."

"I was wondering about the sailor suit."

"Was it a sightseeing tour?"

"Seems so: windows and doors locked from the inside, no sign of forcible entry. There's some disarray but not enough to indicate a struggle, and there would have been; this guy's over six feet four and in good condition, two-forty. For an assailant to get close enough to stick that letter opener in his throat I'm sure he would have left a piece of himself behind. He didn't die quickly. Beside, the angle of the wound tends to indicate self-infliction."

"So, who is he?" Shetland asked.

"Stephen Peel," he said, anticipating instant recognition. "You must have heard of him; he was a pretty popular news commentator and talk show host a few years back. Did you ever watch his show, *Citizens*?"

"I saw it a couple of times; doesn't look the same as he did on TV."

"No wonder. Most of his blood's on the carpet. He knew his anatomy; got the jugular square on, and that ain't as easy as most people think."

"He meant to go all the way then."

"Would seem so. Either that or he was incredibly un- lucky."

"Why do I get the feeling you're not positive?"

"Oh, I'm positive—not officially, of course, not until a thorough autopsy is completed; it's just that I can't get used to the idea of suicide. I mean, I've seen people slash their wrists with pieces of broken glass, kitchen knives and razor blades. Even then I never understood how they could calmly sit there just waiting to bleed to death. It's the kind of bent desperation that rattles the sensibilities, you know what I mean?"

"And?"

"And peculiarities. We had a storm all night. Still, it was eighty degrees and he had a fire in the fireplace. No note, his car left with the door open and the engine running, the back door smashed in—done, it seems, by Peel himself. But this letter opener was as dull as a cucumber. He must have really rammed it in there. When we came in we found one of those big heavy dictionaries on the floor near the door—the spine was broken and pages torn; there's the stand for it on the desk. I wonder how it got over there?"

"Maybe he threw it."

"Yeah, why and at what? For my money this guy was acting like he was running from someone or something. Of course," he said, closing his medical bag, "that's pure speculation on my part and your hassle, thank God."

"Peel married?"

Blake thought for a moment. "Think so," he said hesitantly; "divorced or separated. Oh, by the way, Lieutenant, weren't you one of those rice-paddy heroes in Vietnam?"

Shetland's brow wrinkled with puzzlement. "Yeah; didn't care for it much."

"I did a stint myself as a medic."

"We grunts were very appreciative. Do you want to reminisce, Blake, or is there a point to this?"

"There's a couch out in the living room. I think Peel might have flopped out on it before coming in here. Take a look at it; it should bring back some startling memories." Blake shook his head and snapped the latch on his bag. "Well, that's it for now. I have a feeling Harry's going to handle this one personally, so I'll say hello for you. Want any last looks at the deceased?"

Shetland shook his head and watched as the body was placed on a stretcher.

Blake started to leave. "Be in touch," he said. As he was going out Casey came in; he was less preoccupied. "Sorry I forgot to say hello, Lieutenant," he said. "This sort of thing

11

gets to me. Like to get through them as quick as possible. So what have we got; how do we proceed?"

With his foot Shetland nudged the torn curtain lying in a heap on the floor near the window, as if the answer to Casey's question were just beneath the rumpled folds. "Like Blake said, we call it suicide. For insurance, though, check out the likelies—family, friends."

Shetland took a quick look at that couch. There was nothing unusual about it; it was well used, and the only thing that could account for Blake's strange curiosity was a familiar smell, the smell of fear. It was a special kind of fear of the lonely, lost and terrified. It was the kind of fear that bubbles out of the skin with the sweat, a sweat that carries the stench of body waste, a foul, rancid odor that can't be washed out of clothes and can be smelled on corpses that have been rotting for days in a dung-filled rice paddy. The couch reeked of it. Its presence, more than anything else, alarmed Shetland. He examined the rest of the house, then returned to the study, where he spotted something that should not have caught his attention but did, with riveting effect: a red-bound book wedged disjointedly in with a hundred other books. He dislodged it from the bookshelf and slapped it against the open palm of his hand with a curious anticipation. The edges were vaguely singed; he glanced toward the fireplace, then back at the book. He started to open it when Sergeant Tedeschevich, in the company of an exhausted, soot-covered fireman, came in.

"This is the lieutenant," he said. "He's the man you want to speak to." The fireman stepped forward. "The company commander sent me up here. We found something next door, at the Turners' home. He thinks somebody should come take a look." The fireman was so tired he was acting punchy. As soon as he finished saying what he had come to say he turned and started off, not knowing if anybody was coming with him. Shetland shrugged and followed. The fireman walked like an old man in a dream. "Rough one," Shetland said.

He laughed. "We might as well not have bothered. We had enough equipment to put out a skyscraper and it rained, too, like the dickens, but the damn thing just burned." The fireman fell silent as if he no longer had the wherewithal to talk any more. The Peel and Turner houses were set on five-acre plots separated by a natural boundary of trees. The walk across the Peel grounds and then through the woods was slow and tedious. They came into the open near where Shetland had parked his car, climbed laboriously over a split-rail fence, then crossed the dew-covered lawn of the Turner property. They approached a blackened rectangle in the ground. It was like a giant grave filled in with ash and charred, smoldering rubble. Most of the firemen stood back near their equipment, along with a handful of onlookers, while one group poured a fine spray of water over the wreckage. "It's still hot down underneath," the commander said. "That keeps it from erupting on top." The commander and two of his deputies, Shetland, and the fireman who had brought him over met on the driveway that ran from the street to the edge of the blackened scar. A pathway of plywood boards was set down but nevertheless Shetland was cautioned to watch his step. "A lot of the house has collapsed into the basement," the commander said, "but there's plenty of weak spots with no underpinning to fall through. If you fell through you'd be cooked mighty fine before we could get to you." Shetland took the warning to heart.

The commander's eyes were red and watery from staring into smoke and fire; like his men, he was weary and strung out. "Never seen a fire so stubborn; it wouldn't go out till it burned everything to ashes." He pointed to the rubble scattered in the street and a hundred yards in all directions. "Lightning bombed it like artillery; got hit while we were trying to put it out. Damn lucky we didn't lose anybody." In the same breath he added, "We found them, the people who lived here."

Shetland was led along the board path down into a charred ashen pit. At the bottom, like a coffin sunk into the earth, lay a blackened elongated box; it was a freezer. An unsettling twitch in his stomach warned him; he had been summoned to view its contents. No one said a word as he lifted the lid, releasing the stink of roasted organs. The inside of the freezer was covered with a thickening grease broiled from ham and human flesh. An armless, legless torso, like a melted department-store manikin, rested with ludicrous irony among steaks and chops. Overcome with nausea, Shetland dropped the lid and scrambled up top. He stood, with the others, staring sourly down into the pit, his hands working together feverishly in a washing movement to rub them clean of the oily soot that came from the freezer lid. He let off with a shuddering sound. "Who was the first one to find that?"

"I did," one of the men said. "I really hadn't meant to look in there. Just curious, I guess."

Shetland shook his head grimly. "Did you find any other bodies?" he asked.

The man hissed through clenched teeth, "This fire, this heat—shit, mister, if we find a charred bone it'll be a miracle. Something was left of that body down in the pit because it was in that freezer buried under a ton of burned material from the upper stories. It acted like insulation; kept the worst of the heat away."

"This house was owned by the Turners," the commander said, "a retired couple. We are assuming that's one of them, your guess as to which. What do you want us to do?"

Shetland was still recovering from the grisly shock of the corpse in the freezer. He labored to clear his thoughts. "Is the fire all out?" he asked.

"It's going to be hot for some time," the commander said, "but there's nothing left to burn, so it's out."

They started back along the board path. "Pull your men back to the street, and if you wouldn't mind, until I can get some of my men out here, help keep the area cordoned off and take down the names of those people out on the street. Maybe one of them saw something that could help."

Without comment the fire company commander went to implement Shetland's request. His men were all volunteers. They had worked their regular jobs the previous day and then fought the fire through the night and into the morning. They were dead on their feet but they responded without griping. Finally they were able to leave; a haggard-looking bunch of men, half asleep, clinging to their truck as they rumbled away.

Shetland had patrol units, detectives on special assignments from the Huntington precinct, and a special forensic
team from the county seat plus the county fire marshals at
work. With all the official logistics came the local news reporters. He assigned Scalley to give out a brief statement and
slipped off to supervise the removal of the body from the
freezer. They were just lifting the body bag out of the pit
when Richard Ferrara trotted over. Shetland looked over at
him. "Did you get all the gory details?"

Ferrara glanced at the notebook he clutched in his hand.
"This one's straining the odds, wouldn't you say, Lieutenant?"

Shetland cracked a smile. "And read about it in your
paper tomorrow?"

"You so sure about Peel?"

"What? That he's dead?"

"Funny. That he killed himself. I mean, why not a triple
murder?"

"You volunteering?"

Ferrara shook his head. "It's hard to believe that a brilliant man like Stephen Peel would take his own life."

Shetland reached for his pack of cigarettes, then stopped,
reminding himself that he was trying to quit. A moment later
he was unconsciously pressing the spongey filter tip of a lit
cigarette between half-clenched teeth. "You and Peel were in
the same profession. What was he like?"

"Thanks for the compliment, Lieutenant; similar profession, different league."

"You didn't know him, then?"

"By his work, not personally. Peel just missed a Pulitzer
about five years back and it was a sure bet he'd get the brass
ring on the next go-round, or so the rumors went."

Shetland took a deep drag on his cigarette and held it for
a long time before exhaling. "Go on; I'm fascinated."

"Like I said, the guy was brilliant: journalist, social
commentator with a social conscience. He had enough literary
awards to carpet a basketball court."

"So he dropped out."

"Yes. He was there and then he wasn't. Don't ask me
why."

"Who were his friends?"

"Pick the name of any publisher or network bigwig; he had friends in the profession, the arts, business, politics, and none of them know what happened. That's the main reason I think we're all out here, to find out what happened to Stephen Peel. You can bet the television people won't be far behind."

Shetland rubbed the back of his neck and sighed. "God, I hate mysteries; never could stand to go see them in the movies. But it all fits; his life turns sour, his work becomes meaningless and he drops out."

Ferrara laughed. "The tragic descent? It's a bit shopworn."

"If it explains why the man took his life?"

"Why not, right, Lieutenant? Unless of course it's wrong and somebody took it for him."

After putting in thirteen straight hours Shetland guessed he was tired, but he was too numb to be sure. He drove back to the private house near the harbor in Oysterville where he rented a two-and-a-half-room efficiency apartment over the garage. His suitcases sat side by side near the door where he had dropped them the previous evening; he thought about unpacking, but he needed sleep more than a change of clothes. He poured himself a drink from the bottle of bourbon he kept in the cabinet over the sink; it hit his stomach like a rock dropped into an empty barrel. His total food consumption for the day had been a glass of orange juice and a cup of coffee. There was nothing in the apartment to eat and he had a throbbing headache from hunger. A little rest to catch his wind, he told himself and then he'd go out and get some food. He sat on the edge of the bed, and the next thing he knew he was waking up to the morning sun coming through the window. He was already late, but he managed to grab a bite to eat at a diner a few blocks from the precinct. He read the morning paper in the confines of his tiny green cubicle. A lot of influential people lived year round or part time in the elegant homes that stood on the sandy bluffs and dotted the green hills of Crane's Neck, and suicide and murder were big news items.

The murder story had not been made officially known but it had leaked out nonetheless. It was too soon for a break in the apparently related deaths of Peel and the Turners; in a very real sense they were still sifting through the ashes for clues. Detective Scalley barged into his office, smiling pleasantly. They didn't socialize after hours but the tough, good-natured cop was the closest thing to a friend Shetland had on the force. "Wish you were still sailing, Lieutenant?" Scalley said, plopping himself down into the only other chair in the office besides the one Shetland occupied. "If you don't, you will. I got a bit of trivia for you. Want to hear it?"

Shetland leaned back. "Be my guest," he said.

Scalley whipped out a piece of paper from his inside coat pocket. "I checked through the back files and I found, to my surprise, that there've only been three burglary complaints on Crane's Neck in the past ten years. So, for the heck of it, I checked with records at the county seat, and what I found should make you feel honored. There has been only one murder on Crane's Neck since 1701, and that was one hundred twenty-three years ago. Not," Scalley said glibly, "what you'd call a high-crime area, is it? I utilized some of the taxpayers' money to check out our victims' past. Mr. Turner was one of those captains of industry, banking and finance, semi-retired for the last five years, with the usual mixture of friends, associates, and adversaries, but nobody with a big enough axe to grind to kill him, at least not on the surface. His wife was some sort of educator, retired; again, no likely prospects there."

"I don't suppose there are any underworld connections floating around there," Shetland asked in a vain hope.

Scalley laughed. "How about the Boy Scouts of America, or the JayCees. He was big into them. As for this guy Peel, up until three years ago his life was an open book. After that, I think he threw the book away. Very little during those three years; he lived pretty much a reclusive life. I got the impression that most of his old friends didn't know he was even living out there; his wife sure didn't."

"He must have had some friends."

17

"We're canvassing the neighborhood residents. Maybe we'll get a better picture of this guy's social life from them."

"Any leads on the guy who called us?"

"Negative, Lieutenant. The guy refused to give his name; he just said he had gone over to Peel's house to thank him, he didn't say for what, and that he saw Peel's body through the study window. Then he hung up. Our man who took the call said he thought he heard fire-engine sirens in the background but he couldn't be sure."

"It's logical enough that the caller's one of Peel's neighbors," Shetland said, tapping a pencil on his desk blotter. "There are four homes close enough to Dobbs Lane where the sound of sirens might be picked up inside a house and heard over the phone."

"Assuming the call wasn't made from somewhere along the way between the fire house in Oysterville and the Turner home."

"True," Shetland said, "but I think it's a safe bet to start with those. I'm going out there now to see how the lab boys are doing."

When Shetland arrived he found the county fire marshal with some of his men going over the wreckage to determine the cause of the fire. He talked with him briefly while he drank a container of coffee. "No telling how long before we can pin it down; not much left to work with," Maitland said. "But the initial info gathered from eyewitnesses and certain other sources indicates the house was struck repeatedly by lightning. If nothing else turns up, that will be it."

"Convenient," Shetland said skeptically.

"Convenient?" Maitland repeated with a puzzled look.

"Having a murder nearly obliterated by an act of God," Shetland mused aloud. "Damn convenient and damn lucky."

Riker, who was heading the police forensic team, came over and joined their conversation. "If robbery was the motive we'll never be able to prove it. From a list of possessions we got from the insurance company we haven't found a recognizable article in there. Here," he said, tossing Shetland a lump of silver, "teapot, sugar bowl or the fillings in somebody's teeth?"

Shetland examined it and quietly handed it back. "The freezer survived. Something else might have," he said, shaking his head in discouragement.

"I'm beginning to think," Riker said in an exasperated huff, "that the freezer was one of those little jokes that the Fates leave lying around as sort of a cockteaser." He turned and stomped off.

Shetland kept out of the way while the others picked and pored over the ashes. He kicked around in the scattered rubble in the yard, thinking more than looking. A metallic glint on the opposite side of the Turner's backyard fence caught his attention. Absent-mindedly he investigated. He spotted the garden hose nozzle and a tangle of green hose hung up in the shrubbery, where it had been tossed haphazardly. He climbed over the fence and followed the hose as it trailed off into the woods. It more or less followed a well-worn footpath through twenty-five yards of trees, leading away from the Turners' property. The hose was connected to a sprinkler system hooked up at the edge of a well-tended lawn surrounding a single-story fieldstone home. A man dressed in a commercial pilot's uniform came out through a side door of the house, carrying a black leather bag and a flight case. He was in a hurry. He sidestepped a boy's bicycle blocking the walk and started for the carport in front of the house.

Shetland thought he hadn't been observed, but then the man put his bags down and came toward him. "I didn't think you'd find out," he said, nervously tweaking his thin mustache with his fingers. "You must have traced my call."

It didn't immediately occur to Shetland what the guy was talking about, but when it suddenly hit him he couldn't keep from breaking into a big, toothy grin. The guy looked at him like he was nuts. "You're a cop, aren't you?" he asked suspiciously.

Shetland handed him his business card, which read: DONALD SHETLAND, LIEUTENANT OF DETECTIVES, HOMICIDE, SUFFOLK COUNTY POLICE DEPARTMENT. The guy wasn't impressed. "No badge," he said.

"Sometimes it intimidates people, so we use the card," Shetland said, producing the tin.

The man was upset. "I didn't break any laws, did I?"

Shetland shook his head. "No. Just tell me your name and why you went to see Peel."

"Okay," the man said hesitantly, "but come with me while I put my bags in the car; I've got a flight out of Kennedy soon." They walked together to the front of his house, where his car was. He dumped his luggage in the trunk. "My name is Joe Michaels. I told your people over the phone that I went to Peel's to thank him for saving my life. You see, my family and I were asleep when this tremendous crash of thunder woke us. We saw the fire out our bedroom window, or at least the glow of it through the trees. We knew it was a house on fire. Anyway, to make a confusing story short, my son and I grabbed up the garden hose. We took all we had, and started through the trees, thinking we could help. When we got there the house was pretty well gone, even then. But there was this one section that hadn't been consumed by flames. There was a broken window near the ground, so I thought maybe there was somebody unconscious inside, who couldn't quite get out."

"Were you and your son the first ones there?"

Michaels shook his head. "No. David, my son, sprayed water onto the side of the house—it barely reached it—while I made a dash for the window to get a boost up. That's when I saw this Peel guy standing near the trees, just staring at the fire like he was hypnotized. He must have been there before us."

"He didn't try to help?"

"Nope, just stood there."

"Go on."

Michaels shrugged. "Well, I jumped up and hooked my arm over the window sill, made a gash in it on some broken glass, but managed to get a look inside. Smoke and flames were coming through the wood paneling on the wall and up through the floorboards. A big overstuffed chair started to smolder and then burst into flames while I was looking at it. The Turners had two German shepherds, nice dogs; I heard them barking. I think they kept the dogs in the basement at night. Poor beasts, there was nothing I could do. I was starting to cook on that wall." Michaels paused, shaking his head. "Just as I was about to jump off there was an explosion. Must have been the car gas tank, or maybe the house got hit again by lightning. I came off the side of that house with a thud that knocked me senseless. I looked up in a daze from where I lay flat on my back and saw this wall of fire about to come tumbling down on me. My kid tried to pull me out of there. I couldn't get my breath but I tried to tell him to get away. The last thing I remembered was being picked up like a sack of potatoes and carried out of there."

"Peel?" Shetland said.

"Yeah, Peel. When I came to my kid told me, and I went over to thank him. It doesn't make sense," Michaels said. "Saves my life; then goes home and takes his own. I'm a Catholic, Lieutenant—maybe not a good one, but I'm going to pray that what he did for me and mine will cancel out the sin of taking his own life. It's not right he should end up in hell or purgatory, is it?" A small tear ran down Michaels' cheek. "I didn't know him personally."

Shetland sat eating dinner at the far end of the Pier Restaurant, an old railroad diner stuck out on a pier and festooned with fishnetting, a couple of life preservers on the walls, plastic mermaids and seashells, coils of rope and various other nautical odds and ends. Some of the tables were on the dock underneath a striped awning. It was a warm, still evening and he sat out there in the yellow glow of the oil lamps, picking at his food, staring beyond the glare of harbor lights into the darkness across the bay.

"Hard to put what happened out there aside after working hours, isn't it, Lieutenant Shetland."

Shetland looked up into the face of a very young man dressed in a blue blazer who offered Shetland his hand. "My name is David Sloane," he said with a smile, "reporter for the *Sentinel*. I'm into doing a heartstring piece on Stephen Peel. I need some information and I was told at your precinct that I had to talk to the senior investigating officer."

Shetland interrupted, "The man you seek will be in his office tomorrow morning at eight sharp or thereabouts. But if I were you I wouldn't bother because he probably won't give you any more than what's already been handed out."

"Aren't you Lieutenant Donald Shetland, senior investigating officer on the Peel/Turner case?"

"No, I'm the aforementioned fellow on the case of this fillet of lemon sole."

The reporter's face took on a pleading look. "This is important to me."

"So's my dinner, pal. This fish gave up its life to be here."

"I waited at your apartment for hours but you didn't show up. Your landlady mentioned that you ate here on occasion. I just want to ask one question and then I'll split. I'm doing Peel's slide into obscurity, the why of it. Was it the pressure of being on top, that sort of thing."

"You picked a good choice of topics; dead is about as obscure as I imagine one could get."

"Look, Lieutenant, I need a real grabber for the ending."

Shetland threw up his hands. "All right, one question; then buzz off."

The young man's face brightened. "Thank you," he said. "The note—there was no mention of a suicide note."

"That's because we didn't find one. We assume he didn't leave one."

"That doesn't make any sense," Sloane countered heatedly. "I mean, the guy was a writer. Surely he would have left some sort of written commentary on why he did it."

Shetland continued eating his dinner. "That's what we figured."

"What, Lieutenant?"

"That was the straw that broke the camel's back: he couldn't think of anything to say."

"Why are you giving me the run-around, Lieutenant?"

"Look, you said one question; now we're in a debate about what makes sense. You want a priest or a philosopher, not a cop."

Sloane became adamant. "Don't you see, Lieutenant, there must have been something—a note, a diary."

"Okay, you convinced me; there was a note. Bring it into my office tomorrow and we'll read it together."

The Pulitzer aspirant beat a disgruntled retreat. The reporter's interruption had done more than destroy his already elusive appetite; it had jarred something that had been gnawing at him since yesterday. He had lost track of that red book; he couldn't remember whether he'd carried it out of the study and dropped it someplace or left it where he had found it. The book's significance escaped him but there was no denying that its whereabouts was important to him. Brimming with curiosity, he left the diner without finishing his meal and drove back to Crane's Neck.

Peel's driveway was blocked by a police barricade. Shetland parked his car on the shoulder of the road and walked up to the house. He noticed it wasn't a particularly old house, just a neglected one. In the moonlight it seemed like a face without makeup, weary from resisting the pressure of the woods encroaching on two sides. The doors were padlocked but he had the key and went in through the front. He felt no residual sense of tragedy or sorrow, no mute testimony permeating the walls, just a sobering emptiness. He turned on the light in the foyer, crossed to the study, opened the door and flicked on the light switch. The red book was where he had left it, stuffed between the shelf and the top of the other books. Its discovery seemed to diminish its significance. He picked it up, examining it, turning it over from front to back, and then with a shrug of his shoulders he slid it into the pocket of his coat.

It was then that he noticed the change. It was subtle, like a slight fluctuation of pressure in the inner ear. He felt as if he were no longer alone in the house. Shetland knew the feeling of an empty house, the sense of loneliness that fills the rooms like the air itself. He stepped back into the hallway, turning off the lights behind him, and looked around. Nothing seemed altered, yet there was a difference, as if furniture had been moved around or something had been changed.

The sound of a car door opening and closing drew his attention away from the house. A car was parked in the middle of the road, its headlights out; somebody was standing on the driver's side. He started walking in that direction; whoever it was became startled, jumped back into the car and sped away. He caught sight of a woman in the momentary illumination of the courtesy light, her face hidden by a scarf tied around her head.

When Shetland got back to his apartment the phone was ringing. He nearly tripped over his suitcases getting inside to answer it. It was Blake's boss, Harry Simpson, the county medical examiner. He said that they should meet tomorrow, "early."

Shetland asked, "Do you have something, Harry?"

"Yes, but I won't talk over the phone." He hung up.

Ominous calls in the night weren't Simpson's style. It had been one thing after another since his return. He hadn't had time to ease back into the routine, to get his balance. He was running out of step just to catch up, and it was doing funny things to his head. He needed a good night's sleep to get back into sync. Intuition told him the red book in his jacket pocket was important; the temptation to open the book and have a look inside was almost overpowering but he managed to put it aside, telling himself to get it together, clear the mind, be refreshed for the meeting with Harry in the morning.

Shetland dozed off on the sofa still in his clothes, but his sleep was anything but refreshing. It was a voyage harried by dreams, disturbingly real. He saw the shadowed figure of Stephen Peel standing at the edge of a dark woods, looking on, mesmerized at the whirlwind inferno. There was the roar of wind and flames. The trees swayed like children arm in arm, their bright faces aglow in the firelight. The figure stepped from the flickering shadows into the open, then began to run toward the burning house. In a magician's quick change from one guise to another, it was Peel, then himself, rushing toward the licentious arms of the fire, which harbored murder in its searing embrace. The flames leaped skyward in a terrifying humming gust, then suddenly, violently they reached down, not for Peel but for Donald Shetland. It was he recoiling in horrified disbelief, a guttural cry wrenched from his throat. It was his legs, tangled in the shrubbery, that held him anchored in place as hell reached out to touch him. He felt the rogue impulse to survive burst upon his consciousness like a scream, and drive him flailing, stumbling, away from the hideous fire into the cool darkness.

Shetland was suddenly delivered: it was Peel, not he, running back through the woods, twisting and turning in the glow from the fire that played havoc with light and shadow, turning familiar forms and textures into a deranged kaleidoscope. Peel stumbled off the path and floundered in a grasping jungle of undergrowth. In a matter of seconds he was turned around, lost, confused as to which way to proceed. The overcast sky added to his bewilderment, reflecting and disseminating the light, making it seem as if the woods were ringed by fire. Shetland could feel the panic swelling in his own breast as Peel wheeled about, crashing to the right and then to the left, and stumbled forward, trying to retrace his steps. Again Shetland was drawn back into the dream; he leaned against a tree trunk to catch his breath. His pulse was racing. He became aware that something was approaching; it was near. He searched the darkness and saw nothing. He forced himself to look harder into the black depths of the woods and then he caught a glimpse of a fleeting shape.

Shetland tumbled off the couch onto the floor and woke with a jarring thud. He rolled over, then sat up, eyes looking wildly about. It was morning.

CHAPTER TWO

At SEVEN A.M. a bleary-eyed Shetland walked into Harry Simpson's spacious, wood-paneled office in the County Morgue building and eased himself into a cold leather chair. Harry was seated behind his massive desk, dressed in his white medical coat. He was a big rectangular man who sported a yellow handlebar mustache that fluttered like a pair of wings when his small, almost pouty mouth moved to speak. Glancing up from his papers, he gave Shetland a quick, appraising look, then lifted himself half out of his chair to reach for the mug of hot chocolate on the sideboard behind him. Harry swore by hot chocolate and drank it incessantly; it was the only thing that kept his hands warm after a session with the knife, or so he insisted in squeamish company. Peering over his mug, Harry began to examine Shetland with a critical eye. He was visibly shocked by Shetland's appearance. "Don, boy, if I were you I wouldn't lie down around here. After a two-week sailing trip I thought you'd come back tanned and fresh as a daisy, but you look more like a blown-out dandelion puff. I'm not sure you're up to what I have to tell you."

"I feel worse than I look," Shetland quipped dryly.

"I had to spend a lot of time going through those on this one," Harry said, rolling his eyes toward the bookshelves containing an extensive medical library that lined two walls.

Shetland followed his gaze, and for some reason settled on Harry's golf trophy on the top shelf and the framed medical diplomas on the wall behind it. "Did it help?"

"Not overly. This sure isn't a classic textbook case."

"You trying to tell me something, Harry?"

Harry was not a man prone to melodramatics, but what he had to say was important and he wasn't sure where to begin. Contemplatively Harry held his mug close to his mouth. Finally he took a deep breath and said, "I've already discussed this with your captain." Exhaling, he continued, "He told me to tell you to handle it however you see fit, but it's not to be made public yet, at least not until a complete coroner's report is ready. We might come up with an explanation by then. Mr. Turner's arms and legs were removed at the shoulder and hip joints in a twisting, wrenching movement counter to the normal limb and joint articulation."

"What the hell are you talking about?" Shetland choked, his mouth agape. "Didn't the explosion tear them off?"

"No. I'm saying they were torn off by some mechanical process, and I don't necessarily mean a machine, either. In short, the dismemberment occurred in a manner not unlike a drumstick wrung off a cooked chicken, only the indications are that Mr. Turner wasn't cooked yet; he was still alive at the time it happened. Provocative," Harry said, leaning across his desk, "isn't it?"

"What are you guys doing about an explanation?"

"We're trying," Harry said, none too hopefully, "conjuring up the physical process by which bone, muscle, cartilage and skin, combined as they are in the shoulder, could be separated from the body like that. It's not easy; the lateral tensile strength has got to be equal to that of steel cables. In the good old days it took a team of horses on either side of the victim to draw and quarter him. In short, a lot of power and leverage were required to remove those arms and legs, and one evil, sadistic mind. It's one thing to dislocate an appendage, but as I've been saying, it's quite another . . ."

Shetland waved Harry into silence. "Could we skip the gore? Just tell me what the hell we've got here."

"That's precisely the problem: we don't know what we have."

"Harry, you don't know about problems. Want to know how to start a public panic? Take a savage murder with no apparent motive, then for spice, you add method unknown and splash it across the newspapers in fifty-point pica." Discouraged, Shetland shook his head. "For the time being this information will stay with the captain and me on our end. What about your department?"

Harry showed his displeasure at Shetland's intimation. "Blake knows and some of the others, but there are no leaks in this office."

Shetland threw him a who-are-you-kidding look. "Harry, how long have you been in this business?"

"Twelve years as the county medical examiner and thirteen before that in private practice. You worried about my credentials?"

"Just wondering if you've ever run into anything like this before—I mean, as bad as Mr. Turner."

Harry laughed. "Hell, I've seen them brought in in bags like so much garbage; auto accidents, industrial explosions, the woman in Brightwater they found in the trunk of her husband's car where he'd dumped her all cut up to pieces. That was the year you joined the force. Then there was the guy who fell or was pushed into a commercial printing press during a union problem in Melrose. Talk about messy . . ."

Shetland threw up his hands. "Okay, okay, you've seen worse."

Harry interrupted, "The physical severity of Mr. Turner's destruction isn't the point. It's one thing to fall or get pushed into a commercial printing press in a printing plant; it's quite another when somebody tears up a human being like an unwanted advertising circular. I mean," Harry said, cupping his hands behind his head, "how do you get the printing press through the front door? If you discover a body lying in bed, in a fourth-floor flat, and it's been run over by a bulldozer, you don't look for the bulldozer in the closet."

"And yet a long-distance telephone call from the Turners' granddaughter placed them at home just before midnight, and I figure the time of death at somewhere between midnight and one A.M. So how does that mesh with the mechanical dismemberment of the victim?"

"I got no answers for you, Don."

After the less than comforting meeting with Harry, Shetland walked from the County Morgue across the mall to the new three-story Central Headquarters building. He took the elevator from the main lobby to the second floor, where the homicide division was located. Everything in the new facility was clean and airy except his office; his was the only room without a window. It was a paradox that always struck him more acutely after a visit to Harry's office. With his two file cabinets and desk there was barely enough room for him to squeeze around to his chair and flop onto the crumbling plastic cushion.

He thumbed through his mail and found his requisition for new office furniture and his request for increased office space returned for the second time, stamped: REQUEST DE-NIED. FUNDS NOT AVAILABLE AT PRESENT TIME. PLEASE RESUB-MIT AT APPROPRIATE FISCAL BUDGETING SESSION. Shetland snarled to himself, "I would, you creeps, if you'd tell me when that was." With a shrug he picked up the morning paper and spent a few minutes looking it over. The double story made page one, complete with menacing headlines and photographs of Mr. and Mrs. Turner, Stephen Peel, the charred rubble of the house and the freezer. Shetland didn't have the heart to read the accompanying story on page two. Tossing the paper in the wastebasket, he called Scalley, Tedeschevich and Casey in from the squad room just outside his door for a conference. "Standard procedures," he said, "but this time we stick to it. Do not talk to anyone about the investigation, wives and small pets included. In case you boys missed the dramatic implication and have not figured out that we've got a weird one on our hands, any words uttered to the press other than 'no comment' will result in immediate suspension; that's the captain's orders, not mine.

"Tedeschevich, you and Casey are to work full time on

the Turner investigation. Priority: Pin down if the murder took place in the house or elsewhere. Scalley, you're the middleman. You'll work with Casey and the sergeant and myself on the Peel investigation."

"I don't get it," Tedeschevich muttered sarcastically. "Peel's a suicide."

"Perhaps," Shetland responded, anxious to move on to the particulars.

But the sergeant wasn't buying it. "Come on," he retorted smugly, "the guy iced himself. Why bust chops and waste manpower on a guy who bugged out in a locked room. Where's the percentages?"

"We go at this my way," Shetland glared at Tedeschevich, "and if it somehow gets finked I'll know where to come."

The hostility between Sergeant Tedeschevich and Lieutenant Shetland was no secret to Scalley. A year ago they'd been throwing charges and countercharges at each other during formal departmental hearings on the whys and hows of ten months' work to put the kabosch on a dope and prostitution ring working out of Wyandanch. The thing went bust; somebody had leaked information about the impending arrest and the suspects scattered to the four winds. Seeing a row blowing up, Scalley cut in. "How about a connection?"

Distracted, Shetland turned to Scalley. "Coincidence is suspect, okay? Just go where it leads you."

Scalley stayed behind to talk after the others left. "You've still got it bad for Tedeschevich."

"Does it show? That lying s.o.b. tried to crate me up and stick me underground."

"You know," Scalley said measuredly, "it's conceivable that you both got thumped on a bum charge."

"Is that how everybody sees it?"

Scalley shrugged. "Nobody likes to think the worst."

"Let it ride for now," Shetland said angrily.

"Maybe we shouldn't. You look like something's really bugging you, and popping off at Tedeschevich was a way of venting the pressure."

"What do you know! A resident psychiatrist," Shetland said, half annoyed.

"Excuse me, Lieutenant, I just butted out."

"Hey, I'm sorry," Shetland apologized. "You know me; I'm the original stick up the ass when it gets personal." Shetland sat on the edge of his desk. "I had a dream last night, a real lollapolooza. It was about this guy Peel, or myself—there were moments when I wasn't sure. It was like I was seeing his last night alive on reruns."

It was obvious to Scalley that Shetland was deeply disturbed. "Look, Lieutenant, it doesn't seem so unusual to dream about a thing like that, considering the circumstances."

"I can accept that," Shetland said. "I can even accept that it seemed so damn real. But let me ask you, how many dreams can you remember verbatim a few hours after you wake up, even the most vivid ones?" Shetland sighed wearily at Scalley's hapless look. "I guess we can let that slide too. What have you got for me?"

"Names," Scalley said; "over a dozen for the Turners, people close enough to be in the picture. For Peel there's just two, at least for the past few years." Scalley handed him a sheet of paper.

Shetland looked it over carefully.

"One more thing," Scalley said. "I got a memo from the New Rochelle police. They're hot under the collar about the lack of cooperation they're getting from us on a missing person case. This is the first I've heard of it, Lieutenant."

"That makes two of us," Shetland said blankly. "Who's supposed to be working on it?"

"You are, Lieutenant."

"Look," Shetland muttered, "I don't know what they're talking about. When you have time, look into it and get back to me." Looking back at the list of names of those who knew Peel, he asked, "Who are these people?"

Scalley handed him a clipping with a photograph from the society column of the local paper. "Renée Sebastian, unmarried, age thirty-seven."

Shetland let out a whistle. Even with the grainy texture of the photo offset process, he could see that she was beautiful. "That's thirty-seven?"

"She's a socialite jet-setter with a very select circle of

friends. She has more money than God and nearly as much as the Rockefellers. You've sailed on the Sound—you must have seen her mansion; it's like a brownstone mountain on top of the bluffs of Sebastian Point. There's an invalid brother, but I couldn't find anything on him."

"That's it?"

"She puts out a lot of money to keep her private life just that—private, Lieutenant. Whenever she takes up residence on Crane's Neck there's usually a blurb in the local papers like that one. I talked to a couple of the newspapers and as far as they know she's in England, but they wouldn't make book on it."

Disappointed, Shetland asked, "How about this one—Arken?"

Scalley brightened. "That's a different story, Lieutenant. Jules Arken, born Philadelphia, P.A., age forty-two; occupation, research scientist specializing in a field called bioenergetics. This guy's got degrees like Renée Sebastian's got money. I have a list of colleges and universities he's attended and the position he held just after graduation. Five years ago he was working for the Houston, Texas, Research Institute. The project had something to do with Kirlian photography and its possible industrial application. It was a federally funded project which the feds ceased funding and was discontinued."

"Was Arken let go?"

"No. The institute wanted to retain him in another capacity, but he quit and dropped out of sight for two years. There was no record of what he did during that time period, but three years ago he surfaced again, this time as head of a privately funded institute."

"He came up in the world," Shetland commented.

"Guess who the private funder was?"

"Let me think," Shetland mused aloud, scratching his brow. "Renée Sebastian?"

"He had the whole works, the building and a staff out near Calverton Air Force Base. It was about that time that he became acquainted with Stephen Peel, apparently through Ms. Sebastian. The project was another fadeout. He's been living more or less in seclusion in a cottage below the bluffs of Breakman's Cove."

"Okay, we'll do Mr. Arken first."

They drove out to the northwest side of Crane's Neck, which faced away from the harbor of Oysterville. From here they could look down the Sound toward the sea approach, where a dozen sailboats gull-winged toward them before tacking away about half a mile out to the north. Shetland and Scalley parked on the bluff. "We walk from here," Scalley said unenthusiastically. There was a path leading from the rim of the bluff down the face of the sandy cliff to a narrow stretch of barren gravel beach. The tide was coming in, and a line of dried seaweed along the beach indicated to Shetland that there wouldn't be more than three or four yards of solid ground left between the water's edge and the cliff facing at high tide. They walked westward in the cliff's shadow for a good distance, or at least it felt that way to Shetland's aching calf muscles; then the cliff slid away to their left.

Scalley pointed out over a broad flat stretch of beach glittering harshly in the sun to a line of sand dunes overgrown with brush and grass. "Lieutenant, the cottage should be just over those hills." The cliffs around the cover were lower, but as Shetland looked along their face he couldn't locate any other way to get down to the beach. The trees marched right to the edge of the bluffs, some of their roots stepping out into mid-air. "It's a fair bet to say this Arken takes his privacy seriously," Scalley said, wiping the sweat from his forehead.

"Yeah, but I wonder how his paper boy feels about it." Shetland took off his jacket and threw it over his shoulder and Scalley did the same. Every step they took stirred swarms of flies into the hot stagnant air about their legs. They reached the base of the sand dunes and then walked up a path through the brush. Near the top they were met by a refreshing breeze and the eerie, melodious sound of tolling bells. Shetland and Scalley threw each other a puzzled look and then hurried the last couple of feet to the top.

"Crap," Scalley said breathlessly.

"Are you sure this is the place?"

"Honestly, Lieutenant? No."

John Pintoro

The path they were on meandered down between brush and scrub pine for about twenty-five yards and ended abruptly at the edge of the sand. The beach fanned out like a splayed hand, broken and uneven with sparse patches of saw grass. Below them and about halfway between the bluffs and the water's edge, a ramshackle cottage sat like a discarded beer carton in the sand. Indian ceremonial clay bells hanging beneath the eaves of the cottage rang somberly in the steady breeze that came off the Sound. There were dozens of them, each a different shape, all brightly painted in geometric, animal or floral patterns. Some had feathers attached to their clackers; no two were alike.

The outside of the small, two-room cottage was laden from chimney top to foundation with magic charms, talismans and amulets. Nailed to the sloping roof were wood and metal T-shaped crosses, crucifixes and Stars of David, colorful plaques of birds and geometrical designs, and fierce voodoo masks. The sides of the cottage were covered with an incredible mural depicting terrifying multiarmed Indian gods surrounded by a pantheon of cowering demons. There, in all his bug-eyed twisted deformity, was the Hei-tiki, side by side with the seven-eyed lamb of God. In still more bizarre contrast were witches' circles and the pentagram. Bunches of feathers were nailed to the sides of the building. The wooden slat-rail erosion fence that circled the cottage was draped with voodoo beads and leather pouches. These bags were decorated with black and red feathers and strings of beads and filled with strongly scented powder. Papier-mâché skulls were stuck on top of some of the fence slats. And yet beyond the fence, driven into the sand in what at first glance Shetland took to be a random pattern, stood wooden crosses as tall as a man. Some of the crosses were like the T-shaped ones on the roof; others resembled the Cross of the Crucifixion. Looking down upon them, Shetland soon began to see a pattern in their placement; more than a dozen formed a circle and within that circle the crosses were laid out to show a five-pointed star. Each of the crosses was decorated with voodoo masks and other magical charms.

"I think," Scalley gulped, "this guy's found the ultimate

religion—all of them rolled into one. You don't suppose he's a collector?"

Shetland sighed. "I wonder if the Bureau of Tourism knows about this place or, more important, the Department of Mental Health." Shetland led the way down the path, with Scalley following behind him. They reached the end of the path and made their way across the yielding sand, pausing amid the crosses that stood like silent sentries. Scalley stared at a shiny brass disk that had a single eye enameled in its center, then shook his head and followed Shetland to an opening in the fence which was barred by a log and chain boom. Shetland examined one of the charms attached to the boom. It was a piece of white flint. He rolled it between his fingers, then let it drop from his grasp.

"Lieutenant, do you have any idea what's going on here?"

Shetland shrugged helplessly. "A fortress of defense, I would say."

Scalley looked at him questioningly. "Against who?"

"Whatever Jules Arken imagines will be stopped by this junk." They hopped over the boom, went up to the front door and knocked. There was no answer. Shetland called out but there was still no response.

"I can't see a thing," Scalley said, peering through a crack in the shutters. "The windows are painted over. Christ, nobody can live in there. I must have been wrong, Lieutenant." Suddenly he stopped talking and pressed his ear close to the shutter. "I hear something," he whispered, "scraping— no, more like fingernails strumming on wood."

Shetland stepped closer to the door to listen. He could hear it too, an odd mixture of rapping, tapping, and scraping that increased in tempo, died away then rose again from a different point. Baffled, he shook his head and gave the door a couple of vigorous raps. "Mr. Arken," he called out, "it's the police; we'd like to talk to you."

"Whatever's inside, you've got it agitated. Lieutenant, what about a warrant?"

"You're absolutely right," Shetland grunted. He applied his full weight to the door, which swung open with a bang. Shetland stumbled forward into the darkness. Something cracked and crunched underfoot. He jumped sideways. "I can't see a thing," he called. "Get the lights!" He felt something scurry across the top of his foot and he let out a yell; then he heard Scalley behind him screaming with revulsion.

"Jesus, Lieutenant. Crabs!"

Shetland spun around and another crab squirmed and crunched under his foot. Dozens of crabs scurried toward the light through the doorway. Scalley stood frozen just outside the shack, staring in disgust. "Damn it, Scalley," Shetland roared, "turn on the light." Shetland could hear the crabs all around him in the darkness and feel them underfoot, and he felt about ready to come unglued when Scalley finally moved and hit the light switch.

"Where did they come from?" Scalley stuttered, standing in the midst of the crawling pandemonium. Crabs were everywhere, charging here and there for cover. "Sickening, disgusting," Scalley ranted. The inside of the cottage was like a crowded nightclub full of drunks right after somebody yelled fire, with everybody pushing and shoving and stepping on each other to get to the exit. In a few seconds the shack was nearly empty except for stragglers, the ones that got crowded out or turned around in the mass hysteria or hadn't quite gotten the message.

Sick to his stomach, Shetland exhaled sourly. It was then that he saw the single crab on the floor in the next room, its pincer claws raised above its flat shell of a body as if to reach for something out of its grasp. "There's always one," Shetland muttered, "who doesn't know when the party's over." He stepped into the kitchen to give the ugly brute the bum's rush and found Jules Arken hanging by an electrical cord from a beam in the ceiling. His eyes, murky in death, bulged from Arken's blue and swollen face and his tongue drooped from his mouth like a piece of raw liver. Without the fall to snap his neck, Arken had strangled to death. Shetland turned to summon Scalley into the kitchen, but he was already there.

"He's what the crabs were after, weren't they, Lieutenant."

Shetland nodded at the unpleasant truth.

"Another suicide?"

"Another murder," Shetland said. "Look at the wrists. You can still see the marks where they were tied, and it wasn't no machine that did it either. You'd better go back and radio in."

"Lieutenant, do you want me to tell them anything special?"

"Yeah, see if they can get a hold of Harry Simpson, the county medical examiner. Blake's good, but Harry's got a sixth sense about this kind of thing. Also, I spotted a safe bolted to the floor by the fireplace. Take down the name of the company and the serial number and see if we can have them get us the combination. The reason for this might be in there."

"Anything else, Lieutenant?"

"Yeah. Don't leave me here by myself too long." Shetland stepped to the door to watch Scalley as he made his way back across the beach the way they had come. In a few moments Scalley had disappeared over the sand dunes. The moment he was gone time seemed to stand still. It was a bright clear day and the wind picked up sand and scoured it over the coarser gravel underneath. The monotonous peal of the bells had become part of the background noise, along with the wind that rose and fell in shrieks and sighs and no longer warranted special attention, until suddenly it stopped. The silence struck his senses like the crash of brass cymbals. A strange darkness like the shadow of a cloud swept over the ground about the cottage. Shetland dashed into the front yard and looked up into the sky at the sun glaring down like a burnished steel disk. His nervous system got a jolt that sent his body into shudders; he was sweating and trembling like an old car with a busted suspension bouncing on a rough road. Knees shaking, he started walking slowly out of the yard, then began to quicken his pace. Before he knew what was happening, he was running. He reached the log boom completely out of breath, threw one leg over and then drew it back as if he had just stepped into scalding water. His strange panic vanished with the gloom. The bells were tolling again as

Scalley appeared on the skyline, yelling, "They're on their way."

Shetland was standing in the front yard of the Arken cottage watching the Crane's Neck cops getting in the way. They were acting as if his men were poaching on a private preserve. As far as Shetland was concerned, the town cops were nothing but security guards for the local estates. But even though homicide came under county jurisdiction, Shetland didn't have the authority to send them packing. In his hand he was holding a piece of parchment that Casey had found attached to the back door of the cottage; it was inscribed with Arabic or Hebrew letters. To Shetland the document was a mystery. Harry, who was standing by his side, struck a match to his pipe, then held it for Shetland's cigarette. A billowing puff of smoke rolled from the pipe bowl and swirled away in the breeze. "Six hours," he said. "Died six hours ago, no more." He checked his watch. "That would put the time of death at seven-thirty, eight o'clock this morning. Death by strangulation. Beat up some, though, before he died, by somebody familiar with the martial arts or torture. Both collar bones were fractured; very painful." Harry glanced sideways at Shetland. "You sure you don't want something to calm your nerves?"

"No. My nerves have had enough futzing with, thank you."

Harry laughed. "Delayed reaction, that's all it was. You really wanted to start running when you first got in that cottage. Your brain just had a slight delay transmitting that erstwhile desire to the body."

Shetland grunted noncommittally.

Casey walked out of the cottage with a large manila envelope under his arm. "You were right, Lieutenant: Somebody tried to break into the safe. We found chisel marks near the combination lock." He handed Shetland the envelope. "That's what was in it. Can you believe this place?"

"Do you think we have a choice?" Harry asked.

"I see what you mean," Casey said, and walked away.

Shetland opened the envelope, reached in and withdrew

what looked like an overexposed negative. He and Harry studied the eight-by-ten picture with a peculiar uneasiness; it was some sort of group portrait, the silhouettes of human forms lost in spiraling coronas of color. "It makes no sense," Shetland grumbled. "Why would anybody kill for this?"

"It must show something important," Harry interjected. "Show it to the boys at the photo lab; maybe they can help."

Shetland slid the photo back into the envelope. "This whole business is getting downright freaky," he said.

"Don't relax yet," Harry warned.

Shetland groaned at the thought. "You got something new?"

"I will soon, and I'm afraid it's going to muddy the waters even more."

"I need help," Shetland said; "this thing's turning into a massacre. Pretty soon the newspapers are going to start lumping it all together. Can so many unexplained deaths be unassociated; is there a Crane's Neck fiend on the prowl? Jesus, I don't need that kind of headache."

"There's no proof of that."

"Where the hell do you live, Harry, in a cave? What does proof have to do with what those guys write? They write to sell papers. What do they care that the story will send everybody and his grandmother to the neighborhood gun store?"

"I can appreciate your concern but you can't do much about it. You can't stop the papers from writing what they will and you can't stop the average citizen from thinking what he will." Harry shook his head, there was something in Shetland's noncommittal manner that startled him. "Don boy, is that really what you're concerned about?"

"Yes, of course, Harry. I worry some terrified turkey is going to shoot the postman delivering the mail. I'm afraid if this thing goes on the tennis doubles and golf foursomes at the country club will start forming vigilante groups, and I'm even more afraid that the local lunatics will start coming out of the closet to give credence to the irresponsible newspaper stories. Believe me, Harry, it happens."

"Yes, yes," Harry said with surprise, "but I detect an

ominous note of reservation beneath that steely exterior of yours. Perhaps you think there is a Crane's Neck fiend."

"I didn't say that," Shetland countered defensively.

"You protest too much," Harry said. "But you do think there's going to be more deaths."

"I didn't say that either, Harry."

"Never mind what you said or didn't say, Don. You think there's a connection. Well, would you mind telling me what happened to the M.O. and all that police jargon? I mean where the hell are the similarities?" Harry took a long draw on his pipe. "I grant you coincidence, but how you see a connection is beyond me."

"Harry, are you charging for this mind-reading session or is it off the cuff? Talk about wild speculation, Harry."

"Okay," Harry said, "let it drop. So what now?"

"From you, Harry," Shetland said, "I want to know what you know when you know it."

"And where are you off to?" Harry asked as Shetland started to leave.

"To connect the third dot: to see the Sebastians."

CHAPTER THREE

JESSICA HAD BEEN SUNBATHING in the nude all afternoon and no one had passed on the cliff road above the secluded beach to intrude on her privacy. It was a road seldom traveled by anyone except those going to the Sebastian manor. But when she first heard the faint drone of an approaching car she was not altogether surprised, for sooner or later she had expected to see that particular brown sedan, and when it finally appeared she watched it drive past with almost a sense of relief. She vaguely knew the man behind the wheel who was about to enter her life. The ground near her house sloped gently to the water's edge, but if she looked further down the beach she could see the cliffs of Sebastian Point where they began to loom higher and higher until they reached the prominence upon which the manor itself stood. The cliff road made an out-of-the-way loop before it came to the Sebastian gate. Jessica slipped into her cut-off jeans and halter top, which she tied in the back as she broke into a trot going up the path that was a short cut to the manor driveway.

The brown sedan was parked in front of the locked gate. There was a methodical persistence in the man's bearing as he stared silently through the wrought-iron gate down the long winding drive to the Sebastian mansion, which was partially hidden by the trees. To Jessica his stance seemed stoic, and yet she sensed a vague undercurrent of vulnerability beneath his impassive exterior. "Hideous, aren't they, Lieutenant," she called, referring to the stone gargoyles crouched on top of the pillars that flanked the gate.

Shetland glanced up as he slowly turned around. The woman approaching him had the long thoroughbred lines of a high-fashion model, soft brown shoulder-length hair that a man would give a lot to put his hands into and tough yet sensitive, liquid amber eyes that you could drown in. Barefoot, she trooped up to him as if they were fully acquainted.

They shook hands. "I'm Jessica Cummings and you are Lieutenant Donald Shetland," she smiled. "Don't worry, we don't know each other. Or I should say you don't know me."

"I'm glad you said that, but how did our one-sided acquaintance get started?"

"You trying to see the Sebastians, Lieutenant?" Jessica said, avoiding his question.

"Do you work here?"

"I'm afraid not."

They stepped toward the gate. "It's locked," he said, shaking it with both hands. "Aren't these things supposed to have a buzzer or something so you can call up to the house to announce your presence?"

Jessica pointed to the pillar on their right. "Over there, Lieutenant—it's hidden under the wisteria vine, but I wouldn't bother if I were you."

"Why not? Am I dressed inappropriately?"

"No one's allowed to visit the house when Renée's not at home."

"I gather from that, Miss Cummings, you're telling me the lady's not home."

"She went out early this morning with her chauffeur and her bodyguard."

"A bodyguard? Is he a professional or a rent-a-cop?"

"I'm afraid I wouldn't know, Lieutenant."

"I'm surprised. Is Miss Sebastian in need of a body-guard?"

"She thinks she is and that's the same as real need, isn't it?"

"You have a point, Miss Cummings, but what about the brother? Is he antisocial or isn't he home either?"

"Oh, yes, Aaron's always home, but you definitely won't get to see him."

"So I won't spend all night trying to figure out how you know about me and everything else when I should be getting my rest, why don't you explain it? Start with this rather suspicious encounter."

"There's no mystery in that, Lieutenant. The Sebastians knew Stephen Peel. I figured somebody from the police would be around sooner or later to talk to them."

"Then you know the Sebastians personally?"

"I didn't say that."

"I gather you like one-sided acquaintances."

"I have a house along the beach; you can see the road from there. I saw Stephen Peel drive up to the manor many times, the same way I saw you just a little while ago."

Shetland nodded. "So far I can follow this. Now tell me where we haven't met before."

"You're not going to like it, Lieutenant."

He shrugged. "You can't please everybody."

"About a year ago, Lieutenant, during a certain brouhaha in the police department, we had our first encounter. I was standing next to a certain public official about whose parental heritage you were giving a very colorful description."

"You're one of Assemblyman Dority's people." He exhaled as if all his enthusiasm for the conversation had suddenly died.

"I'm his administrative assistant."

"Must pay pretty well for you to afford a house on Crane's Neck."

"You're getting nasty with those innuendoes. Not everyone on Crane's Neck lives in a mansion."

"What's Dority got to do with this?"

"My coming here to see you? Nothing. But with the

Sebastians, plenty. The state assemblyman wants to be state senator and he's been spending a great deal of time befriending the money and power behind those gates because he figures it's the shortest route to the Republican nomination. He's right too; the Sebastians wield a lot of clout in this state. There isn't any favor he wouldn't do for the Sebastians."

"Like run interference with a pesky police lieutenant?"

"Especially one he likes as much as you."

"Assemblyman Dority isn't stupid; he knows the quickest way to land his ass in a sling is to openly interfere with an ongoing police investigation."

"To quote you, Lieutenant, he isn't stupid. But from your own personal experience you ought to know he throws a pretty mean monkey wrench. He'll find ways."

"How informative, Miss Cummings, but this makes you what? A concerned citizen, a turncoat, or a counterfeit traitor?"

"Let's just say it comes by way of an apology for our last encounter. Even under the circumstances I think Ray overstepped the bounds of propriety in his dealings with you and the police commission."

"Overstepped propriety? Your boss tried to gut me with innuendo and without a shred of evidence, so he could parade a crooked cop's scalp in front of the voters." Shetland's face darkened with anger at the memory and for a brief moment Jessica was frightened but yet intensely attracted to this man. Just as quickly his anger seemed to pass.

"I'm glad it didn't work out that way."

"Yeah? Listen, I'm not interested in your apologies. I only want to talk to the Sebastians. How much mileage does Dority think he can get out of preventing that? I mean, how much could five minutes' worth of conversation mean to the Sebastians?" Jessica was about to say something, but Shetland cut her off. "In any case you'll have to excuse my boorishness if I consider the possibility that you might be one of Dority's monkey wrenches." Shetland walked past her toward the car.

Jessica turned and followed him. "Look, Lieutenant, I was only trying to help."

"Thanks," Shetland said, opening the car door and getting in. "I appreciate it."

"There was something more I wanted to talk to you about."

"Look, Miss Cummings, I have a carefully nurtured hatred for your boss. I wouldn't want to start associating anything nice with him."

"Okay. It was a long hike up here—at least give me a ride back down the hill."

Shetland closed the door and stuck his head out the window. "I think not. I'm the sort of person who can resist anything but temptation. When you do see your boss tell him I haven't forgotten." Shetland kept looking at Jessica Cummings through his rearview mirror as he drove off until the curve in the road blocked her from his sight.

Shetland drove straight to the county seat in Hauppauge, to the new forensic lab where Scalley, at his instruction, was to hand-deliver the mysterious photo. He met Scalley in the quadrangle in front of the criminal court building. "Finch has got it now," Scalley said, "and apparently it's something special."

"Did he say anything?"

"Nope, just looked at it bug-eyed and asked how I came by it."

"Look," Shetland said, "I'm in a rush, see what you can find out about a bodyguard employed by the Sebastians."

"I could use a name."

"If I had one I'd give it to you." Shetland was lost in thought for a moment. "Four people dead; there's got to be a connection. Tell Casey and Tedeschevich to work on that angle. I know," he said, cutting off Scalley's protest; "you've already checked."

"Okay," Scalley said with marked skepticism. "However comforting it might be, I bet you we come up empty-handed."

They parted company on that pessimistic note.

The photo lab was located in the basement of the smoked-glass-and-concrete police forensic building. The head man was a tall lean character named Willy Finch. When Shetland entered Finch's office the latter was in the midst of his coffee break; the photo was on his desk. "It's Kirlian photography," he said matter-of-factly.

Trying not to look any more ignorant than it took to get Finch to explain, Shetland nodded. "Then you know what it is?"

"With a disclaimer. Kirlian photography is basically high-voltage picture-taking without a camera. The method was perfected by a Russian technician, Semyon von Kirlian; hence the name. It's not a new process but until fairly recently there hasn't been much work done with it."

"And the disclaimer?"

Willy didn't answer immediately but took the picture in his hands and studied it carefully. Finally he said, "Kirlian works something like this. You take unexposed film, place it over electrodes, then take the object to be photographed and lay it on top of the film, and finally you send a high-voltage, low-amperage current through the electrodes. If everything goes okay—and there are a lot of things that could foul up the whole works, such as barometric pressure, humidity, et cetera—you get a picture of the object's outline in a light corona. In short, it's not like walking into a room with your Brownie and photographing a crowd of people. The subject has to be next to the film. The disclaimer is that this photo has all the earmarks of a portrait in three dimensions. So, Lieutenant, I say it's butter and the facts say it's margarine."

Shetland threw up his hands in defeat. "That's as clear as everything else in this investigation." Frustrated, he asked, "Can you at least tell me what causes the lights, what the damn thing is showing, and whether it's valuable?"

"Hold the phone," Finch said and walked out of his office to get more coffee for himself and some for Shetland. "I hope you've got some time," he said when he returned, "because I think there's something you should know. First, I have to assume the picture is Kirlian-produced by a technique I haven't heard of which makes the rest of what I've got to say even stranger.

"Theories abound about what is the precise nature of the corona that surrounds animate objects. These ideas run the gambit of possibilities from bioenergetics, an energy field distinctive to living matter, active biology, to biomagnetic, exclusive to mentating biology, a kind of mind-body energy that the theory's supporters claim explains such unsolved scientific curiosities as precognition, mental telepathy and telekinesis." Shetland followed as best he could, remembering that Jules Arken had been a research scientist in bioenergetics. "The properties of the energy field are unknown, so," Finch continued, "the theories and theoreticians can get pretty far out. They see, in the strange mystical light of the corona, proof positive of the human soul."

Shetland reclined in his chair.

"You're not laughing, Lieutenant. Since you aren't I think I'd better proceed." Willy opened his desk drawer and withdrew a magazine which he spread open on the desk. "This," he said, "is a recent article on Kirlian photography in a scientific journal." He turned the pages and went on, "Here is a Kirlian photograph showing what is called the ghost images. As you can see the experiment involved a leaf. Observe carefully," he said, following the outline of the leaf with his finger. "The tip is cut from the leaf, then the leaf minus the tip is set down onto the photographic surface. The ghost image of the missing portion is still apparent in a less intense coronic light."

"How?" Shetland demanded.

Willy's deadpan expression suddenly became alive with speculation. With expansive hand gestures he said, "Is it merely a matter of physics, photography and electronics, or are we looking at something much more? I don't know and I haven't heard of anyone who claims to understand it completely. There is evidence that human emotional and psychological moods are reflected in the corona. Anger produces more reds that extend a greater distance from the body; anguish and desperation also produce changes in the corona. That brings us to the photo Scalley brought me." Willy shuffled the magazine out of the way and stood the Kirlian photograph on its edge in front of them. "Okay," he said. "Take note of the ghost images that appear to the left of each individual. I have no explanation for that, so don't ask how they got there. Observe the coronas for the five individuals, especially around the cranium. The distance the coronas extend from the body surface is greater by far than I've seen on any other Kirlian, and the coronas themselves are almost violent in their intensity. Pay special attention to this particular individual." He indicated a figure. "Pardon the pun, but he or she outshines them all. If the corona is biomagnetic in nature, then we are looking at a psychic giant."

Shetland's mouth was dry as he questioned, "And if the corona really is the soul?"

Willy laughed nervously. "Then, Lieutenant, we behold a god or the devil and his disciples."

They both stared at the picture in speculative silence for several minutes, then Shetland heaved an exhausted sigh. "Okay. You've reeled out the theories: now what's your opinion?"

"Hey, I'm the wrong guy to ask if you're looking for, quote, rational answers, unquote. I believe in UFO's, the powers of the occult, and astrology, and I don't let black cats cross my path."

"Let's just say I'm in the mood for a little titillating horror—give."

"It's your time, Lieutenant. Let's take the more sober of my fantasies. I've read the papers and picked up the rumors; for my money you've got a mind-manipulating killer. Don't jump on me yet, Lieutenant. ESP, telekinesis and that whole bag of mind power is generally accepted by science as having some validity, more or less of it depending on who you're talking to. Let's go back to my psychic giant."

"Don't misunderstand me," Shetland said. "I don't think you're as nuts as I'd like to, but couldn't you picture me putting the cuffs on somebody's thoughts for murder one? It's got to be unconstitutional at the very least."

"Now you're the one who's going over the deep end, Lieutenant. Try thinking more in terms of a Manson type of thing; look at all those people he had under his control robbing and murdering for him."

"Finch, they didn't put Manson away for wishing those things to happen, and besides, I don't happen to have a

Manson-type suspect or anything vaguely resembling him. So if you could come up with any other reason why somebody would get murdered for the picture I would appreciate it."

"There's only one other possibility."

"Well," Shetland said.

"But it's a bit thin. What little money there is available for research in this field comes, to a great extent, from the military. They're looking for a fast, inexpensive way of detecting stress points in machine parts and building materials. A private company that could discover a reliable method for doing that would certainly have an edge over its competition in getting military or government contracts. There are also some people working to develop a medical use for Kirlian, called Corona Discharge Photography. One such device I'm familiar with would be used as a diagnostic tool, a sensor, to monitor moisture levels in human skin. There's even been some research using Kirlian as a device for early detection of cancerous tumors."

Shetland rocked in his chair. "Now that's the kind of stuff I'm looking for," he said enthusiastically; "murder for profit and greed."

Finch shook his head in disagreement. "You're the detective, Lieutenant, but I still think it doesn't hold up. I mean, this stuff's no big secret. Even the work the military is doing isn't classified and they've got top-secret stenciled on G.I. underwear."

"But you said Arken's method was new, something you've never seen before?"

"True, Lieutenant: I have to admit, the field's so wide open it's hard to tell what uses it could be put to."

Arken's murder by someone hoping to profit from the industrial use of his invention looked like a good possibility to Shetland. Perhaps, he thought, death was an accident. Maybe Arken's assailant had only meant to frighten him, not kill him. It was alone in his apartment at night that he pondered Finch's mention of a lunatic gang along the lines of the Manson clan. The police had checked out that possibility and come up with nothing. Casey was on the night shift, and Shetland called him. Casey answered the phone with a yawn.

"Casey? This is Lieutenant Shetland."

"Lieutenant, how did it go with Finch?"

"Okay. He gave us some possible leads. I'm calling about that Wyandanch motorcycle gang."

"What about them, Lieutenant?"

"You sure we checked them out thoroughly?"

"Positive. There was no way we could place them anywhere near Crane's Neck at the appropriate time. Twenty goons on Harley Davidsons would hardly go unnoticed in that kind of neighborhood."

"Who else did we check?"

"Every offbeat group in Suffolk and Nassau counties and we're still checking Queens and the rest of the five boroughs."

"Okay. But run them through again. See if you can find any groups that might have moved into the area recently, living in houses or communes—way-out types into drugs."

"That reminds me, Lieutenant, I was about to call you myself. We found a stash of drugs under a loose floor board in Arken's cottage. Mostly pot and hash, but we also think we got some Angel Dust. Lab's testing it to be sure."

Shetland let out a low whistle. "It takes a mean bunch to push that poison."

"I would say so, Lieutenant—mean enough to murder for the hell of it."

"Narcotics owes us for all the manpower we've given them. It's time to collect."

"Already done, Lieutenant. Pidgeon and Reese are checking their files for likelies."

After hanging up the phone, Shetland felt fidgety. He made a quick trip to a hamburger joint and polished off a greasy bag of hamburgers and french fries for supper, but when he came back he sat down feeling more on edge than when he went out. The red-bound book kept him company. It lay tauntingly on top of the busted TV. The question of why he hadn't turned it in to the police property office or returned it to Peel's den gnawed at him. Perhaps there was something in it, he thought, remembering what the kid from

the newspaper had said about a diary. He retrieved the book
from the top of the TV and sat down at the table to examine
it. It was Peel's diary, and Shetland studied it carefully, looking for a phrase, a word, a clue. It took several hours for
him to glean and underline the passages that drew his attention in light of what he now knew or thought he knew. His
eyes were burning with fatigue and irritation from the smoke
of the two packs of cigarettes he'd consumed. His stomach
was drowning in a swill of coffee, but he kept reexamining his
marked passages separately from the rest of the journal.

March 15, the Ides of March. I have chosen to
record in this journal, not a record complete with precise
data of events as they unfold, nor a scientific investiga-
tive report to be examined and scrutinized by others (for
I am of the mind that no other eyes shall see what is
written here—a dark premonition perhaps). Rather I
want to bear witness and transcribe the change of perception, the psychic metamorphosis of my own mind. It
has happened and it continues to happen. Boundaries are
no longer distinguishable; what is wood will be stone,
and in turn flesh and that which is I shall transcend. . .

April 3, 2 A.M. After the gathering this evening I
feel we have knocked at the door to a dark and foreboding house. I stood like a child who has accepted a dare
to enter the place where the fragmented horrors of old
nightmares await, and yet I eagerly seek to enter for I
am aware of the light and warmth within, ordinarily hidden by a barrier thrown across the mind as impenetrable
as any wall of rock. We have not been able to get beyond
autoscopy, transcendence.

Shetland figured that whatever Peel was up to had begun
before Peel had started writing the journal; he also got the
impression that some recent occurrence, not specifically
alluded to, had in Peel's mind necessitated keeping the journal.
The word "barrier" and metaphoric allusions to uncrossable
frontiers appeared throughout the text. The names Renée and

Jules appeared only once, and questions rumbled in Shetland's head like distant thunder. What was the "barrier" and what lay beyond?

Stephen Peel, Jules Arken and Renée Sebastian; did those three names correspond to three of the five persons in the Kirlian? And who were the other two? Which one was the psychic giant? Pages were missing, lines and sometimes whole paragraphs smudged and erased. The gaps might have told him something he could use. Shetland glanced at his wristwatch. "Damn. Four A.M. and around and around the merry-go-round the monkey chased the weasel. Monkey's got a headache and a backache," he groaned, flubbering his lips in exhaustion and pushing the journal across the table.

CHAPTER FOUR

SHETLAND HAD A DIFFICULT TIME dragging himself out of bed the next morning. He showered and shaved and had his usual breakfast of orange juice, dry toast and black coffee. It was only after the third cup of coffee that he began to feel he wasn't sleepwalking and was able to think about getting dressed.

Shetland left his apartment and drove out to the West Side Bay Country Club in the town of Head of the Harbor. Crane's Neck was just across the narrows of the upper bay. The club was exclusively conservative Republican; its members consisted of judges, lawyers, businessmen, politicians and Harry Simpson. Because Harry was a valued member, at first the club management was reluctant to disturb his golf game until Shetland showed his badge and said it was official. Harry would have agreed with their reluctance. When he strolled into the clubhouse he was wielding a nine iron in his hand and had an unpleasant grimace on his face. "It may not be your day off," he snarled, "but it is mine. I had an hour's wait to get onto the fairway so this better be important."

Shetland said, "Relax, Harry. Let's go sit down and we

can discuss it." They chose a table on the terrace, which over-looked the golf course. "Harry, did you find any drugs in Peel's or Arken's systems, something special perhaps?" Shetland asked.

His question caught Harry off balance. Guilt for having withheld information made him defensive. "Did you get that from Blake?"

"No."

"Then how?"

"Lucky guess," Shetland said.

"Bull," Harry retorted, "you should be so lucky."

"Was that the surprise you had for me?" Shetland said.

Angry, Harry said, "That was part of it, but there's more."

"Why are you sitting on it?"

"The only thing I'm sitting on, Lieutenant, is this chair when I should be out playing golf. I told you that it was coming and that we have every intention of delivering, but in a complete package. There are certain problems."

"Like what?"

"You'll find out when I give you the rest."

"Why so ticked?" Shetland said, backing off.

"I don't like leaks in my department."

"There are no leaks, Harry. I've already told you that."

"You didn't ask me about drugs; you said special. That could only come from a leak."

"Believe what you like, Harry, but I want to know what you've got and no bullshit about Christmas wrapping."

"Come in tomorrow."

"Why not today, Harry?"

"Because," Harry shouted, "I can't get a clearance before then!"

"A clearance? From whom? Since when does the chief medical examiner need a clearance to perform his duties?"

Harry insisted they were going over the same ground. "Tomorrow you'll know everything."

It was Shetland who was angry now as he warned Harry, "I became a cop because I hate mysteries. If anything stinko is going down then I'm going to tell the newspapers all about my hatred of mysteries. I got caught once, but never again."

"Nothing like that's happening, I promise you, Donald."

Harry was upset and wanted to end the conversation, but Shetland had a few more questions. "Transcendence, autoscopy—have you ever heard those terms?"

Harry's gaze narrowed, drawing his brows and the flesh over the bridge of his nose into mountainous wrinkles. "They're terms used by some to describe so-called out-of-body states." He seemed even more uncomfortable than before. "Perhaps," he said, "you've heard or read about the controversy raging between the medical and legal communities over a proper definition of what constitutes a clinical state of death and the medical advances that have spawned that controversy. For the past twenty years modern medical techniques have been relentlessly pushing back the boundaries from which a patient can be retrieved from death. There are those who claim that we have reached beyond death. There are a growing number of cases in which patients have reported conscious experiences during a technical state of death; one of the most common is a feeling of hovering over one's own body. That phenomenon has been labeled autoscopy. Supposedly the patients are able to describe in detail what was happening; the doctors and nurses working to revive them, the procedures they used, the reaction of other patients in the room.

"In the other most common phenomenon, transcendence, the patient's consciousness migrates into an alien dimension. Descriptions of transcendence vary to some degree but in general they're quite similar. The patient is unaware of what's happening to his body, and the conscious travels down a long tunnel, until it's confronted by a light that grows so bright that its brilliance is almost blinding. Some claim they are met by dead friends and relatives; they communicate by a form of thought transference. In both autoscopy and transcendence the patients claim they're overcome with a euphoric sense of warmth, joy and happiness. In transcendence they come to a barrier, a stream, a gate."

"A door?"

"You just turned three shades of pale," Harry said.

"You just slammed the brakes on my merry-go-round, that's all."

"I hope that's not supposed to make sense to me," Harry said, getting up from the table. "Either way, I'm finishing my game. Be in my office tomorrow around eleven and I'll give it to you straight and you can tell me why you wanted to know what those words meant."

Shetland watched Harry climb into a golf cart and putter off across the fairway when a familiar voice said, "Lieutenant's pay must be pretty good." He turned and found himself staring into deep amber eyes. Jessica Cummings was standing less than a foot from him. She was in a tennis outfit, and a thin film of sweat, the residue of a hard match, covered her arms and legs and made her hair curl in ringlets about the sides of her face. Shetland could smell her natural scent; it was more arousing and enticing than perfume.

Jessica was pleased to note the way the gruff-mannered lieutenant was looking at her, and without asking his permission she sat down. "If I had a suspicious nature," she taunted, "I might conclude that cop plus country club equals hanky panky of the seamiest sort, or at least that the man's ethics are questionable. But unlike some people I don't jump to conclusions. Having had the unfortunate displeasure of becoming acquainted with the man, I give him the benefit of reasonable doubt."

Shetland's expression showed that he was more amused than annoyed at Jessica's acerbic wit. "What do you know," she said, "the nasty policeman is smiling."

"Why is it so important to you?"

"Why is what so important, Lieutenant?"

"The Dority thing and me."

"It's not," she retorted, "and neither is your opinion of me. I just don't like anybody slapping me down for trying to be friends. It's not a pleasant experience. But as I just said, I like to give people the benefit of the doubt, so this is your last chance to be decent and accept my unwarranted apology with grace and sincerity."

"I accept it."

"That's a fine fellow," she said and got up to leave.

"What happens now?" he asked, getting up and following her.

"I'm going to shower and change, then you can drive me home. I came here with some friends; they won't mind."

"And?"

"And nothing," she said. "You go on about your business, which I would imagine is Renée Sebastian. It's not every day one gets a chance to kill two birds with one stone." She laughed. They headed past the tennis courts toward the clubhouse dressing rooms; Shetland stumblingly taking two steps for each of Jessica's long, lethal strides.

"Jog, don't you," he puffed. "Swim too? I know you play tennis; how about track?"

"I'm sorry," she said, slowing her pace. "I am imposing and I thought you might be in a hurry. You can wait for me over there," she said, pointing to a bench. With the feeling that he had just been put out of the game by the coach, Shetland cooled his heels in the shade for a quarter of an hour.

When Jessica came out of the dressing room she was wearing a pale blue jumpsuit, her hair was curly and flowing free and her skin had a warm, vibrant, just-scrubbed glow. Shetland couldn't help but feel that even walking by her side was some kind of vulgar mistake. Fortunately they got to his car without anybody noticing it. Jessica kicked off her sandals and sat facing Shetland, her legs tucked up underneath her. "You look uncomfortable," she said, and then, without giving him a chance to respond, she asked, "Why do you want to talk to Renée Sebastian? Is it because she knew Stephen Peel?"

"I'm driving you home; I didn't say I was going to see the Sebastians—you did."

"But you are, aren't you?"

"Not that it's any of your business, but yes."

"Why then?"

"You said it yourself: they knew Stephen Peel."

"The paper said his death was a suicide. I mean, what's the point?"

"You want the truth?"

"It would be nice, Lieutenant."

"Okay. The truth is, Miss Cummings—"

"My first name's Jessica."

"All right, Jessica. The truth is, I'm just taking advantage of probably my only opportunity to see how the other half lives. I want to get into one of those big mansions while the owners are still in residence—before they unload it on the state as an historical landmark and get themselves a tax write-off. I always feel like an unwanted relative when I visit the Vanderbilt estate."

"You're in a good mood, Lieutenant. But seriously, Stephen Peel used to visit Renée a lot. Sometimes he'd stop his car on the road above my house and get out to take in the view."

"Did you ever talk to him?"

"No. He wasn't the kind of man you just walked up to and started a conversation with; he always seemed lost in thought."

"And you didn't want to interrupt him?"

"What about the story in the paper this morning?"

"Which story?" Shetland said.

"The dead man the police found yesterday in the cottage in the cove—Jules Arken was his name. Any connection?"

Changing the subject, Shetland said, "Do you have someone, a boyfriend, a lover?"

"Why don't you want to talk about it?"

Shetland laughed and shook his head. "I've already told you it's none of your business. If you want inside dope, join the force."

"What division would you suggest, Lieutenant?"

Shetland rolled his eyes and said, "Vice."

"I get to you, don't I."

"Yeah," he mused, "and don't act so smug, because I haven't exactly been hiding the fact." He turned off the cliff road onto the dirt driveway that descended to Jessica's house through a tunnel of overhanging trees. "Stop here," Jessica said, leaning forward.

"There's no extra charge to the front door."

"That's okay. I like the walk."

He shrugged and swung the car in a half-circle, stopping

when the car's nose pointed toward the road. "Would you turn the motor off? I'd like to talk a moment."

Shetland nodded and with an exaggerated motion shifted into park, turned off the ignition and put on the emergency brake. "Something's wrong," he said, noting the serious look on her face.

"We're frightened out here," she said. "Four deaths in two days. And I don't mean just concerned, I mean scared. We're closing into ourselves in a sense, pulling the blankets up over our heads. All I have is my parents' house and my job . . ."

"And a few bucks," Shetland said.

Jessica ignored the interruption. "I have friends too, but nobody close enough to depend on, at least not any more. Despite appearances to the contrary, I'm the original gutless wonder, so some night I might sleep with you because my kind of bravery doesn't cut the muster against this sort of thing. I know it sounds like a cheap come-on but I perceive in you a man with an open mind. Think about it," she said, getting out of the car, "and so will I." She turned and strolled along the narrow road that led down to the beach as if she had just suggested a polite Sunday picnic, leaving Shetland totally bowled over.

"Are you serious?" he called after her. She nodded as she walked into the dappled shade of the overhanging trees.

Shetland shrugged in dismay, started his car and in a few minutes passed through the open gates of the driveway leading to the Sebastian manor. His tires crackled over the gravel drive that ran through a belt of unlandscaped woods; the mansion loomed ahead as he rounded a bend. The house, set in the midst of a broad, rolling expanse of lawns and shade trees, faced the Sound. Shetland parked behind a silver Mercedes limousine, got out of his car and marched up to the tall reedlike character who had observed his approach with the interest of a guard dog. Shetland took the man's measure in a single glance; he was about six feet two, with perfectly coiffed blond hair, innocent baby-blue eyes, gaunt features, understated movements, and a .45 automatic tucked tastefully beneath the lapels of a very expensive summer suit.

Shetland instantly felt hostile toward the man and could

sense that it was mutual. He had dealt with this kind before. The classy thug had "professional" stamped on his contemptuous smirk and Shetland didn't bother asking about a permit for the gun when he flashed his badge and asked to see Miss Sebastian. Shetland followed him around the outside of the mansion to a terrace. "She's not in the house. We'll have to call down to the pool to find out if she wants to talk to a cop."

"Unless," Shetland corrected, "I have a warrant. Then the call is just to let her know I'm coming, right?"

Ignoring Shetland's remark, he picked up a white phone on a table. "Miss Sebastian? It's Rudy. There's a Lieutenant Shetland here to see you."

Shetland took in the opulent view of the formal walled gardens. The rising terraces were landscaped with flowers, ornamental shrubs and trees, and reflecting pools. Beyond the gardens a moundlike hill rose out of the field. The hill was crowned by an oak grove whose antiquity was obvious even at a distance. The grove stood like an ancient hill fortress, a barbaric anomaly against the civilized foreground.

Turning in the opposite direction, Shetland looked out over the waters of the Sound to the coastline of Connecticut, twenty miles away, stretching east and west as far as the eye could see. It was a magnificent vista and for a moment Shetland's thoughts were distracted from the coming interview. Standing on the terrace, he remembered viewing this same awesome promontory from the water on the night he returned from vacation. He had left Bridgeport at dusk, traveling under sail, trying to cross the Sound and reach Oysterville Harbor before the storm broke. He had almost reached the coast of Long Island when clouds from the northeast swept in low over the water, blocking out the full moon and throwing everything into pitch blackness. Lowering his sail, he had tried to make his way along the coast under power. It was a guess as to how far off shore he was and he was nervous about getting around Sebastian Point without running aground or tearing out the bottom of his boat on the submerged rocks just off the point. He missed just such a catastrophe by the slimmest of margins when lightning brightened up the sky and threw the point into silhouette; it was like a nautical mirage in which the mansion grew up from the sheer cliff and appeared as an imposing citadel.

"Wealth is a whole 'nother world unto itself, isn't it, cop. It galls and impresses, it makes you think that there but for the grace of God go I, but the truth makes you scream."

"Hm, this is true," Shetland mused. "But then again, I'm easily impressed."

"She's waiting," Rudy said coldly. "I'll show you the way." Rudy escorted him to the free-form swimming pool and then, without saying a word, drew back to the edge of the path they had come down and stood, waiting, those baby-blue eyes never averting their gaze from Shetland's back.

The place seemed deserted and Shetland was about to comment on that fact when he heard water rippling and noticed the porcelain form of a nude woman swimming underwater, with a copper-bodied male in close pursuit. Her hair fanned out in long black streamers just before she surfaced and climbed up the ladder. She paused at the top, thus keeping her companion from getting out of the water. Her skin was the color of milk and red roses and her eyes seemed to possess no color of their own, only that which they captured and disseminated, like opals, into fiery violets and searing greens. From her position on the pool ladder she began to toy with the man in the pool, whom she called Markos, pushing his head underwater with a backthrust of her leg, ignoring Shetland's presence. Then she relented and allowed Markos up, seizing the thin gold chain around his muscular neck to assist him onto the deck. Renée told Markos that he and Rudy were to amuse themselves someplace. The Mediterranean threw Shetland a look of distaste and then walked off. Shetland watched with surprise as Rudy turned and followed Markos, his hand making a caressing pass over Markos's genitals. While Shetland was momentarily distracted Renée slipped into a dressing gown and made herself a drink from the liquor cart.

"Does the sight of men touching and fondling each other disturb you, Lieutenant, or does the special way that men have intercourse intrigue and excite?"

Shetland let the goading remark slip by. "Miss Sebastian,

now that I'm duly shocked and morally incensed, would you mind telling me why you feel the need to rattle my cage? I'm sure you don't treat the postman like this—or do you?"

"Ask your questions, Lieutenant, and then go."

"Fair enough. You provided funds for Jules Arken to carry out specialized research in bioenergetics. Do you know exactly what he was working on?"

"I would imagine, Lieutenant, that you could get a more concise answer by looking at the research institute's records."

"True," he nodded, "but the records seem to have been misplaced along with the names of the employees. The building the research facility was housed in was left completely empty, clean as a whistle. Down to the wastepaper baskets and the garbage disposal bin. The rental agents, who were pleased at such tidiness, said that their maintenance crews had almost nothing to do when they went in to refurbish the interior."

"I have no idea what Jules was working on."

Shetland laughed. "You gave him three quarters of a million dollars out of personal funds in less than eighteen months and as far as you know he could have been running a pizzeria. I can't help but notice that you don't seem terribly perturbed by his murder."

"Was it murder? I haven't read the news accounts. And as far as my concern over his death goes, Arken was a brilliant man involved in fascinating work. The combination was worthy of financial assistance. But personally I hardly knew him."

"You know, Miss Sebastian, there's an easy way and a hard way of doing things in this life. Why are you bent on the latter?"

"If you want a false anwser, Lieutenant, just say so and I will be happy to supply you with one."

Shetland was at a loss to understand Renée Sebastian's hostile attitude. If she were trying to hide something she was being awfully blatant about it, perhaps too blatant. He backed off. "How did you meet Stephen Peel?"

Renée thought for a moment, then said, "He came to one of my parties."

"On an invite?"

"I really can't recall, Lieutenant."

"Did you become good friends?"

"Lovers is the appropriate term, Lieutenant. For a short while, then just friends."

"I hate to be crude," Shetland said, "but here again it could be said your manner of mourning lacks a certain finesse."

"It's not the dead who need mourning, Lieutenant. To save you the breath of asking, I do not know why Stephen chose to end his life. It's been some time since I've concerned myself with his personal problems. If he were despondent or depressed about something, I couldn't even begin to guess what it might have been. I think our interview has come to its end."

"Not quite," Shetland retorted, his patience running out. "If you don't stop trying to rawhide me, Miss Sebastian, I'll haul you and those two gay blades down to the station house for a more formal interview, and if you don't think it can't happen, push it." For an instant she seemed cowed; she finished her drink and poured another. But when he asked to talk with her brother she came back at him with a vengeance.

"Aaron suffered a terrible accident a long time ago, Lieutenant. He hasn't seen an outsider in twenty years. Your request is absolutely out of the question. And now, I'll give you a warning. I can buy enough trouble to bury you with." She picked up the phone and called for Rudy to come down to the pool and escort the lieutenant out. When she hung up her anger had vanished. "Do you understand?" she said calmly. "I don't wish to be bothered by you or any member of your police force again."

"Do you really believe that's going to happen?"

"It better, Lieutenant," she said, then noted his distracted look. "What's the matter?" she demanded.

"I'm sorry," he apologized. "I just saw somebody watching us from the hill near that grove. Looked like a woman, but she's gone now."

"You're mistaken," she snapped sharply. "Nobody's allowed near the grove; Rudy sees to that."

Shetland didn't argue the point, partly because of her adamant insistence to the contrary and also because the glimpse was fleeting and it could have been a trick of the eye. A few moments later Rudy showed up, out of breath from running.

"Let us hope, Lieutenant, we do not meet again," Renée admonished. "I found you most disagreeable."

Shetland came away from the confrontation feeling as if he had just been mauled, and for no apparent reason. It was impossible to tell where he had struck a nerve, for she had been defensive from the word go. In either case he wasn't looking to have a run-in with the Sebastian fortune, wielded vindictively by Miss Sebastian. He believed her when she threatened him with trouble, but still he was curious. Mentioning Aaron seemed to upset her the most and he decided to do some investigating. The best place to do that without causing a stir was the newspaper morgue. He would begin with Aaron's accident.

He found a small article in the October 9, 1957 issue of a local paper that mentioned the crash of a corporate plane on the island of Martinique and provided a list of passengers. Aaron was among them, as was his father. The article was written on the day of the crash and gave few details. Oddly, he didn't come across a follow-up article until the issue of December 29. In it he learned that five of the six passengers were killed instantaneously but that a sixth, seventeen-year-old Aaron, miraculously returned from the dead. Since he'd sustained third-degree burns over sixty percent of his body in addition to extensive internal injuries, doctors held out little hope for the young heir to the Sebastian millions. After six hours of surgery and intensive medical treatment their prophecy came true: at 4:21 A.M. on October 10, Aaron Sebastian stopped living. At 4:24, in what attending physicians described as a miracle, he awoke from eternal sleep.

The long hiatus between stories disturbed Shetland. He checked with several Nassau and Suffolk County papers, looking for somebody who might have been around when the story broke. As luck would have it, one assistant managing editor had been with his paper in 1957. Shetland and the editor talked in the latter's office. "As I remember it," the editor said, "we tried to get a follow-up but nobody was giving. At one point we assumed that Aaron Sebastian had been killed in the crash with the others and that the story was being covered up because of a corporate power struggle. Nobody printed that or the nasty rumors concerning certain members of the family and the reason Aaron was on that plane with his father."

"What rumors?" Shetland asked.

The editor screwed up his face evasively. "Look," he said, "the biggest tramp of a gossip columnist didn't print that junk and it's been twenty years. I don't want to comment on it. Besides, I wasn't exactly important around here at the time and the information I had was probably inaccurate."

"You know this is a police matter," Shetland said.

"It sounds more like a fishing expedition, and I really can't remember anyway," the editor interrupted, ignoring Shetland's threat and politely ending their conversation.

Shetland had to admit, as he thought about the conversation on the drive back to Oysterville, that the guy had a point. He *was* fishing, and perhaps in the wrong pond. But the hook seemed firmly implanted in a fateful October day twenty years ago and the line which was made to appear broken in the murky waters of time still sprang taut when he jiggled it. He wasn't sure what he would eventually drag up when he reeled it in.

It wasn't much to go on, as Scalley pointed out when Shetland handed him Xeroxed copies of the newspaper articles and told him that he wanted to know all the details surrounding the crash and as much as he could dig up about the Sebastian family. "Anything and everything, and on the financial we're specifically looking for companies owned by or affiliated with corporate holdings of the Sebastian family that might be involved with or benefit from a new Kirlian photographic process."

"Would you run that by me again, Lieutenant? What kind of process?"

"Discuss the details with Finch; he's our resident expert

on Kirlian. But the companies will more than likely be involved with manufacturing industrial components for machinery, automobiles, military vehicles and aircraft. Or check out companies involved in manufacturing prefabricated building or construction materials—and, oh yes, companies experimenting with and/or manufacturing medical equipment. The possibilities are endless."

Scalley seemed exhausted just from listening to his instructions. "Lieutenant, you see before you one man. What you ask is a tall order. It would take an army of IRS auditors six months just to find out who owns what and why. I mean, what do I tell the captain if he finds out that I'm wandering around in left field researching corporate structure and finance and asks me why?"

"Tell him the truth, that you haven't the vaguest idea."

Scalley broke into a big grin. "It's going to be your tush he's going to barbecue over a slow fire. Any particular place you'd like me to start?"

Shetland nodded. "Just go with what you've got. Telex the Martinique police and request any information in their files, assuming they keep their files that far back. Try the local newspapers and the hospital records. You'll have to scrounge for the other sources because I'm warning you now, don't expect much cooperation."

The weather turned unseasonably cool overnight and Shetland woke to a Sunday morning steeped in a viscous, gray fog. Through his window, from which a patch of bay was usually visible, he could only see to the street. The fog was at its worst near the shore, and it didn't improve much inland. Traffic was light but it crawled, and he was late meeting Harry, who sat in his office guzzling hot chocolate as if it were going out of style. "It's a piss-poor day, but I guess it's appropriate for this sort of thing," Harry said, sliding a folder across the desk toward Shetland. "It's all in there."

"Save me the trouble," Shetland retorted, pushing the folder aside.

"We found heavy traces of a hallucinogenic drug in the blood cells and brain tissue of Peel and Arken. We couldn't pin it down, so while our own laboratory worked on it we sent samples to school labs, drug companies, and to Washington. It turned out to be an exotic compound derivative of a fungi and it's a military secret. We still don't know who I.D.'d it but whoever it is, did it fast. Six hours later we were getting phone calls from Washington informing us that agents from the FBI and the military secret police were on their way and we were to sit on the matter until they arrived. To be perfectly honest with you, I didn't know what the hell was coming off so I did what I was told. In fact, I was so scared, not fully knowing why, that the thought of doing any different never entered my mind."

"Good for you, Harry."

"Same to you," he sneered. "The long and the short of this is that the drug was used by the Army in an experiment to, and I quote, study and evaluate methods for nonlethal neutralization of an enemy in the field, unquote. That's all they said except that the project had been deemed a failure for reasons they didn't elaborate and was terminated on a date they also didn't see fit to enlighten us about."

Shetland slumped into his chair. "How the hell did the military get involved in this?"

"That's what the FBI would like to know. When the experiment was ended the drug was supposed to have been destroyed. As you can guess, they're not too keen on this information becoming public, especially in such a roundabout way. So you can see the dilemma they put me in."

"This is all I need," Shetland moaned, "secret agents and conspiracies."

"It's not as bad as it seems. They're going to work very discreetly at their end to find out how the theft occurred. All they asked was that the precise nature of the drug and its military connection be kept quiet for the time being."

"Why so decent?"

"They're scared that if they crack down too hard with the secrecy bit, some liberty-and-truth-in-government nut might balk and blow the whistle on them. And why? Well, there's the obvious: I suspect they've been using the standard military guinea pig, G.I. Joe, with disastrous results. I don't think they'll interfere," Harry said, "but I don't think they'll cooperate either."

"I'm content if they stay on their side of the fence." Shetland slouched in the chair, his elbows planted on the armrests and his chin snuggled contemplatively against his clenched fists. He mumbled the phrase, "Mind-altering," as if he were examining a physical object, turning in over, putting it down, then picking it up again. Finally he looked up. "What does this super drug do to the person taking it? Is it similar to a trip on, say, PCP?"

"Phencyclidine and this drug both fall into the category of hallucinogens. Both would produce illusions, hallucinations, time and distance distortion. But that's where the similarities end. Under the Controlled Substance Act this stuff would come under the psilocybin-psilocin category. It's made from the poison of mushrooms, and induces a sort of textbook case of schizophrenia. It produces twin identities, the normal you in touch with the world of sensory perception and everyday realities and then the other, totally unaware of and separate from the normal three-dimensional constraints of our world. This out-of-touch identity exists on a cognitive plane where time, space and dimension are distorted by a rather exotic hallucinogenic sensory perception where you see anything from birds with incredible plumage to rainbows. That's straight up and right out of the bottle. This stuff, I can't be sure because I don't know what the results of the experiment were or how they monkeyed with it. They could have combined it with almost anything: phencyclidine, mescaline, lysergide, or one of the synthetics like diethyltriptamine. Or perhaps, and this is my guess, some totally new concoction of their own. But the government guys were shook that the stuff was still floating around and not at the indignity of being ripped off, you can bank on that."

"How long would the effect of a dose of this stuff last?"

"It's variable, depending on the person taking it and the dosage."

"What would be the effects of an overdose?" Shetland asked.

"Like with all hallucinogens, psychosis and possible death."

"It's this particular drug I'm interested in, Harry."

Harry frowned angrily. "I've just finished explaining to you that our own people were only able to pin down the psilocybin-psilocyn. We simply don't have the facilities for any more than that. So the answer is I don't know."

"Would this twin identity in the land of Oz be capable of committing a violent act against the better nature of his other half?"

"You're thinking Peel murdered the Turners in some kind of berserk trance. No," Harry said, "it works in stages. First, complete relaxation; then lights and visions; then the two identities become aware of each other. That's when the schizophrenia sets in and the danger, but for the individual under the influence of the drug, not normally for others."

"It didn't fit anyway," Shetland sighed disgruntledly. "I'd still have to explain how he managed to pull the guy apart like a cheap watch."

"And the animal wounds. Surprise!" Harry added sardonically. "Half a dozen puncture marks in Turner's skull made by the canines of a large dog or similar animal. Ten times that number on the torso and neck. For a moment there we thought we had the murderer, but as it turned out it's only an accomplice. We checked with some experts and the fact that arms and legs were removed from the body before the fire and in the particular manner that they were, put the kobosch on that. They say the largest dogs, even wolves, don't have the power in the neck, shoulder, and jaws or the skeletal structure to inflict that sort of damage." Harry was visibly disappointed that his revelation elicited no more than a raised brow from Shetland. "You don't seem surprised. I thought you'd be bowled over when I told you like this."

"I'm getting to the point where if anything normal happened in this case I'd fall over in a dead faint." Shetland wanted desperately to talk about Peel's journal; perhaps Harry might see something that he hadn't and yet when he started to tell him about it, something inside of him wouldn't let it come out.

THE SUMMONING

The fog suited Shetland's mood when he came out of the meeting with Harry, dismal and alarmed, not at what had been said, but at the difference between his attitude and Harry's. As bizarre as this business was, Harry was taking a straight-on view; he, on the other hand, had begun to consider other possibilities—fruitcake possibilities. It occurred to him that Harry's view was likely to be the majority's and it bothered him less that he might be going over the deep end than that Harry might be wrong. He went back to his office to catch up on some paperwork. Half an hour of that and he was ready to climb the walls. He took a walk, but everything seemed to close in depressingly with the fog. A few cars sped by, their passengers hidden in grim sanctuary. A man stepped briskly down the street ahead of him, Sunday paper tucked under his arm; but by and large the world had shuttered itself indoors, turning inward against the miserable weather and the quiet fear that seemed to hang oppressively in the gray haze, as if the plague across the harbor had slipped in with the mist. When he saw the phone booth he had no second thoughts; he didn't want to be alone tonight. His hands fumbled nervously with the telephone directory. Cummings, Jessica: she was listed. His finger bent on the page. He repeated the number several times in his head, set the directory down, fed coins into the slot and dialed. The phone rang once, twice, five times; the receiver was lifted off the hook. "Hello," she said.

Forgetting to give his name, he said, "How about dinner tonight?"

There was amusement in her voice. "Sure, Lieutenant."

Loneliness for a long time had been Shetland's constant companion. It had never been a friend but until recently it had never been his enemy either. Now, being alone was the the same as pain and Shetland felt that in an uncanny way Jessica sensed that. It made him feel awkward with her, and yet at the same time he wanted to be near her. When she hopped into his car she was dressed for an expensive evening. "How did you know I wasn't taking you to a hamburger joint?"

"Are you?" she said, smiling coyly.

"No," Shetland muttered. They dined at a French restaurant in Port Jefferson. Because Shetland usually ate alone, what was generally as natural as breathing became an intimidating exercise. Despite the fact that he was about as uneasy as he could ever remember being, he enjoyed himself immensely. Jessica was beautiful and pleasant and he gorged himself on her presence like a starving animal. It showed.

"Lieutenant, you are a peculiar man. You're so openly enamored of me. Most men try to be a little more subtle about such things."

"You make it sound like I'm completely transparent."

She threw him a knowing, whimsical smile.

"To be truthful, there haven't been a whole hell of a lot of women in my life."

"You don't strike me as the shy type."

"With your common felon I can be the life of the party. With women, attractive women like you, I'm not so sure of myself."

"So there haven't been any women in your life."

"I didn't say any women. I just haven't been beating them off with a nightstick."

"Is that because you're all professional? A cop married to the force?"

"No, we're just going steady, although there's this cute little squad car I'm developing a thing for."

Jessica frowned. "They say humor is a form of self-repression."

"Yeah, and they also say firemen like putting out fires because they're too repressed to start them. And guns and nightsticks are really phallic symbols and cops are suffering from fear of castration so they like to keep a couple of spares handy just in case, et cetera, et cetera, ad infinitum."

"Why are you a cop, anyway?"

"Just something I fell into and found I was good at. Guess I could have gone either way once, I've always had a certain insight into the criminal mind." At that moment the waiter appeared and asked if they would care for an after-dinner drink.

"A daiquiri for me," Jessica said.

"Nothing for me."

When the waiter left Jessica reached across the table and laid her hand on his. "Tell me, how does it feel to shoot somebody in the line of duty?"

Shetland sighed. "Truthfully, I wouldn't know. I've never had to."

She sat back with a look of amazement and disappointment on her face. "You never killed anybody?"

"No, not as a cop. Maybe in the Army, but I don't know that for sure and that's the way I like it. I hate to say this, but your interest in this subject borders on the kinky. Is that why you're interested in me?"

For a moment Jessica seemed distracted, then she looked up at him. "I'm not sure why I'm interested in you. I might have a father fixation; you remind me of my father except you don't remind me of him at all. Also, I saw the way you defended yourself during the police commission investigation. When somebody went for a vital spot you sort of bristled up and lashed back—sometimes effectively, sometimes not, but the total was convincing because of the vulnerability. Your courage was instinctive, not affected. That's what first intrigued me about you. There are other things."

"That doesn't put me in a very complimentary light. You're saying: take a tomcat by the scruff of the neck and try to drown him in a pail of water and he'll scratch you."

"That's more or less what I'm saying, except he'll try to do more than scratch."

When the waiter returned with Jessica's drink Shetland changed his mind about having one. "A bourbon and water," he said, starting to light a cigarette, then hesitating. "You don't mind me smoking?"

"A gentleman," she said, nodding her consent.

Except for the muted light emanating from the concealed electrical fixtures in the ceiling the restaurant was illuminated by real candles. To Shetland the golden glow of candlelight and the soft brown shadows seemed to fall upon Jessica's face in such a way as to make it a portrait by a great master, suffused with timeless beauty. "You're staring, Lieutenant."

The waiter brought his drink, and Shetland was glad for the interruption. He settled back, took a sip of his bourbon and reorganized his thoughts. "I don't know much about you. You said I remind you and don't remind you of your father. What was he like?"

"Do you really want to know?" she asked skeptically.

"No."

"I didn't think so. What do you do for fun, Lieutenant? Your life can't be as mundane as you make it out to be."

"Hey, how about taking off the spurs. I have a boat."

"A sailboat—am I correct, Lieutenant?"

"Yeah, a twenty-two footer."

"What's her name?"

Shetland had a funny look on his face. "I bought it second-hand," he said. "I ever bothered to change the original owner's name for her."

"Which is, Lieutenant?"

Water Beetle.

"That's precious, the *Water Beetle.* And is she your pride and joy, to which you devote all your spare time?"

Shetland was getting annoyed. "If you mean do I have apoplexy every time a square inch of paint chips and peels, the answer is no. It's a nice boat; I like it."

"I don't mean to sound patronizing, but by the scowl on your face it's obvious that's how you took it."

"Pardon me. It just sounded like you were making fun of me."

"Well, I wasn't. Everybody has at least one thing they hold dearest above all others. I have my house by the Sound. What's yours, Lieutenant?"

Shetland grinned. "I do have something like that." He held his hands out over the table in front of him as if to mold the image. "I have this bank. I keep it on a bookshelf in my living room. It's a white porcelain reproduction of a commode, in miniature of course, called The Oysterville I-Haven't-Got-A-Pot-To-Piss-In Savings Bank."

Jessica laughed. "That's precisely the kind of thing I meant."

They talked for another hour, then Shetland drove

Jessica home. She gave him a light kiss on the cheek. "I had a good time," she said and got out of the car. Shetland watched as she made her way across the driveway to a path that led to an arched footbridge. Beneath the bridge a shallow stream passed over a rocky bed, ran in front of Jessica's house, and angled sharply to Shetland's right before vanishing into the trees above the beach and emptying into the Sound. Jessica crossed over the bridge, turned around on the other side, waved, went in the front door, and was gone. As he turned his car around in the tight space and drove off, Shetland suddenly felt let down.

CHAPTER FIVE

I T WAS A HOT MONDAY in more ways than one. Shetland had barely enough time to glance at the morning newspaper with its front-page pictures of the four victims and a space for a fifth with a question mark in it before he was swallowed up in meetings, plenary sessions, and P.R. briefings. A third-floor conference room was chosen for the meeting. Top brass, including the commissioner of police for Suffolk County, were in attendance, but the chief spokesman for the department was Captain Rutledge. The captain cut a commanding figure. He was husky with white wavy hair and penetrating, steely eyes. Shetland was there to add the latest information on the investigation and to clarify the finer tactical points. On the other side, led by Assemblyman Raymond Dority, were half a dozen district representatives, the Oysterville Town Council, members of the Chamber of Commerce of several surrounding communities whose summer tourist trade was suffering from all the publicity about the murders, and representatives of a number of concerned citizens' organizations who, for the most part, were concerned with self-preservation.

Except for the time of the opening statement, when some questions had been directed at him, Shetland had sat for the better part of two hours with nothing to do but listen to accusations and counterstatements. His eyelids heavy, he watched as Assemblyman Dority, exuding three-piece-suit credibility, again took up center stage. "It is curious," Dority said, "that in this congressional district, which pays the highest property tax in the state and one of the highest in the nation and therefore is entitled to the finest public service, should, in its greatest hour of need, find that its police force is lacking."

Captain Rutledge shot to his feet. "With all due respect, Assemblyman, the department rejects all such assertions of laxity in the discharge of its duties to the public."

Dority continued, "I must note, Captain, that it is precisely that point which has brought this concerned citizenry and their duly elected officials here to this conference." Dority held up two fingers in a "V."

Just then Scalley slipped into the room and sat down next to Shetland. "Why's he giving the V-for-victory sign?" he asked.

Shetland leaned over and whispered, "Your age is showing, Tom. I would have said that was the peace sign."

Just then Dority's voice boomed, "Two weeks and not a single positive statement indicating a resolution in the near future or the distant future of the heinous murder of two of this county's most prominent citizens. In fact, a third murder was committed in the midst of the investigation of the first two."

"Ah," Shetland chuckled under his breath, "we're both wrong. He was just showing us that he knows what two looks like."

"He's looking at you," Scalley said.

Shetland forced himself to look attentive.

Dority was holding a newspaper in his right hand and vigorously striking it with his left. "Now we see in the newspapers disturbing articles appearing about the as-yet-unreleased coroner's report. Is there any wonder that people are near panic?"

Again Captain Rutledge interrupted, "The department

sympathizes with the public's concern. Our intention at this meeting is to alleviate some of those fears and apprehensions, but there are limits as to how much detail can be released about an ongoing investigation without hampering and surely jeopardizing that investigation."

Dority's voice became almost conciliatory. "Captain, I have always supported the police in all areas, including public relations within the community; I think my record speaks for itself on that matter. But when it becomes apparent to me that the officer in charge of handling these investigations is floundering, trying to go in all directions at once, invading, in an offensive manner, private sectors and in general squandering the vast resources at his disposal without obtaining the least results, then I am forced to conclude that we are dealing with a cover-up of incompetence instead of any legitimate concern over proper procedures." Dority pointed to the five members of the Oysterville Town Council and the three members of the Crane's Neck Civic Association, and then moving his arms in a sweeping arc, said, "I've talked with the members of the respective communities involved and together we have decided we will not tolerate or endure a deranged lunatic cutting a bloody trail of murder through our communities."

"I'm foursquare for that," Shetland muttered under his breath to Scalley, "and now that we've told the killer where he can get off I say we call this bull-throwing contest to an end."

"Even now," Dority thundered, "the officer in charge shows his disinterest by his behavior at this meeting."

"That means you," Scalley said.

"I know who it means, but I'm diplomatically trying to ignore him."

The captain's voice boomed, "I will not tolerate the baiting of one of my officers."

Dority slammed the newspaper down on the seat of his chair. "Then we must insist that the senior investigating officer, Lieutenant Donald Shetland, respond to the allegations made here and not hide behind the chain of command."

"So much for diplomacy," Shetland groaned, and stood up. "If the good assemblyman would rein in that political bandwagon he just ran me over with and be more precise in his charges, then I would have something specific to answer to."

Before Shetland could get another word out, Captain Rutledge, his broad chest thrust forward, came between Shetland and Dority. "Thank you, Lieutenant," he boomed, then added in a firm whisper, "good-bye, Lieutenant. And that means sixty seconds ago."

Shetland didn't need a second verbal command to leave the meeting; the gentle shove toward the door was sufficient.

Scalley joined him in the hallway. "You lost your temper in there."

"I didn't lose my temper, I knowingly threw it away and the captain threw it back. You'd think a guy with white hair wouldn't be so intimidating. This business of the brass trying to good-face a bad situation by holding that farce of a meeting has got me all torn out of shape."

"To like being a cop means taking the good with the bad," Scalley said philosophically.

"Who likes being a cop? If I could have gotten into the plumber's union I'd be making twice what I am now and I'd only have to deal with leaky pipes and cockroaches." Inside the elevator, to Scalley's alarm, Shetland broke into laughter. "I can't believe it. They held a referendum and the killer got a no vote. That had to be Dority's idea."

"You can't blame them, Lieutenant, can you?"

"Like hell I can't. Tom, you know what's going to come out of this? The department will staunchly defend itself and then turn around and jump on my case. They'll disrupt everything and accomplish nothing. The public will be happy but in as much ignorance as it was before. Dority will have scored some brownie points with the powers-that-be and then the police department will be guilty of trying to make itself look good."

The elevator door opened and they stepped into a hallway crowded with reporters waiting for the statement that was to be released after the meeting upstairs was over. "See you around," Scalley said, and ducked into the men's room to avoid the onrush of reporters.

Shetland threw up his hands. "Hold it; I know you've all been waiting patiently for word. Sergeant Tom Scalley, who, as you saw, is momentarily indisposed due to a call of nature, will be out in a minute to give you that word." The reporters started gathering around the men's room door. "That's it," Shetland said, hurrying the group along. Then he sidestepped them and walked toward the squad room.

Sergeant Pidgeon was leaning over his desk. "Where are they going, Lieutenant?"

"Tom decided to hold his own conference in the john, and they apparently think he's got something important to say. But they'll be back."

As the morning ground on Shetland hung around his office not getting anything done because of all the commotion and confusion. To add to the turmoil, somebody from Internal Affairs was rumored to be floating around in the stationhouse, which was rapidly turning into a madhouse. Reporters trooped in and out of the squad room, asking the same questions and getting the same answers they had received five minutes earlier. Soon they just walked in, stood around for a few moments, then walked out without saying a word. Finally Pidgeon, who was at his desk, had had enough. "If you shit-heads would stop bugging our asses until we have something, then we might have something," he shouted.

What Shetland didn't need was a punch-out contest: press versus police. He came out of his office, temper in check, and said, "Please, I must insist that you confine your wanderings to the hall outside." Disgruntled, they complied.

Fifteen minutes later Scalley walked into Shetland's office with an angry, puzzled look on his face. "You're not going to believe this, Lieutenant, but those crazy newspaper reporters barged right into the men's room, demanding to hear my statement." Shetland couldn't help smiling. "It's not very funny, Lieutenant; there were women reporters. Five seconds earlier and I would have been caught in the act. I didn't even try to convince them they had made a mistake, I just shoved my way out into the hall and ran. I still can't believe it—right into the men's room, cameras flashing, the whole bit. Jesus,

81

those people will do anything for a story. Anyway, Lieutenant, I came in to tell you Martinique doesn't have a telex so I sent a Mailgram and I'm waiting for a reply, but that's not the main reason I'm here either. It's New Rochelle. They can't be positive who's supposed to be handling it here, but in either case the girl's family's got a lot of clout up there and they want action."

Shetland ran his fingers through his hair. "I haven't got the time for this," he sighed, "but you'd better fill me in on the case."

"Gloria Ester Savien, that's the girl's name. Age nineteen. Comes from a well-to-do, socially prominent family. She disappeared about a month ago, right after she had returned from vacation. She and some of her girlfriends rented a cottage on Crane's Neck for the month of June. Apparently they got into a drug scene, according to the girlfriends, with some of the locals—nothing big, a little grass. They paired off with some guys and got out of touch with each other. You know, two's company, and if they were a little more into swinging three wouldn't have been a crowd. Well, the Savien girl did too, except she paired off with a woman. Her friends never really met the woman; they just saw her from a distance a few times on the beach."

"Then how were they sure it was a lesbian thing?"

"They weren't, Lieutenant, not until the Savien girl disappeared and the parents came across love poems she had written to this woman among her personal belongings. There was an unfinished letter, with no name or address, indicating the girl's intention to be with this woman again. And that's the story."

"Well," Shetland said, "somebody in this office must have taken the call. Who?"

"I asked around and nobody remembered it. But I did some checking with some of the young men involved. They said a cop had come around asking questions a short while back. They couldn't remember the guy's name but—you aren't going to like this—they said he was the thin, lean and hungry type."

"Nothing in our file," Shetland snarled.

Scalley could see Shetland was desperately trying to contain his temper but it came through in his voice.

"No report to me, that bastard," Shetland muttered.

Scalley reminded the lieutenant that he had been on vacation for two weeks, and Shetland seemed to cool down somewhat. "All right," he said, "maybe the weasel reported to the captain and the file got mislaid. Look into it. When will Tedeschevich be back?"

"Around two."

"Good; that should give me some time to cool off. Scalley, inform the sergeant of the situation and tell him to be in my office with a mighty fine excuse when I get back."

Shetland took a ride out to Calverton, hoping that through the rental agent's records he might track down former employees of Arken's research center. The agent didn't have anything but Shetland got the man to give him a quick tour of the building. The two-story brick structure was in sight of the Calverton Air Force Base security fence. The cigar-smoking rental agent said, "As you can see, Lieutenant, it's clean as a whistle. They had all kinds of electrical equipment; even put in sinks for a lab on the second floor. It's amazing how nice they left it, considering the monkeys."

Shetland put a restraining hand on the agent's shoulder as they headed for the stairwell to the second floor.

"What's the matter, Lieutenant—seen enough?"

"You just said monkeys?"

"Yeah, that's right. They had a hell of a time getting permission to house them on commercial premises. I got the permits in my files: three dozen rhesus monkeys. You want to see them?"

"Do the permits say what the monkeys were for?"

"Experiments, that's all it says."

Shetland checked with the Brookhaven Town Zoning Board and found the permits for the zoning changes. They had been granted for purposes of postmortem research. That was all he could find out.

When Shetland returned to his office Tedeschevich wasn't there but Scalley was. "What did you find out, Lieutenant?"

"I found out that Arken's research had something to do with dead monkeys."

Scalley frowned questioningly. "Monkeys, Lieutenant?"

"Yeah, monkeys. Is that the report on the Savien girl?"

"Yes. Somehow it got filed, I assume by accident, not in the file cabinet itself but in the crack between it and the wall."

"Optimist," Shetland said, opening the report folder. Something was attached to the main body of the report. "What's this?" Shetland asked and then began to read aloud. "Duke University, Parapsychology Laboratories Summary Report. Test subject: Gloria Savien, female, age thirteen." Scalley tried to interrupt to explain but Shetland waved him off and continued reading. "Psychokinesis negative. Subject showed no ability in mind-matter manipulation. Extrasensory perception positive. Subject consistently anticipated the target with seventeen hits in twenty on ESP cards; demonstrating a strong example of displacement. Comments: Though the subject's demonstration of extramotor perception is negative, her performance in other spectrums of precognition are far above probability of chance. Therefore I recommend further study. Dr. Harold Clark, Duke University, Department of Parapsychology."

There was more, but Shetland stopped reading and looked up at Scalley. "I repeat, what's this all about?"

"Lieutenant, I asked myself that same question so I checked back with New Rochelle and they told me that the parents of the Savien girl demanded that be included with the report. They said that their daughter has been gifted since she was a child. They believe that because their daughter is sensitive she can develop a very deep and emotional rapport with certain responsive types of personalities. They insist that their daughter's relationship, despite those letters, is not homosexual, but based on this psychic compatibility."

Shetland rolled his eyes toward the ceiling. "Whatever makes them happy, but the fact remains that their daughter is still missing. Psychic simpatico," he muttered; "the next thing the Saviens will demand is that we hire a fortune teller to track down their daughter."

"Close, Lieutenant, but not a fortune teller, a psychic."

"What?"

"The Saviens have hired a telepathic detective by the name of Carla Weiss."

"I think I've heard of her," Shetland said; "she's Danish or German."

"She's Dutch, Lieutenant."

Shetland was both curious and skeptical as he laid the report folder down for a moment.

"If you can believe what you read in the newspapers, this Carla Weiss is supposed to be pretty good at finding kidnap victims, missing persons and the bodies of murder victims. More than that, Lieutenant, the Dutch police have credited her with solving two murders. She's worked for police forces in France, Belgium and some Eastern-bloc countries."

"Scalley, are you sure about this?"

"Yes, positive, Lieutenant."

"And the New Rochelle police are willing to work with her?"

"Unofficially, Lieutenant, and that only because I suspect she's going to be working here on the Island."

Shetland broke into a smile. "The captain should wrench a few lug nuts over this bit of news. And wait until the newspapers get hold of it; everybody from the captain on up to the commissioner will have a fit."

"What about you, Lieutenant?"

"Truthfully, Scalley, I don't know. I'd use a crystal ball if it would help, but if I know the ways of this department, if we so much as acknowledge that Weiss exists we'll all end up in the pine barrens handing out speeding tickets to the bunny rabbits." Shetland picked up the report again but didn't open it. "Scalley, just out of curiosity, check Weiss out through Interpol, the Dutch police and any other department she's worked with for confirmation on her credentials. If they back the claims made about her—"

"Maybe we could convince the brass, right Lieutenant?" Scalley interrupted.

Shetland nodded. "Why not. We've used people with Weiss's talent before in this country; in the Boston Strangler case, for instance. But don't advertise what you're doing.

We'll just keep this between us for the time being." Shetland sat back in his chair with his folded hands pressed to his chin and mentally reviewed the maddening events of the day, to which he now added the ludicrous way this report was handled. He could feel the frustration build up inside of him, filling his chest, then gathering like a fist-sized knot in his throat. He wanted to yell but he took in a deep breath and then sighed. "A report on a sloppy investigation has been handsomely misplaced, apparently by Sergeant Tedeschevich. That man has got to be the most thoroughly competent incompetent or something else." Shetland's temper had cooled when Tedeschevich entered his office from the squad room and stood next to Scalley. "Is this the explanation I asked for?" Shetland said, looking at the sheet of paper in Tedeschevich's hand.

"Yes, Lieutenant, and I'm sorry about any confusion that my actions may have caused, but when you read this you will see that the whole situation boils down to a misunderstanding." Tedeschevich handed the papers to Shetland, who put them off to one side of his desk.

"Why didn't you keep me informed?"

"You were on vacation and my judgment was that it was just some dotty kid skipping out on her parents; no big deal, nothing to call out the dogs for. So I turned it back to our missing persons department."

"Why didn't you inform New Rochelle of what you had done?"

"I'm sure I did."

Shetland began to strum on the top of his desk with his fingers. "I guess we're dealing with a differing interpretation of what constitutes a big deal. In the initial report you filed, or I should say misfiled, you state that the Savien girl stayed at the motel on Coast Road and that according to the hotel management the girl went out one day and never came back, leaving all her belongings in her room. I would like to know, here and now, why you didn't transmit this information to New Rochelle and why one of their police officers had to come down here on his own time to find it out."

"Lieutenant," Tedeschevich snapped, "I wrote that explanation out, assuming you would read it first."

"Are you objecting to this informal inquiry?" Shetland asked.

"You're damn right, Lieutenant, because this doesn't sound like an informal inquiry to me," Tedeschevich snapped.

Shetland began looking about the room. "Sergeant, do you see a stenographer taking down what we say? Or maybe you think the room is bugged and the captain is listening to everything we're saying? If that's the case we can go out in the parking lot."

"Of course the lieutenant's being facetious, but I think he understands my meaning."

"No, Sergeant, I'm not being facetious, and no, I do not understand your meaning."

"I merely wish to protest the manner in which this interrogation is being conducted."

Shetland shook his head in bewilderment. "Okay, Sergeant, we'll do it your way. I'll read your written statement and after that we'll have this informal talk. That's it; you can go." Tedeschevich hesitated. "Is there something else, Sergeant?"

"Yes, Lieutenant. I think at this stage of the game matters of my conduct in this case should be put before the captain without any further exchange between us."

"Sergeant, are you claiming bias on my part?"

"Lieutenant, I'm not claiming anything other than my rights."

Shetland was angry but he managed to present a calm exterior. "You're dismissed, Sergeant."

"Lieutenant, may I know what you intend to do about my request?"

Shetland shuffled some papers on his desk. "You may. And when I've decided I'll let you know."

Sergeant Tedeschevich turned around and walked out of the office.

"What was that all about?" Scalley asked.

"Damned if I know, Scalley."

"Lieutenant, I read his initial report on the Savien girl,

and I'll be damned if I'd want the captain to see that kind of police work if I were responsible for it. The note the girl supposedly left telling her family that she was leaving to be with her female lover was typewritten and unsigned. Tedeschevich sent the note up to New Rochelle without giving the slightest indication that he considered it suspicious. And then in his personal comments on the report, he made out like there was no question in his mind that the girl was just another runaway."

"It's obvious he was only going through the motions on this one."

"It doesn't make sense, Lieutenant. Instead of trying to bury the whole matter the sergeant wants to make a big deal out of it. It doesn't figure."

"It does," Shetland said, "if the sergeant's gambling that I'll let it drop before I get involved in another official investigation."

"You really think that's what he's up to?"

"I don't know, Scalley. I'm admittedly prejudiced against him so I think it's best I don't go around attributing seamy motives to his actions. Now, I'd like you to do something for me. Catch up with the sergeant and inform him that on my orders he is relieved of all other duties except the Savien case until he's cleaned up the botch job he's made of it to this and the New Rochelle police department's total satisfaction. I know I should personally bring this matter to the captain's attention immediately but I haven't got the time. Mrs. Peel's flight from California should be arriving at Kennedy Airport in about an hour and a half; if I rush, I'll make it there in time to meet her."

"I suppose," Scalley said, "she's coming here for her husband's funeral. Has the coroner released the body yet?"

"No, but I'm sure there are matters to settle about her husband's estate that she can look into while she's waiting to bury him. Well, I've got to get going."

"Lieutenant, can I ask one question? It's sort of personal."

"Sure, if you don't mind if I don't answer it."

"Would you push this thing with the sergeant if you felt the situation warranted it?"

"To tell you the truth, I don't know."

Shetland had made several long-distance telephone calls to Mrs. Peel in the past week and through those conversations had learned that she had been living in Los Angeles since separating from her husband three years earlier. She owned and operated several boutiques. Reluctantly she agreed to the peculiar plan whereby Shetland would meet her at the airport and drive her out to Crane's Neck so they could talk alone in the car for a few hours without the intrusion of reporters and lawyers. To avoid the news media, he had persuaded the airline to allow them to meet in the crew's lounge. There was a brief introduction, then a hurried walk to the employees' parking lot and a quick getaway before their ruse was discovered by the press. Mrs. Peel was in her early forties, attractive with an air of self-assurance that gave Shetland the initial impression that she was emotionally detached from her husband's tragic death. Only when they were swallowed up in the anthill surge of homeward-bound commuter traffic did her icy aloofness melt; her eyes filled with tears that would not be shed and her head fell wearily into her hands. "I feel like I'm burying my husband for the second time," she said. Her voice was thick with emotion. "It's just too much," she sighed without further explanation of her peculiar statement.

Shetland had never found any comfortable way of doing this sort of thing except to proceed as slowly and with as much compassion as possible and still get the job done.

"I don't know how I can help," she said. "Stephen's life for the past few years is a complete mystery to me."

"I'm not sure you can help, and I'm not sure I even know what I'm looking for, but there are some unanswered questions about your husband's death—"

"Are you suggesting that perhaps Stephen didn't take his own life?" she interrupted.

"There's no question about that," he said. "It was suicide." She became visibly disheartened. He didn't want to pepper her with a lot of questions and he simply allowed their conversation to flow as it would. It was painful and labored at first, but eventually he got around to asking what sort of man her husband was.

"If you mean," she said with hurt anger in her voice, "was he suicidal, the answer is no. Not the man I married and lived with for seven years." At that point she began to open up and Shetland listened quietly, without interrupting. "To love people the way he did you had to love life. Life was sacred to him and the quality of life paramount. He worked and strived, in his career, to achieve a meaningful existence, not only for himself but for others. Stephen was a man of passion and compassion. Those are hardly the qualities of a suicidal man." The tears she had been holding back suddenly flowed. She wept and her voice quivered but she didn't falter. She spoke randomly and then began to zero in on the breakup of their marriage. She spoke of a swimming accident that her husband had suffered. "It was an unfair, irrational happenstance. Stephen liked to swim and he liked Coney Island because it was always full of people. It was a warm hazy Sunday in late July, and . . . it was like innocence being violated. Stephen was out swimming and suddenly, without the earth trembling or dark foreboding clouds ominously filling the sky, they dragged him up onto the beach not twenty feet from where I lay on the blanket. He was unconscious, his eyes were closed, and water was trickling out of his mouth. The lifeguard tried to revive him right there but it didn't work. They carried him off the beach and rushed him to the hospital; I rode with him in the ambulance. He stopped breathing, so they gave him oxygen and worked over him. When they reached the hospital one of the ambulance attendants shouted that he just went under, he was dead. They hauled him into the emergency room anyway and worked like maniacs. A minute passed, then two. Mindlessly I watched, feeling nothing. The only thing I really remember was somebody telling me that my husband was responding; he was alive. I don't believe the implication of that registered; death was something you didn't come back from. They took him up to a private room and an hour later I was able to see him. His eyes stared, not at anything in the room, but almost as if they were turned inward. I had the feeling right then that something was wrong; something was different about him. Later when he had recovered but was still in the hospital we had a long talk. I should say he talked and I listened. He was like a mystic proclaiming the revelation of God in death. He said he had seen the true light at the end of a tunnel. He said dying was not a terrifying or painful experience as he had thought it would be. He said when he went under it was very dark at first, but it was a warm, comforting darkness; he said he felt very secure and described it as what a human first must experience in his mother's womb. Then he said the dark began to fall away; he said it was like coming out of a tunnel. Voices were summoning him toward this light which Stephen described as a brilliant illumination beyond all earthly imaginings and which, despite its intensity, was not harsh or blinding. He said how he was able to see the hospital staff working to revive him. He described the scene later on to his doctors and it was accurate—frighteningly so, I might add—down to what the doctors and nurses were wearing and the conversations they had. Stephen said that at this point in the experience he had no desire to return to the living and he tried to tell the doctors that but they couldn't hear him or the voices he heard beckoning him to the other side; one was that of his grandmother. Stephen was quite devoted to her when she was alive. Eventually his grandmother appeared from this light that now totally encompassed him, not as an old woman but young, as Stephen had seen her in the family photo albums. He said his joy and contentment at this point was overpowering. He followed her to a river of blue and gold and many other colors. He said it was like a liquid rainbow, and on the other side of this river lay a paradise beyond the powers of the human mind to create or speech to describe. He was led across that river to a place he wouldn't talk about other than to describe the terrible anguish he felt when he was forced to return to the living. I've told you this, Lieutenant, because I can't think of anything else in Stephen's life that might explain his act.

"They saved the body and the intellect," she said, "but the soul was gone. The hard truth came a short time later. The

Stephen I loved was no more. All that remained was the shell inhabited by a wretched, twisted obsession with death. I talked with psychiatrists, and they told me that a profound personality change in such cases was not uncommon. Three weeks later our marriage, in everything but name, was over. After that I never saw or heard from Stephen again." Mrs. Peel regained her composure but the rigidity was gone. She wiped the tears from her eyes and asked Shetland for a cigarette.

"Just like that he walked out? Your relationship had gotten that strained in such a short time?"

Mrs. Peel laughed. "There was no strain and there was no relationship. Stephen completely shut me out. He didn't want any help or any part of me any more. I found myself despising him because he turned everything we had together into nothing so quickly and seemingly without remorse. I hated him for changing, even if it wasn't his fault. It's like having the rules changed in a game and suddenly you go from being a winner to a loser. At least that's how I looked at it. I couldn't feel sorry for Stephen and I think that later on that bothered me the most. But it's over with and maybe Stephen's return was a mistake and maybe the error's been corrected. I don't hate him anymore; I can even feel pity. Not for Stephen Peel, because he died three years ago, but for that bewildered being, a thing of death exiled in life. It's over," she repeated and then for the first time since they met she managed to smile philosophically.

"I don't think I'm going to feel comfortable in Stephen's house but I'm afraid I'll have to endure it, at least until I know when the body is going to be released for burial and the lawyers can be more specific about how long it's going to take to settle Stephen's estate. I've been told by the lawyers that the estate, after taxes, is well over three hundred thousand dollars. It sounds terrible to say, but I could use the money."

Shetland smiled. He had begun to like Mrs. Peel. "On the contrary, I think it would be more terrible to say you couldn't use three hundred thousand dollars. I'd have been sick with envy."

The slight laugh that she allowed herself was warm and

friendly, which made the prospect of her staying at Stephen Peel's house even more loathsome to Shetland. It was something he had not allowed himself to dwell upon, but he simply did not like the place. It was nothing tangible, just a feeling that something there was wrong, out of sync. "Maybe," he said, "for your own emotional well-being you should put other considerations aside and take a room in town. You said it yourself; you're bound to feel uncomfortable with old memories and the like."

"Thank you for your concern, Lieutenant, but I'm sure once I get used to it I'll be all right."

Shetland nodded and said no more about it. When they arrived at the house her lawyers and some reporters were waiting. "I was hoping you'd miss that," Shetland said.

"That's okay. When they find that I have nothing to tell them I'm sure they'll go away."

"You won't reconsider, Mrs. Peel?"

She looked at him questioningly. "About staying at the house? No. But it will be all right."

"What now, Mrs. Peel?"

She sighed, "I bury a stranger and then I go home."

Shetland helped her with her bags, then in the midst of pushing and jostling said good-bye.

The disturbing stories in the newspapers and the nasty rumors that had been circulating through official and public channels from the beginning were rudely and shockingly given the stamp of truth when the coroner's report was released. Whitewashing euphemisms and befuddling medical jargon did little to blunt its alarming effect. The moribund fear that had settled over the town of Oysterville and the surrounding communities turned into silent panic. Phone calls demanding action from the police came in torrents, along with pressure from the top brass in the department, political cajoling and threats.

When Shetland got to his apartment he was too keyed up to sleep and he spent a good part of the night staring out the kitchen window at the park across the street. The small-town scene gave him a comforting feeling. The park lay alongside

the Oysterville harbor, and had a walkway with benches close
to the water's edge where people could sit and watch the boats
come and go. There was a baseball diamond with bleachers
at one end and a music shell at the other. School bands gave
concerts there all through the summer. When Shetland turned
away from the window and wandered about the apartment
his mind formed disturbing images of Peel, Arken and the
Turners, and always there were the questions to complete the
grim montage. The images and questions seemed to pursue
him through the two and a half rooms until finally he threw
on his jacket and went out for a walk.

He stepped softly down the outside stairs so as not to
disturb anybody in the house, then down the driveway and
across Bay Avenue. A few blocks to his left was the main
street of town. The traffic light at the intersection of Main
and Bay blinked red and then green but there was no traffic
to follow its commands. Though first light was already high
in the sky and the lamp-post lights in the park had shut off,
night would stay a little longer because of the fog, the fog
that always formed in the evening over the Sound and then
crawled up the rivers, inlets and bays and into the streets of
the coastal towns as morning approached. Sometimes it was
no more than a thin mist; this morning it was thick, like a
white wool blanket drawn up over the face of a disturbed
sleeper. The dampness put a chill in the air that sent shivers
through Shetland's body. He pulled up his jacket collar and
rubbed his hands together as he picked up his pace. He crossed
the eastern corner of the park and then the parking lot that
serviced both the park and the dock area. He reached the
gate that led onto the piers, pushed it open, stepped through
and then closed it behind him. Just inside the gate he paused
to look inside the guard shack to identify himself to the
watchman. Seeing that there was no one about, he walked
halfway out onto the section of the pier that jutted out into the
harbor. There was an open shelter at the end of the pier,
where there were usually a couple of anglers with pails full
of live bait, fishing for the flounder that were abundant in the
water around the pier supports. This morning there was no
one. He went down the gangplank to the floating dock, his

feet making a hollow, clomping sound on the weathered boards. His boat was tied up at the last in a long line of slips. As he stood at the end of the floating dock looking at his boat, his hands shoved into his pants pockets, he could feel his troubled thoughts swirling around him like the fog. Shetland began to talk aloud to himself: "Stop giving yourself problems. A place for everything and everything in its place. Terrific, but every time I think I've got it all separated and go for a solid lead something happens and my fingerpaints get all mushed together and there's no more sharp colors, just muck-brown."

A prickly feeling at the back of his neck stopped his conversation with himself, and he turned around. There was a man standing inside the gate. An anxious moment passed and then a flashlight was turned on him. Blinded, Shetland called, "Hey, I'm not doing a floor show out here. Turn that thing off."

"Sorry, Lieutenant. I didn't know it was you." The flashlight went off. The night watchman came toward him. Shetland had talked a dozen times with the old man; he knew he was a retired fireman but he couldn't remember his name or if he'd ever known it. "How's it going?" Shetland asked.

"Fine as always, Lieutenant. You taking your boat out today? Once the fog lifts it should be good sailing weather."

"No, I'm just out for a stroll."

"Haven't had too many people doing that lately because of all the trouble, but then I guess you know about that better than me, right, Lieutenant?"

Shetland would have liked to say, "You wish," but he nodded with a knowing look on his face.

The night watchman stood face to face with Shetland and was about to say something when he averted his gaze. In the momentary pause Shetland turned to look where the watchman's eyes were directed. "Here she comes," the watchman said.

Straining to pierce through the masking fog, Shetland caught sight of a boat's running lights approaching from the other side of the harbor. All pretense of conversation died as he intently watched the glimmering specks thread their way between the channel marker buoys. In a few moments the faint throb of diesel engines could be heard. The running lights faded momentarily as the vessel passed through a dense patch of fog, and then a broad white lapstrake bow emerged from the gray mist. Without seeing her identifying marks Shetland knew the craft. She was the *Carlisle*, something of a port celebrity and the only deep-water lobster boat still working out of Oysterville Harbor. The *Carlisle*'s engines grew louder as she pulled abreast of the floating dock some twenty yards out in the channel. A figure appeared in the dimly lit wheelhouse and waved to them. Shetland waved back and then the boat slid past, white water breaking in front of her bow and churning up as she turned her fantail stern to them. In a few moments all that was visible of the *Carlisle* were her running lights and then they were gone too.

CHAPTER SIX

EARLY THE NEXT MORNING Shetland was called into a meeting with Captain Rutledge. He assumed it had something to do with the statement that was to be released to the press later in the day. Just as he was going in, Ray Dority, the state assemblyman, walked out of the captain's office. They brushed past each other without exchanging a word. Dority gave Shetland that same vivisecting smile he had given him all during the police probes over a year ago. For an instant Shetland was overcome with the urge to punch his shit-eating grin right to the back of his head, but he restrained himself. When he walked into the office and saw Steve Jackson from Internal Affairs sitting on the edge of the captain's desk and the captain looking perturbed, Shetland put himself on guard. Jackson noticed Shetland's apprehension and excused himself, telling Captain Rutledge that he'd get back to him later.

"Jackson's presence," said the captain in a matter-of-fact way, "has nothing to do with you."

"Since I didn't ask about Assemblyman Dority either,

should I think he's here on a goodwill tour of inspection?" Shetland asked.

"The assemblyman was simply sharing the concern of his constituency in consulting on their behalf with the police department as to the progress of the ongoing investigation."

Shetland couldn't help but laugh. "Captain, the only constituency Dority's concerned about are the handful that can further his political career, most of whom live on Crane's Neck. The rest he could give two figs about, except on election day."

The captain closed his right hand into a fist and cocked his arm as if to send that fist slamming down on his desk, but instead a thick index finger shot out and pointed at Shetland. "I don't want to hear this," the captain said, the tone of his voice unchanged. "I understand you have a man —Scalley, I believe—who is wandering somewhat far afield in this investigation. With all hell breaking loose over our heads I don't think it wise that valuable man-hours be expended in looking into something that happened twenty years ago with a family that, at this moment, has no connection with our investigation. Unless you have information to the contrary, I suggest you reel in your man."

"Not to be argumentative, Captain, but since I didn't give you that information I'd like to know how you came by it."

"Lieutenant, I have been trying to overlook the fact that I didn't read it in your reports; how I came by it is not important. What is important is that the public maintain confidence in its police department and not get the impression that we are negligent in our duties. You were at the meeting—most of it, at any rate—so I shouldn't need to tell you this."

"Begging the captain's pardon, but I think the matter is important; it puts my position as senior investigating officer in question."

"Look, Lieutenant, I don't want to go to war over this. As your commanding officer I am advising you that our resources in manpower are spread thin as it is, and unless you have a good reason to justify continuing the investigation

relating to the Sebastian family, I'm ordering you to call
Scalley off and assign him to more fertile fields of endeavor."

"I don't suppose the captain could suggest where I might
find this fertilized field of endeavor?"

Captain Rutledge's face darkened with a menacing flush
of anger and his index finger pointed to the door. "You can
start outside this office."

"Captain, I apologize for saying that, but since we're
worried about credibility, think of how it's going to look to
the public if we back away from a legitimate course of investigation. They're bound to say we did it just because the
Sebastians have power and wealth and friends like Assemblyman Dority to run interference for them. And there is a
connection."

The captain shook his head. "Certainly not enough of
one, Lieutenant."

"Maybe not, Captain, but to point out the obvious, we
can't be sure unless we look into it."

"Since you want to talk about legitimate, Lieutenant, by
your own obstinacy you've forced me to lay it out to you
straight. There is legitimate cause for concern about the manner in which you have been conducting yourself in this whole
matter. I know your department got this Savien case because
the missing girl's family insists there's foul play involved,
though more than likely it belongs to missing persons. But
that doesn't mean we are going to go along with every
fanciful whim that they or the New Rochelle police department has. And so there'll be no misunderstanding, the particular whim I'm referring to is Mrs. Carla Weiss. Department personnel and department procedure are all that are to
be used in the investigation."

"Captain, I know it's against procedure, but since you've
got this crystal ball . . ."

"That's enough, Lieutenant," the captain said sharply.
Shetland expected the captain to blow his top but, instead,
his mood changed. The sternness in his bearing gave way to
the strain of pressure. "Look," he said, "I have no bone to
pick with you. I have long since accepted the fact that you're
something of a maverick. If I hadn't, you'd still be a de-

tective first grade. You've been given orders—act accordingly."

"Captain, are those orders subject to interpretation?"

"They most certainly are not, Lieutenant."

"Captain, the way you phrased that—"

"Lieutenant, get out of here—now!"

Shetland returned to his office and called Scalley in. "Somebody has been shooting his mouth off to the captain about what we've been doing down here, and in detail."

"Are you accusing me, Lieutenant?" Scalley asked.

"I'm not accusing anybody, Scalley."

"That's what it sounds like."

"Damn it, Scalley, I can't help what it sounds like."

"I'm the one you've been working with and I'm the one you're addressing your accusations to."

"It's not an accusation." Shetland was surprised. "You're a bit thin-skinned, aren't you?"

"Yeah sure, Lieutenant, and I'm offended that you think that I might be the one."

"Scalley, whatever you perceive my thoughts to be, please be offended later." Shetland closed the door to his office. "What I want to know from you is, have you been discussing your assignments with Sergeant Tedeschevich or anyone else?"

"No, Lieutenant."

"Okay, Scalley. Then you tell me how anyone else but you and I should know the details of those assignments?"

"I can't say for sure, Lieutenant, but the sergeant and the rest of us work in relatively close contact. If one of them were so inclined, I don't imagine it would be very hard to figure out what I was doing."

"In such detail, Scalley? Has anyone shown a special interest in what you've been doing? The sergeant, for instance?"

"No, Lieutenant, not particularly, not any more than Casey or the others."

"Come on; think, Scalley. Try to remember . . ."

Scalley cut him off angrily. "Lieutenant, there's nothing

to remember. I do my work; I don't watch who's watching me."

"Damn," Shetland said, "now can you appreciate my predicament? My gut reaction is to say Sergeant Tedeschevich is behind this—and don't get that look on your face, Scalley. I don't like the guy either personally or professionally—with good reason, I think—and yet there is a question of whether certain information is accessible to him."

Scalley cut in, "And that brings you back to me, right, Lieutenant?"

Shetland sighed. "Maybe it should, but if I didn't know you better than that I'd have to pack this detective business in."

"Should I take that as a vote of confidence, Lieutenant?"

Shetland glared at Scalley. "Don't get a stick up your ass. Whoever is doing this has gone beyond a screw job; he's deliberately trying to derail this investigation. Maybe this all has to do with I.A. nosing around."

"Isn't that good, Lieutenant? If there's something wrong at least we know that Internal Affairs is aware of it and doing something about it."

"I'm afraid, Scalley, I don't have as much faith in I.A. as you seem to. To put it plainly, one of us apples in this barrel is rotten and I don't think I.A. knows which."

"That doesn't put any of us in a very comfortable position, does it, Lieutenant?" Scalley was not the sort to lose his temper but suddenly he exploded with anger. "I think this situation stinks. You ask accusing questions of me and I'm supposed to understand, and okay, so I understand, and then maybe it's the sergeant or Casey and it's not even clear what's going on or why." Scalley took a deep breath and exhaled in frustration, then added in a calmer voice, "With everybody under suspicion, how are we supposed to work?"

"First of all, by not running away with ourselves. Nobody's under suspicion of anything yet. Second, we work like we always have. All I ask from you is that you be more conscientious of who's minding your business. If the I.A.

investigation has anything to do with us we'll hear about it soon enough."

"That's how we leave it, Lieutenant?"

Shetland chewed pensively on his lower lip. "I'm afraid so."

"I still think it's a stinko situation."

"I grant you, Scalley, it ain't a bed of roses."

A few moments after Scalley left Shetland's phone rang. "Lieutenant," said the caller, "my name is Richard Bates. I'm the legal representative for the Savien family."

"What can I do for you, Mr. Bates?"

"The Savien family has retained the services of Mrs. Carla Weiss—"

"Yes," Shetland interrupted, "I'm aware of the fact."

"Perhaps you know who she is and what she is?"

"Yes, Mr. Bates, I do."

"Good. Then I will get directly to the point. Mrs. Weiss is staying at the Land's End Motel. I would like to arrange a meeting with you and Mrs. Weiss to discuss setting up a cooperative effort in finding the missing Savien girl."

Shetland slumped down into his chair, exhaled heavily and said, "I'm afraid, Mr. Bates, such a meeting would be inappropriate and unadvisable from the department's point of view."

"Lieutenant, I appreciate the situation this might put the department in, but I also feel that any method, no matter how unorthodox, that can successfully return this girl to her family warrants at least further exploration."

"I'm afraid, Mr. Bates, that even if I agreed with you I don't have the authority to get this department involved in the situation you are describing."

"Lieutenant, I don't mean to be argumentative but I was informed otherwise."

"I'm sorry, Mr. Bates, but I don't see any way we're going to be able to get together on this."

Bates paused, then tried to conceal his irritation as he said, "I'm disappointed, Lieutenant, not for myself but for the Savien family. I'm sure in their state of mind they're not going to understand this refusal on your people's part to aid in finding their daughter. Good-bye, Lieutenant."

Shetland set the phone down on its cradle and said aloud to himself, "I'm not sure I do either, Mr. Bates." He leaned forward and nestled his cheek on his clenched fist. He stared at the phone, then glanced up toward the ceiling. The captain's office was just above him. He said, "Screw it," got up from his desk and walked out of his office.

In any other locale the privately owned Land's End Motel would have been a dive, but because it was near the water, with its own boat ramp, and since the seafood served in its restaurant was among the best on Long Island, it drew enough summer tourists and local patrons to make money. Carla Weiss had taken the room next door to the one the Savien girl had occupied. When Shetland knocked, a young man in a dark suit answered. "Yes, can I help you?" he said.

"I'd like to speak to Mrs. Weiss."

"I'm the attorney representing the Savien family and I've already explained to the press that we're not looking for publicity. I know you're only trying to do your job, but I must insist that the family's rights be protected." With that, the door closed in Shetland's face.

Shetland was about to knock again when the door opened and the lawyer, confused and sheepish-looking, said, "Are you a police officer?"

Shetland nodded. "I was the one you talked with a quarter of an hour ago over the telephone."

"Incredible," the lawyer said, and with a sweep of his arm he ushered Shetland in.

When Shetland entered the small motel room he saw Carla Weiss sitting on the edge of the bed. She was using several magazines as a portable desk on which she was feverishly writing a stack of postcards. She was an attractive woman with curly salt-and-pepper hair framing her face. He guessed her to be somewhere in her early fifties.

"This is Lieutenant Shetland, Mrs. Weiss," Bates said.

Mrs. Weiss looked up from her work momentarily and said, "Please, Lieutenant, have a seat. I'll be with you in just a moment. My family insists on postcards when I travel, mostly my daughters and youngest son. They get very upset with me if I forget, which usually I do unless I buy them and fill them out and get them in the mail as soon as I arrive."

"There's no rush, Mrs. Weiss. This isn't an official visit."

"I didn't imagine it was," she said with a pleasant laugh and a patient shake of her head. "Perhaps, Mr. Bates, the lieutenant would like some refreshments while he waits."

"Would you care for something?" the lawyer asked.

"No thanks."

Bates seemed uncomfortable. "I was hoping," he said to Shetland, "that your arrival was an indication that you had changed your mind about working with Carla, but now I get the impression that's not the case."

"Your impression is correct, Mr. Bates, but as far as the department is concerned, you and Mrs. Weiss are tourists."

"Considering the circumstances, I would think the police would gladly accept help from any quarter, especially from a woman of Mrs. Weiss's reputation."

Shetland shrugged. "The department's got its problems, Mr. Bates, but in their defense you have to realize that they are subject to pressures that they have to yield to occasionally. Regardless of Mrs. Weiss's reputation, this is a delicate area."

"I of course expected this sort of attitude," Bates countered sharply.

"Look, Mr. Bates, you got half of what you wanted. I'm here to talk with Mrs. Weiss."

"I'm afraid, Lieutenant, some unofficial chitchat wasn't quite what I had in mind."

"If that's not satisfactory I can go out that door with less difficulty than I had coming in," Shetland snapped.

Suddenly Mrs. Weiss got up off the bed and before Bates could respond, she handed him a stack of postcards. "Would you be so kind as to mail these for me and check to see if everything is ready in the next room? We'll want to get started as soon as possible."

Restraining his anger, Bates took the postcards and stalked out of the room.

"Despite what you said to our young lawyer friend, to me your presence here indicates a man willing to accommodate the necessities of an unusual situation."

"Within reason, Mrs. Weiss. If there's no publicity I can't see where anyone need get hurt by our working together. If in fact we *can* work together."

"You have doubts, Lieutenant?"

"The newspapers seem to be willing to give you more credit for your services than the law-enforcement agencies you've worked for previously."

"I see that you've checked me out—is that what it's called?" she asked.

"Yep, that's what it's called."

"And you got negative reports but you still came here. Why, may I ask, is that, Lieutenant?"

"Let's just say I've smelled sour grapes before."

Mrs. Weiss broke into a broad smile. "Yes, sour grapes, professional pride, bureaucratic arrogance. You see through that and yet you are still skeptical. Good. That's the way it should be. You will look upon what I do with a discerning eye and in that way you will see it is not a parlor game."

"Okay, Mrs. Weiss, for the time being you lead and I follow. Where do we begin?"

"Lieutenant, I always begin with a cup of tea, so we will go to the restaurant and then we will talk." She hooked her arm through his and together they walked out of the motel room. When they got outside they saw Bates and another man moving suitcases and clothes on hangers from a car into the room the Savien girl had occupied. "Those are the things sent back to the family, the things the missing girl left in her room. I will explain the purpose of them being here later."

In the restaurant they found a table where they could see the Savien girl's room. With a straw, Shetland stirred the mass of ice in his glass of Coke while Mrs. Weiss sipped her tea. Finally, she said, "I should perhaps tell you something about myself, Lieutenant, other than what you've probably already read in your reports and the newspapers."

"It's not necessary to divulge personal details of your life, Mrs. Weiss."

"Oh, but I think it is, Lieutenant. Should you decide to help, then it will benefit both of us if there is no misunderstanding as to what I am or claim to be. Sometimes the papers have referred to me as a professor or doctor. I am neither. I am a schoolteacher: I teach French and English to thirteen- and fourteen-year-olds. I have seven children of my own. The oldest I had when I was just seventeen; he's nearly thirty now. My youngest is six. I have two grandchildren."

"I see why you were writing so many postcards," Shetland said.

"Some of those were for my students; all of them are very bright, inquisitive children and, of course, to them America is of great interest."

Shetland noticed that Mrs. Weiss's eyes became expressive and her face enlivened. "I gather," he said, "that you like children a lot."

"Of course, of course," she smiled, "they are the purpose of life. People always ask religious and philosophical questions—what is the meaning and purpose of existence?—and their answers are complex and esoteric, when the true answer is simply: children." A mischievous glint came into her eyes. "I'm afraid, Lieutenant, I was one of those women who enjoyed being pregnant. I definitely would not have been popular with the League for Zero Population Growth."

Shetland burst into laughter. "I suppose not, Mrs. Weiss. I guess they'd brand you as something of a rogue."

"Yes, yes, a rogue," she chuckled, "the merry pregnant lady. Thank God none of my three husbands were alarmists."

"Three husbands?" Shetland said.

"I know, it sounds like I enjoyed being married too, but I was a widow in each case."

"I'm sorry about that, Mrs. Weiss."

"I've had much good in my life and some sorrow, but I have also been fortunate to have known three men intimately and I have learned a great deal from each of them and have grown as a person because of them. Everything in life runs its course," she smiled, "but, of course, it's best if it doesn't run too fast."

"You know, Mrs. Weiss, your way of putting things makes just about anything sound almost sane. I guess I can't help but like somebody like that."

"From the first, I knew we would be friends," she said warmly. "I was not wrong about your vibrations—very positive, very instinctual."

Suddenly Shetland stopped stirring his drink and his eyes widened. "My vibrations?"

She smiled knowingly. "Yes. They are on a very basic elemental plane, almost primitive."

Shetland wrinkled his brow skeptically and narrowed his gaze. "It sounds like I'd get into trouble giving off those kind of vibrations."

"That, Lieutenant, would depend on who's picking them up. I find them very intriguing."

"Well, I'm glad at least I don't have to apologize for unknowingly flirting with you on a subliminal plane, but I'm not sure what this has to do with why I came to see you."

Mrs. Weiss's smile turned into a laugh. "Have I embarrassed you, Lieutenant?"

"Yes, Mrs. Weiss, I think you have."

"Good. We have touched each other personally; as I said from the beginning, that is important. We will both be more receptive to each other's thoughts. Now perhaps we are ready to talk about why we have come together in the first place. I consider the power that I have as a gift. I attach no spiritual or supernatural connotations to it. I have studied it and tried to understand it in the context of this world. Wherever possible, I use it to help and I do not try to exploit it for personal gain. I take money only to defray the cost of travel or time lost from my job. Perhaps, Lieutenant, you should tell me what you are thinking."

"Mrs. Weiss, I suppose I should ask you a lot of questions but I'm not sure I know enough to even begin. Yet I am curious. I noticed a look on your face when we passed the Savien girl's room. Something seemed to be disturbing you."

"Very observant, Lieutenant, and quite correct in your interpretation. I was disturbed. On the plane coming here I was eager to get started, but now not so much."

"What changed your mind?"

Mrs. Weiss had a curious kind of smile that was almost a frown on her face. "I don't think you need me to tell you that. You may not have paid heed to it, but what most people have come to call the sixth sense has already been sending you warning signals. Be quiet and very still and listen; that's what I do. We have five senses we normally call on: taste, smell, touch, sight and hearing. But let's say I let one of those senses dominate the others; let's say I'm a very verbose person—I speak loudly, I yell. When I yell I cannot hear, and if I'm always doing this eventually I get to think no one is saying anything. If I never stop yelling I soon forget altogether that there is such a thing as hearing. A poor analogy, perhaps, because vocalizing is not one of the senses, but let us hope it suffices to illustrate my point."

Mrs. Weiss took a sip of her tea and then continued, "All higher forms of animals have the five senses and, to a greater or lesser degree, the sixth. The information thus collected from these senses is subject to interpretation by the mind. Yet, sophisticated and unique as it may be, the mind is nothing but an organ within the body, like the heart or the kidneys or the liver; a product of evolution like the arrangement and size of the teeth in our jaws. Most animals are specialists, with one sense predominating over the others. The dog smells his world, the cat sees his world and the bat hears his. Humans are less specialized; we tend to utilize five of the six senses equally, but the sixth is, in a manner of speaking, the quiet one, the one paid the least attention, though it is the one with the most to say to us."

"Well, Mrs. Weiss, I'm willing to give the new kid on the block a chance if it can help find out what happened to the Savien girl."

"New is a misnomer, Lieutenant, as is the term 'sixth sense.' You see, the power of the cognitive to transmit

thought and derive information from the physical environ-
ment is not an evolutionary advancement, and therefore it is
not the sixth sense but the first. I imagine it has been with
us since the first life wriggled and squirmed in the primordial
sea of creation. I see it as the nucleus from which the first
primitive mind was born. It's a wholly heretical concept if
you're a strict evolutionist. This power, being an integral part
of life, has grown up and advanced, and in the human race it
has reached the pinnacle of refinement, a great attribute
which, as I said, we totally misunderstand and ignore, at the
very least. At the very worst, we clothe it in mystical super-
stition." Mrs. Weiss emptied her teacup to the last drop and
said, "I think we should begin."

Bates was waiting for them in the Savien girl's room. The
shades were drawn and the curtains pulled. "Everything's the
way it was," he said, "when the girl was reported missing."

Mrs. Weiss looked around. "Please turn on the bedside
lamps. The air conditioner makes too much noise—please
turn that off." Then she turned to Shetland. "Shut the door,
please."

The moment the air conditioner went off the room fell
into silence and began to grow stiflingly warm. Bates moved
along the darkened edges of the room and came and stood by
Shetland.

Mrs. Weiss stood at the foot of the bed for a long time
and stared down at it as if she were looking at someone lying
on it. She glanced at the chair drawn up next to the bed. On
this chair was an open suitcase containing some of the Savien
girl's clothes. Inside the lid, tucked away in a pouch, were
some letters written by the girl about the mysterious woman
she had been seeing. A troubled look came over Mrs. Weiss's
face, then startlingly she almost lunged around the bed and
stood before the suitcase. Mrs. Weiss held her hands out in
front of her, palms toward the suitcase. Hesitantly, as if going
into a fire, the hands reached into the suitcase and began
picking through the articles of clothing, touching them with
deftly moving fingers, then rolling them around between the
palms. Mrs. Weiss turned her head slightly to one side and
shut her eyes tightly, then ran her hand over the suitcase and

up the inside of the lid to the pouch. The thumb and index fingers recoiled. "Claws, ripping the ground," she said in a calm voice. "I see an ancient cathedral standing upon great pillars supported by those claws. No. No," she said, her voice changing in mood and tempo, "they're not claws, they're roots, massive tree roots like the fingers of a giant hand spread and clutching fast to the earth." Her hands jerked back spasmodically. "They're holding the girl." Her eyes popped open for an instant and stared unfocused, then they settled on the corner where Bates and Shetland stood quietly. "That's enough for now."

Bates started to open the drapes. "No," Mrs. Weiss said, "leave everything as it is. We'll go next door."

As they entered Mrs. Weiss's room she said, "Gentlemen, please excuse me, but I feel a little fatigued and I should like to lie down for a spell."

Shetland said, "We'll wait outside, Mrs. Weiss."

"No. Actually, if you have no objection, I would prefer that you both stay here. I will only rest for a few minutes." When Shetland nodded that they would stay Mrs. Weiss stretched out on the bed and folded her hands across her stomach, but did not close her eyes.

"Mrs. Weiss, the family is expecting a phone call from me today. What should I tell them?" Bates asked.

Lost in thought, Mrs. Weiss at first said nothing. Then she mumbled under her breath, "Very confusing," and a prolonged silence followed. Finally she said, "Tell them we will try again."

"Mrs. Weiss, they'll want more than that."

"Then tell them we'll find their daughter."

Bates was still not satisfied but he left Mr. Weiss to her thoughts and went off to report what he could.

Shetland sat smoking in the chair beneath the window until Mrs. Weiss sat up in the bed and looked straight at him. "Is she dead?" Shetland asked, tamping his cigarette out.

Mrs. Weiss chewed thoughtfully on her upper lip. "Once, a long time ago, I was in a classroom. I was instructing one of my students in the proper reading of an English translation of a Dutch passage, when I saw a young girl. I could

see she was trapped in a drainpipe. She was crying and calling for help. I recognized the young girl: the newspapers had
reported her missing over a week prior to that incident, and
had printed her picture. I saw the girl calling out for help
but I knew she was dead. I saw this river and on its banks
the entrance to that drainpipe. The river was close to the
picnic grounds from which the girl had disappeared. When
they found her she was dead. The authorities said she had
died from suffocation several days before my vision. So to
answer your question, Lieutenant, I think the Savien girl is
dead. I saw her buried in soft earth, tree roots growing over
and about her, imprisoning her in her grave."

"Why didn't you tell that to Bates?"

"Because, Lieutenant, although I saw her quite vividly
in that grave, she was not dead."

Shetland leaned forward. "Good Lord. Are you saying
she's buried alive somewhere but nobody's made any ransom
demands?"

"Please, Lieutenant. It's not as simple as that."

"Where was the grave?"

"Close to here, that's all I know."

"Please, Mrs. Weiss, I'm going with you on this, but
just saying she's close to here is too vague."

"Lieutenant, I promise you we'll find the grave when I
try again."

"We have a saying in this country, Mrs. Weiss; now
is as good a time as any."

"It's a good saying but not in this instance. I will explain. When I was staring down at the bed I saw the Savien
girl. She was unclothed and lying on her back. She had just
made love. She was confused and frightened and I could feel
her will was not hers any longer. She knew she was going
to die."

"Okay, what does that mean?"

"You don't understand, Lieutenant. I wouldn't have
picked that up if her death hadn't come to pass."

Puzzled, Shetland sat back. "Now you're saying she *is*
dead?"

"I also saw a person lying next to the Savien girl. She

had made love to the girl, but I couldn't see this person's face; it was a blank. That shouldn't have been either—there should have been a face. I was seeing an image of something that took place in the past. Just as when you watch an old movie on television that has been cut in order to fit into the TV programming schedule, something here and now is tampering with the image. I must have time to consider and understand it; then I will try again."

Leaving Mrs. Weiss alone, Shetland strolled down to the boat ramp behind the motel, where he met Bates, who was watching the seagulls soaring in circles above the trash dumpster, like horses on a carousel. Shetland walked up to him. Without averting his eyes Bates said, "Let me be the first to apologize; I'm sorry I jumped on you, Lieutenant."

"Same here."

"I just talked to the Savien family. If something doesn't break soon I think they're going to come unglued. Gloria was their only child; you can't blame them. But getting involved with this, it's too weird."

"You don't buy Weiss?" Shetland said, unsure of how he'd answer the question himself.

"To be frank, Lieutenant, no."

"Then why go along with it?"

"Oh, I tried to convince the Saviens this wasn't the way to go, but when I got the impression that they were perfectly willing to allow me my opinion and get someone else to handle it for them I backed off. But I think I've come to the end of it. I'll try one more time to convince them to let the police handle it, or at least to hire a legitimate private detective agency."

"Why don't you hold off," Shetland said.

Bates shot him a surprised look. "Are you telling me you have confidence in this seance, or whatever it is Mrs. Weiss is doing?"

"I won't go that far, but I'm saying I wouldn't be here if I had a solid lead on what happened to Gloria Savien. And I can't see what a private detective agency could do that we haven't. Like it or not, Mrs. Weiss is the only game in town."

"Okay, Lieutenant, I'll go along if you will, but I still think it's not going to do any good, not even for Mrs. Weiss. Did you notice how pale and worn out she looked after the first attempt? I actually got scared for a moment that she was going to keel over dead with a stroke or something."

"Yes," Shetland said, "but she seemed to have recovered pretty fast once we were back in her room."

"Did she say anything while I was gone, Lieutenant?"

"Nothing positive. I think she's concerned about the apparent failure of her first try."

"I'm concerned about the whole thing. I don't know much about this thing, but with everything that's been happening to you people out here I don't see a bright prospect for Gloria's safe return, do you, Lieutenant?"

"Did you know Gloria Savien?"

"I met her a few times. She was kind of moody and withdrawn, but if you made the first move she would respond and become friendly. I found her to be a very pleasant and intelligent girl."

"I guess," Shetland said, "her disappearance came as a shock to you, especially considering the circumstances."

"I wouldn't say that, Lieutenant. Since she was an only child, the family made a big deal over Gloria. She seemed to handle that okay, but it was this other thing—her gift, as they called it. The family treated it with almost divine reverence. That's a tough tag for any kid to grow up with, especially since nobody really understood it, I think not even Gloria. That was the part of her she kept secret from most people."

"So," Shetland said, "if she found someone who understood, then she was bound to be drawn to that person."

Shetland and Bates started back to the motel room. When they rounded the corner of the building Bates threw up his arms and shouted, "My car's gone. I don't believe this! I left it parked in front of our rooms and somebody's ripped it off."

Shetland got the license plate number and walked over to his car to call it in on the radio. Bates went to check on Mrs. Weiss.

Shetland had the mike in his hands when Bates came back out of the motel room, calling to him and motioning with his arms. Shetland dumped the mike back in its cradle and went to see what was the matter. Bates handed him a postcard containing a note from Mrs. Weiss. "Please excuse my behavior, Mr. Bates. I went looking for you to ask permission to use your car but couldn't find you and I had to go for a drive. I have all the necessary qualifications and documents to drive in this country."

"Now what, Lieutenant?" Bates muttered in exasperation.

Shetland couldn't help smiling. "Unless you still want to report a stolen car we wait until she comes back from her joy ride."

Shetland went back to his office. He waited an hour, then called the Land's End Motel. Bates was anxious but not overly upset. "She hasn't come back yet, Lieutenant."

"Okay, Mr. Bates, you have my office number and I'll leave word here to get any messages to me in case Mrs. Weiss wants to talk to me when she comes back." Shetland hung up.

Around two in the afternoon he got a phone call from Jessica, who was in a lighthearted mood. "Having a rough day, Donald?"

"Something like that," he sneered into the phone; "I ran into your boss this morning."

"I'm at home," she said, "and here I'm the boss."

"Don't you ever work?"

She laughed and despite himself he began to feel good.

"Come over as soon as you can," she said and hung up.

Shetland hung around the office for another half hour, trying feebly to get with it. Finally he gave up and walked out without telling anyone where he was going.

The heat was oppressive, and to alleviate his suffering he threw his jacket over his shoulder, loosened his tie, opened his shirt collar and rolled up his sleeves. It was considerably cooler in the shade on the wooden footbridge that spanned the small stream in front of Jessica's house. He walked into the shade of the front yard at the same moment Jessica emerged from the side of the house. "I heard a car," she said, "but I didn't expect to see you until later; playing hookey?" Tilting her head she said, "You look terrible."

"Thanks; you look swell."

They walked arm in arm into the back yard, and she seated him at a picnic table and then whisked off into the house, returning momentarily with a pitcher of lemonade and glasses. "We can talk while I finish up." She got down on her hands and knees and started digging in an irregular plot of earth. He asked what she was doing. "Gardening. What does it look like?"

"Certainly not gardening," he retorted.

"I have to admit harvest time is a rather disheartening search through the weeds for a pinky-sized cucumber—the sole survivor of my agricultural endeavors—but it's healthy exercise."

"So's breaking cement."

"My, aren't we in a wonderful mood. Is something wrong?"

"How old are you, twenty, twenty-one?" he asked.

She threw him a curious glance over her shoulder. "Twenty-two," she said. "And you?"

"Thirty-four? Thirty-six!" he grumbled.

She feigned a startled look. "My, nearly forty."

"Nearly thirty-seven," he corrected, "and don't change the subject."

"I thought birthdays was the subject."

"How did you get hooked up with Dority?"

"After college I applied for the position."

"How did you get so high up in such a short time? You couldn't have campaigned for that schlep."

"I could have but I didn't have to; the position I first applied for was the one I have now." She stood up, brushed the sandy soil from her long tanned legs, came over, sat down across from him and poured herself a drink. "I bet," she said between gulps, "you didn't know your girlfriend had pull or clout, or whatever it's called. I wish you'd get off the sin-of-the-employer-is-shared-by-the-employees bit; it's absolutely unreasonable."

"I think," Shetland mused, "that's what the Nazis said at Nuremberg."

"Look, if you've just come here to irritate me I can call this little gig off because I'm in the mood to play around, not get kicked around."

"You're right, I'm lousy company," he said and started to leave.

"You're damn right I'm right, but you can stay anyhow," she said with a pleading look.

"I didn't really want to go," he said sheepishly, and sat down. Their conversation turned back to her gardening and then she excused herself again to get cleaned up and change her clothes. During her absence Shetland stretched out under a tree in a spot overlooking the beach and the Sound. It was ironic, he thought, to find peace and tranquility in this place. He began to relax as the sultry breeze coming off the water quickly lulled him into a daydream; the pressure was off. It wasn't long before Jessica made her appearance in a slinky yellow dress with a plunging neckline. She danced barefoot across the yard, a martini in each hand. Handing Shetland his drink, she flopped down beside him.

"That's what I call a sophisticated outfit," Shetland said.

"I wore it just for you, for my sophisticated older man. And I think the martinis add just the right touch. I told you I wanted to play around," she said, snuggling closer.

"To play time," Shetland said, lifting his glass in a toast. "You have a nice place here. It has an air of seclusion that's very peaceful."

Jessica looked about in regal surveillance. "I'm quite lucky to have a sanctuary where I can banish the unpleasant things of this world," she sighed philosophically. "It's an illusion, of course, but it's believable enough most of the time." She turned and began examining his face with a critical gaze. "You're not very handsome; you have good masculine features but they're not coarse enough to be appealing in a brutish way and you certainly aren't a pretty boy."

"That's me," Shetland murmured, wilting under the unflattering appraisal, "plain Jane."

Ignoring his discomfort, she continued, "From the very

first moment we met and you snarled at me you looked like one of the unfortunates of the world, a man with no place to call his sanctuary. I think that's why I instantly took pity on you. Does that bother you?"

"On the contrary, I crave pity; I like when people feel sorry for me. I mean, look where it's gotten me," he said, spreading his arms to take in his surroundings.

"Strong men crave pity? I wouldn't think that's right."

"Strong?" Shetland said questioningly. "Why, because my job requires that I scrounge around in the gutter?"

"To deal with ugliness, to live with it, doesn't that require strength?"

Shetland had to laugh. "You don't deal with ugliness, you sweep it under things. Like a garbageman, you pick it up one day and it's back the next. You get your money and a backache, that's all."

"Bitter?"

"No," he shook his head, "just resigned. I think I'd rather go back to downgrading my looks."

As afternoon slipped effortlessly into evening, Jessica prepared a steak on the outdoor barbecue, and served it with salad and ice-cold beer. Shetland, a man who strongly resisted unwinding, found himself more relaxed than he'd been in months. As they walked barefoot on the beach under a star-filled sky, the water, a black mirror, lapped rhythmically against the warm sand. Looking out across the darkness to the diamond necklace of neon lights strung along the Connecticut shoreline, Jessica stopped and turned him to face her. Then, without speaking, she stepped back and slipped out of her dress. She moved closer and put her arms around his neck and kissed him gently on the lips. Shetland responded by grabbing her up in his arms and crushing his open mouth hard against hers. His hands began to explore her body, caressing her buttocks and fondling her breasts. He wanted to be gentle but his body trembled with an urgency that made his movements clumsy. Fumbling to remove his own clothes, he forced her to the sand, first to her knees and then onto her back, pinning her helplessly with his full weight. He shifted slightly to his side so he could caress the roundness of her breasts and run his hand up the inside of her firm thighs. His mouth settled on her breast and he began to suck and bite the nipple until it grew hard, drawing mixed whimpers of pain and pleasure from Jessica.

She placed her hand on the back of his head and pressed his mouth harder against her breast. "Love me, Donald," she whispered, "now."

When he entered her, Jessica let out a sharp cry of pain, and her body arched against his weight. She threw her arms around his back and held him tightly until her body relaxed.

"Are you all right? Did I hurt you?" Shetland asked breathlessly.

Her cheek moved close to his and in a weakened voice she said, "Yes, I'm all right. Please don't stop." Slowly at first, then with increasing violence, she raised her hips to receive the full force of Shetland's rhythmic thrusts. Pressing her fingers down into his back, Jessica bit savagely into his shoulder, her body arching and jerking upward in the frenzy of climax, even as his body shuddered in release.

Jessica's virginity was perhaps more of a shock to Shetland than it should have been. He was not only curious about it; he also felt guilty for the crudeness of his lovemaking. He tried to apologize. She said that was the way she wanted it, dismissing him as if he had played no part in it. She sat up, folded her legs close to her body, wrapped her arms tightly around them and thoughtfully laid her chin upon her knees. She seemed engrossed in meditation.

"What are you thinking?" he asked after a long silence.

"Crazy thoughts," she said, smiling.

"I like crazy thoughts."

"I read somewhere that the only thing that's constant in the universe is change, that there's really no such thing as boundaries. You know, it said that atoms are always being exchanged all around us and that we're a part of it. I told you they were crazy thoughts."

"No; go on. I think I'm fascinated but I'm not quite sure I know what you're saying."

Jessica scooped up a handful of sand. "Right at this very instant some of the atoms in the sand are trading off with some of the atoms in my hand. It's the same with the water and the air, with everything; even with you and me. If the very atoms that make up our flesh and bone leave to become somebody else's flesh and bone and in turn are replaced from some other source, then no borders exist in the physical world. And what about the mind—thoughts and dreams, things we call imagination and reality—suppose it's all the same but in different guises."

"Rock into paper," Shetland remarked cryptically.

She looked at him questioningly.

"Just something I read; it suddenly makes sense now in a wild sort of way," Shetland explained.

"You don't sound happy about it."

"I guess some things are better left nonsensical."

"What time is it?"

Shetland glanced at his watch. "Nine-thirty."

She grabbed her dress, hugged it to her bosom, got up and started running toward the house. "Come on," she shouted, "we have to get fixed up."

"I'm no damn nudist," he yelled. "Let me get dressed." In a panic he started grabbing for his clothes, his shoes and his gun, which he found half buried in the sand.

"You should really worry after what you just did to me, right out in front of the whole universe."

A few minutes later Shetland stumbled into the house looking like he had just been rolled. He demanded to know what the rush was. Jessica came down the stairs in a bathrobe, having just taken a quick shower. "You've got just enough time to take a quick shower yourself," she said, "before the others arrive."

"Others?" Shetland grunted, just as somebody knocked at the front door. The moment Jessica started for the door Shetland bolted up the stairs as if she were about to let in the bogey man. Voices began to fill the downstairs rooms while he dawdled in the bathroom. When it became obvious that he was hiding out, Jessica rapped on the door. "They're all waiting for you," she said, giggling under her breath.

When he could no longer put it off he made his appearance. Jessica was dressed in a long wraparound skirt and

puffy-sleeved peasant blouse. She had a choker around her
neck. She whisked him through the introductions with pain-
less ease, then sat him down in a cushiony armchair and
slipped a drink in his hand as a pacifier. When he drank that
she refilled it, and soon he began to relax and enjoy the party.
The atmosphere was pleasant and cozy with a crackling fire in
the fireplace and soft music playing in the background. Some
of the guests slow-danced in the middle of the room and
others conversed in small, informal groups. Shetland watched
Jessica moving like a queen among her guests. She played
hostess like a game of chess, giving each person individual
attention in order to move the pieces strategically around the
board. Between dances she would bring some of her more
intimate friends over to meet Shetland. She was a master at
choreographing encounters. He met a friend of hers from
college days, an attractive and intelligent girl named Teresa
who, like him, was obviously enchanted with their hostess.
The party was a mixed bag of personalities and professions.
There was a department-store window designer, and a professor of anthropology whose political and socioeconomic
philosophy was a strange mixture of Marxism and Social
Darwinism. There was a bank clerk who was into astrology
and a female riding instructor who impressed Shetland as inclined to use her whip on something beside horses. If there
was any rhyme or reason to this gathering Shetland couldn't
see it.

As the evening proceeded the tone of the party changed
from Brahmsian to Wagnerian and the gathering began to
grow wild. The music went from soft to acid rock; and the
shimmering glow of the fire, which had formerly seemed to
encourage reflective, contemplative feelings, suddenly lent itself like a psychedelic light-show to the new depth and intensity of the beat. Perhaps it was due to Shetland's generally
suspicious nature, or his growing sense of paranoia, but when
some of the guests started lighting up joints he became
nervous and uneasy. Jessica was connected with Dority, he
reminded himself, and the uncomfortable thought that this
might be a setup crept into his mind. Jessica was a chameleon
personality, vulnerable one minute and assertive the next. But

still it seemed vicious and ludicrous on his part to believe she was capable of that kind of double dealing, and he began to wonder what kind of nasty mind it took to come up with ideas like the ones he'd just had. He slipped away from the party and went outside for a breath of air. Jessica, sensing something was wrong, followed him. "Don't like my friends," she said, stepping out of the darkness.

"Don't like myself."

"Negative feelings about oneself are very destructive; it's better to pile it on others. You know what I mean: I'm okay but I'm not so sure about you."

Shetland laughed and put his arm around her waist; together they walked back into the house. He told himself nobody could be a cop twenty-four hours a day, and nobody expected it either. A little grass was a harmless wink at the law, but nevertheless he kept to himself, hiding behind the shield of disinterested ignorance of what was going on, hear no evil, see no evil. Despite a bit of lingering anxiety, his attitude worked and he was able to relax and enjoy himself again—until someone named Cox walked up to him and offered him a joint.

"No thanks, it's against my religion," Shetland quipped.

"It's better than booze, man," Cox persisted.

"I know it's good but you wouldn't want me to commit sacrilege, would you?"

"Man, I'd get out of a religion like that."

Shetland tried the straight approach. "Look, I'm an off-duty cop," he said. "I don't mind shutting my eyes to it but I can't participate."

Cox grinned. "Don't jive me, man; this is a cop-out like that religion bit."

Shetland walked away from Cox and joined Jessica with some of her other friends. She had watched the encounter with strange amusement and when Cox followed him, becoming almost belligerent in his insistence, she didn't intervene. "Look, man," he said, slurring his words slightly, "your attitude is like refusing to drink with a guy in the Old West."

Shetland glared at him so he'd get lost but he persisted, getting louder and drawing the attention of other guests; all the while Jessica kept smiling and looking away. Paranoid or not, Shetland grabbed the guy by the scruff of his neck, spun him around and with his arm twisted behind his back slammed him against the wall in the spread-eagle position, shouting, "You jerk, you're under arrest for possession of marijuana."

Cox squealed, "Okay, you're a cop, you're a cop. I believe you already."

"Sorry," Shetland said; "you had your shot at redemption. You have a right to remain silent."

"Come on, man, I'll lose my job if I get arrested."

Shetland felt like the biggest ass in the world. "Now do you get the message, turkey?" he growled, releasing his paralyzed victim.

The party was over. The place emptied as if somebody had just announced that there was a bomb set to go off in thirty seconds in the building. Shetland slumped on the now empty sofa, wishing he could shrink down between the cushions. Jessica said nothing as she straightened up a little and then went into the kitchen. Shetland took that as his cue to leave and, sulking, started to go. "Where are you going, officer?" she said. "I just put up the coffee."

"Let me guess," he said; "mine's cream, sugar and arsenic."

"If you like, but I wouldn't let that bother you. It was getting boring. Besides, if you left it would be breach of contract."

Shetland's brow rose in puzzlement, when it suddenly dawned on him what she was referring to. "You sure you want me to stay?"

"Perhaps and perhaps not, but I don't think there's any way you can refund my payment so I'm afraid you'll have to stay the night and protect me."

Shetland supposed he should have felt flattered, but he didn't. "From what?" he asked almost as if he believed she had a secret to tell.

"Whatever is out there, the fear that gathers as intimately about us as our shadows. Give it whatever name you want, whatever name it answers to."

"Hey, quit it; you're giving me the willies. Let's change the subject. What was with that guy? I've never seen a belligerent weed freak before."

"Cox was drinking; he doesn't normally do that but I think he was afraid."

"Don't seem to be able to get away from that topic."

Jessica served the coffee in the kitchen. "You forgot," she said; "not everybody's used to this sort of thing."

"Don't look at me when you say that. I'm no more used to it than you. Despite popular opinion murder is not the most common complaint your average police department deals with."

"Murder?"

"Isn't that what's got you keyed up?" Shetland asked. "What else could it be?"

"That feeling I was talking about—a fear, an anxiety that puts a bit of madness into all of our actions. It's sort of like mentally running scared. It's like a cold draft in a dark room."

Shetland shifted uncomfortably in his chair. "I think you like giving me the willies. Look, I don't know anything about cold drafts and all that, but we've got a looney on the loose. Isn't that enough to deal with without dreaming up worse horrors?"

"It's more than that. We're alone—why do you avoid saying what you feel?"

"Damn it," Shetland grumbled. He jumped up, grabbed Jessica and pulled her out of her chair.

"Where are we going?"

"Upstairs to bed. If you're going to spend all night giving me goosebumps I want to be under the covers."

CHAPTER SEVEN

WHEN SHETLAND WOKE UP in Jessica's bedroom he knew it was late. Jessica was sitting at her vanity table, her robe around her hips, brushing her hair. She smiled at his reflection in the mirror and said, "Good morning."

Shetland pushed himself up and cushioned his back with pillows against the headboard. He looked at the glow of yellow sunshine in the window and said, "Are you sure it's not good afternoon?"

"Almost, but not quite," she laughed.

"I got to get the lead out," Shetland groaned.

"You were tired and you needed the rest, so I let you sleep, but don't worry; I called in for you."

"Did you say where I was?"

"Of course, in case they wanted to get in touch with you."

"You think that was wise?"

She glanced over her shoulder at him. "Worried about appearances, Lieutenant? In this day and age?"

"Just a thought."

125

"I would say that chivalry before you get out of bed is more than just a thought."

Shetland rubbed his eyes and stretched. "Egads, I've been unmasked; you've discovered that behind my worldly façade lurks a backward child."

"Changing the subject," Jessica said, "who's Mrs. Weiss?"

Shetland was surprised. "Carla Weiss? That's the lady —where'd you hear about her?"

"One of your men asked me to give you a message— a Sergeant Scalley. He sounds very nice."

"Well, what's the message?"

"Answer my question first."

"Oh, no, the message first. I'll think about the other."

"Lieutenant, you're impossible, but all right. Actually the message was from a lawyer named Bates. Whose lawyer is he? Mrs. Weiss's?"

"Jessica, please finish the message without the questions."

"Let's see," she sneered, "where was I. Oh yes, Weiss and lawyer are still at the Land's End Motel. Let's see, Land's End; that's just across the bay from here." Jessica pulled her robe up over her shoulders and tied it in the front. "You know, Donald, this sounds a little strange—a mysterious married lady, a lawyer, a cop and a motel room. Are you into a *ménage à trois?*"

"Pervert," Shetland groaned, "give me the rest of the message."

"Mrs. Weiss returned to the motel room about nine o'clock this morning. She's all right but she wants to meet with you again as soon as possible. That's the whole message, Lieutenant. Now the answers to my questions. First, who is Mrs. Weiss; second, when was the first time you met her?"

"She just came back this morning and Bates didn't say any more than that?"

Jessica frowned. "You're being evasive, Lieutenant."

"I met Mrs. Weiss and Mr. Bates yesterday."

"Yes, go on," Jessica said excitedly.

"I'm trying to, if you'll just stop interrupting." Shetland

thought for a moment. "What's the proper terminology? Psychic, telepathic? Anyway, Carla Weiss is supposed to be able to solve crimes by mental powers alone."

"You're kidding. And she's going to be working with you?"

Shetland sucked in his breath. "Saints preserve my pension, no."

"Then why's she here and why should you be interested in her?"

Shetland moaned, "It's too complicated to tell without a fortifying cup of coffee; make me some and I'll talk."

Jessica frowned. "Some detective you are. Look to your right and you will behold on the night table a full pot and all the necessary utensils."

"I'll be! And all this time I thought I was imagining I smelled fresh-brewed coffee." He poured himself one cup, then another.

"I bet you're addicted to that stuff."

"Does a vampire need blood?"

"It's really not that good for you, you know."

Shetland chuckled. "Neither is a biological blowout, which is what would happen to every cell in my body if I didn't get a caffeine fix at regular intervals."

"You were saying about Mrs. Weiss."

"Oh, yes. Well, she's here on a case concerning a missing girl, a case which my department is also involved in. Officially she's working for the girl's family and the department's not to become involved."

"I see. And unofficially?"

Shetland shrugged. "I've been told by the captain in no uncertain terms to mind my own business."

"And are you going to mind your own business?"

Shetland didn't answer.

"Silence speaks louder than words, Donald. You're considering it, aren't you? I'm truly surprised; I didn't think you were the type to put credence in that sort of thing."

Shetland looked into Jessica's eyes. "I've got to get up." Jessica stood up and Shetland threw his legs over the side of the bed. He got up and gathered his clothes together. Jessica followed him into the bathroom. "Are you going to see Mrs. Weiss now?" she asked.

Shetland stared into the mirror, stroking his chin with his hand. "I need a shave."

"Can I go with you?"

"You got a razor?"

"Nothing suitable for a face."

"That's okay. I've got an electric shaver in the car."

"Can I?"

Shetland looked at her as if he hadn't been paying attention. "Can you what?"

Jessica glared with frustration. "Can I go with you?"

"Sure, but it gets awful boring in a police station."

"Donald, that's not where you're going and you know it."

"All I know," he said, marching her out of the bathroom, "is that I've got to get ready."

When Shetland came downstairs Jessica was still in her bathrobe. "No work today either?" he asked. "For a swine Dority's an understanding boss."

She kissed him and said, "Take care, Donald Shetland," as he went out the door.

There was a steady wind blowing in from the Sound but it disturbed the surface of the water very little and brought no moisture with it. When Shetland pulled up to the Land's End Motel Carla Weiss was standing by the boat ramp. The wind tossed her hair into a frantic tangle, but she was calm and her thoughts were collected. Her smile when she greeted Shetland was subdued. "Gloria Savien is dead; there's no question in my mind about that." Shetland was startled more by the positive manner of Carla's pronouncement than by its content; privately he had long since accepted it. Shetland didn't ask how she had come to that conclusion or where she had been and what had happened while she was off by herself.

A wave of helplessness and depression swept over Shetland. "Why haven't you told Bates?"

She didn't answer right away but continued to look out

over the water. Then she said, "Mr. Bates is too skeptical, which makes it, for him, a very uncomfortable situation to be in. I want to find the girl's body and then at least that part of the tragedy will be done with. She's somewhere over there," Carla said pointing toward Crane's Neck. They walked in silence back to the motel room to pick up Bates and then they went to the restaurant to have lunch. Bates asked Carla about the car.

"How did it happen?"

"Thoughtlessness on my part; I let my mind go astray and I'm afraid the automobile followed."

"Where did the accident occur?"

"I'm not familiar with the area, so I really couldn't say."

"What did the police say when you reported the accident?" Bates pressed.

Mrs. Weiss looked concerned and turned to Shetland. "Since only me and an embankment on the side of the road were involved I didn't report the accident to the police. That was wrong?"

Shetland smiled. "Yes, but don't worry; the D.A. will be lenient."

Bates grumbled, "I wish I could say the same for my insurance company."

"I will be leaving for Holland tomorrow, but please send me the bill there."

Bates dropped his spoon into his soup, spraying his expensive suit, shirt, and Italian silk tie with New England-style clam chowder. "Mrs. Weiss," he said, bolting upright in his seat and ignoring the damage to his clothing, "I'm stunned. No, I'm shocked. You came here to help find the Saviens' daughter. I can't begin to tell you how high the family's hopes were when you arrived. It will crush them if you leave so soon without achieving anything."

"Please don't get upset, Mr. Bates," Carla said.

"Mrs. Weiss, I have every right to get upset. First of all, I'm the one who has to deliver your message. Secondly, I was against this business from the start but the family insisted and you were paid to find Gloria Savien."

Mrs. Weiss took Bates's comments with composure. When Bates finished she countered quietly, "That I was paid for travel and living expenses I grant you, Mr. Bates. That I was paid to find the Savien girl I don't grant. The terms for my remuneration, as I expressed to you personally when you came to visit me in Holland, was that I would try and find the Savien girl. I gave no promises, written or verbal, to any other effect."

"I would hardly call what you've done so far, trying," Bates returned angrily.

"Since, as you say, you were against this from the start, you are hardly the appropriate judge as to what I have done so far."

"Come," Shetland said, interrupting them, "let us reason together."

Mrs. Weiss looked at Shetland and smiled. "One of your presidents said that."

"Oh, you heard that one, huh?"

"Yes, but it's very appropriate nevertheless. And reason is precisely what we need here. I will try again once more tonight. If I fail my presence here will be of no further value to you, Mr. Bates, to the Saviens, or to the police."

Bates crumpled up his napkin and threw it down on the table. "You'll have to excuse me," he said disgruntledly; "I have to change my clothes." He stomped out of the restaurant.

"I may be reading you wrong, Mrs. Weiss, but are you concerned about your safety?"

"Yes I am, Lieutenant."

"Then why make a second attempt?"

"I am not a young woman, Lieutenant, but I am in perfect health."

"Then what is it?"

"That's precisely the point: I don't know. Yesterday when we were in the Savien girl's room and all her things were set out and I touched them, it was like holding an electrical cable in my hands. I could feel the current throbbing, vibrating beneath the insulation; the more I handled and examined them the more fearful I became the insulation would crack and crumble away. That's how it felt—if I didn't let go I would be destroyed." Carla set down the spoon that she had been using to whip her melting vanilla ice cream into a milky puddle, raised her hand and closed it slowly into a fist. "My own subconscious closed against it, fighting my conscious will every step of the way. Lay them down, put them aside, it demanded, as if it already knew the nature of this power and the consequences of unmasking it."

"How the hell did you get into this kind of thing, anyway," Shetland said with concern, "when you could be back in Holland with those kids you love so much, looking for a fourth husband."

"It is not easy for me, Lieutenant, to deny help to people who are in need, especially help that I am uniquely qualified to give."

"I don't care; you're the one who told me to listen to that inner voice, and that's exactly what you're not doing."

"I will dare to venture one more peek at the Gorgon's face, Lieutenant, and if I don't turn to stone I will tell you what I've seen."

Shetland didn't know what to make of Carla. Bates's view was the logical one—she was a fraud. But if she was a fraud she seemed to have lost the pea to her own shell game, for when they returned to the room Gloria Savien had occupied she was visibly scared. Shetland felt committed to helping her now.

Bates joined them a few minutes later. He was dressed casually in a short-sleeve shirt and was nursing a drink. He went to a chair in the opposite corner of the room and flopped down into it without saying a word. Shetland stood by the door. Carla stayed near him for several minutes, then hesitantly walked to the foot of the bed and stood where she had the previous day. Without being asked, Bates shut off the air conditioner; then there was silence. The melting ice shifting in Bates's glass made a tinkling sound that reminded Shetland of the bells hanging from the eaves of Arken's cottage. Carla went to the suitcase on the chair and this time reached directly for the letters that were in the pouch on the lid. She held the letters tightly, then crushed them to her chest. "I see her," she said. "It's night and there is a full moon but she cannot see the moon because it is blocked by clouds or trees. She is lying down upon a stone. There are others standing around her. Why can't I see their faces? They're going to kill her. She seems resigned, almost eager for death."

"What kind of rubbish is this!" Bates shouted.

Shetland glared at him. "For God's sake, shut up. This is what you wanted, so let her do her thing. Mrs. Weiss, try to see the other faces or at least where this place is."

"It's very dark," she said and then fell silent.

"I feel like a complete fool and I've had enough," Bates said and got up to leave, but Shetland stopped him.

"A little while ago, Bates, you were having a fit because Mrs. Weiss was giving up."

"So I was wrong."

Mrs. Weiss moaned softly.

Bates rolled his eyes in disbelief. "I'm afraid to look, but I think she's going into a trance." Then Bates gasped, "She's bleeding."

Shetland turned around. Carla was clutching the letters so hard that her fingernails were digging into the flesh of her palms and drawing blood. She was standing rigidly. "God, I don't believe this. She's put herself into a trance," Bates said.

"She didn't do that before," Shetland said. "Something's wrong."

"Well, she's doing it now, Lieutenant. It's probably part of her grand finale."

"No, dammit, something's wrong." Shetland didn't waste any time arguing with Bates, but went to Carla's side. Her eyes were staring and blinking rapidly and her face was chalky. "Mrs. Weiss, wake up." Shetland grabbed her hands to pry them apart. Her flesh was cold and clammy and knotted by straining muscles and tendons. With all of Shetland's strength he could not pull her hands apart. "Damn it, Bates," he shouted, "help me."

Bates let his drink drop to the floor and rushed forward. Together they struggled to pry Carla's hands apart, but to no avail. Then suddenly the tension in her arms relaxed. The effect was that of a rope snapping in a tug of war. Bates lost his footing, stumbled back, and sat down hard on the floor. Shetland's landing was cushioned by the bed. Mrs. Weiss stood with her shoulders thrown forward looking about in bewilderment. Gloria Savien's letters, crushed and red with blood, rolled from her open hand and fell to the floor. Mrs. Weiss took a teetering step back from them. She lowered her head, drawing her mutilated hands to her face. Her legs buckled, her body sagged and she started to swoon. Shetland sprang from the bed and caught her before she fell. With Bates's assistance he helped her back to the bed.

"Lie down, Carla," Shetland said.

"Sit me in a chair," she said in soft gasps; "sit me in a chair." They did as Carla asked, then Bates went into the bathroom for a wet cloth to wipe the blood from her hands. "There's nothing in the cabinet to tend her wounds," he said.

"She needs more than a couple of Band-Aids anyway; we'd better call an ambulance and have her taken to the hospital."

"Maybe we should ask her how she feels first."

"Ask her how she feels?" Shetland snorted, rearing up. "Damn it, Bates, if she feels half as bad as she looks she belongs in a hospital."

"Lieutenant, I was only concerned—"

"I know," Shetland said. "About the publicity."

"That's not it at all," Bates insisted. "She might have had an epileptic seizure, a stroke or a coronary—we don't know."

"And neither does she, so she goes to the hospital."

"That won't be necessary," Carla said. Her voice was stronger and the color had returned to her face.

But Shetland still thought she should go to the hospital. "Carla, whatever just happened to you might happen again— you had a pretty rough time there for a moment."

"Lieutenant, I'm not the heroic type. Believe me, if I felt myself in further danger I would willingly go to the hospital, but it's not necessary."

Bates suddenly changed his mind. "Maybe the lieutenant's right, Carla; maybe you should seek medical attention."

She waved her hand in front of her face. "No, but thank you both for your concern."

"All right, Carla, no hospital. Is there anything you want?" Shetland asked.

"Yes. I think a stimulant would be in order."

"A stimulant? What kind?"

"Whiskey," she said.

Bates wheeled about and started for the phone. "I'll call room service."

"Hey, concerned person, you want somebody to see this place the way it is right now?" Shetland said.

Bates stopped and looked about. "I see your point, Lieutenant. What do I do?"

"Go for it yourself."

While Bates went for the whiskey Shetland finished cleaning Carla's wounds, then went to his car for the first-aid kit he kept in the trunk. When he returned Bates was already there filling three glasses from a bottle of expensive Scotch. Shetland put ointment on Carla's hands and covered them with sterile gauze and tape. Bates handed out the drinks. The Scotch helped, but it was obvious to Shetland that they had all been pretty badly shaken by the incident and a second round was needed before frayed nerves were mended. When Shetland judged Carla to be strong enough he suggested they move next door.

There she eagerly went for the bed and stretched out on her back, her arm covering her eyes. "What happened?" Shetland asked, sitting on the edge of the mattress.

With a great sigh she said, "I don't know, except just before, I remember the darkness sweeping forward, almost as if to attack me. I remember feeling dread, not at the darkness but at something approaching behind it. I recoiled from it." Her voice grew thick and drowsy. "I really can't be sure; it's all so vague."

"You really threw a scare into me, Carla; I think for both our sakes you should drop this whole business and go home as soon as possible," Shetland said, gently taking her hand in his.

"No arguments, no arguments, Lieutenant. This time I go

home. I'm so very tired . . ." Her voice trailed off and she fell asleep.

Shetland eased himself off the bed and turned to Bates. "I want you to get her out of here, and I don't want to hear any bull about how upset the family will be or remuneration or anything else."

Bates's face was pale and drawn. "You'll get no arguments from me," he said. "Whatever took place here, it's time to end it, for everyone's sake."

CHAPTER EIGHT

SHETLAND ATE LUNCH with Harry in a restaurant near the county seat. The place was crowded with county workers and employees from the state office building across the street; the din of conversation and the clash and clank of plates and silverware was nerve-wracking. Harry added his bellicose thundering to the general background row. "Pressure is all I'm getting," he complained. "They're acting like I made up that coroner's report off the top of my head and now they want me to make up the answers. You know, Don boy," he said, threateningly waving the piece of roast beef skewered at the end of his fork, "fire's a pretty thorough destroyer. You saw it; I don't have to tell you what it does to human tissue." Now he began to swing the fork like a baton-twirling cheerleader. "I'm not saying we can't find the answer, but it's going to take time and those meatheads had better get used to that."

"Harry, I've got my own problems. I don't need yours." Shetland unenthusiastically turned over the top of his hamburger bun and squirted extra ketchup on it.

"That's a joke," Harry countered. "Half the pressure comes from your people—you in particular. And the worst part is that I get no help." He finally stuffed the piece of beef in his mouth, but it did nothing to mute his tirade. "A couple of suspects, some fingerprints."

Bored, Shetland asked if Harry was getting any help from the Washington boys. Harry stuck out his tongue and quietly let out a Bronx cheer. "I asked for a chemical analysis of that drug and some information on its effects." He rolled his eyes and in a squeaky sarcastic voice mimicked what they had told him: "We have to get clearance; we'll have to get back to you." They probably need a security clearance to tell you where to take a leak."

"At least," Shetland mused, "they're keeping out from underfoot—so far, at least," he added, crossing his fingers.

Harry sat back, exhausted and annoyed. "Are you getting anywhere?"

"A lot of provocative leads but that's it—nothing seems to tie in. I've got a hunch this was a long time in the coming, but I got monkey wrenched when I tried to explore that possibility. I think the captain's beginning to believe his own press releases about the prospects for an immediate breakthrough and indictments." Shetland chuckled. "Even if we had a likely candidate for Arken's murder we haven't got enough evidence to write up a parking ticket. Part of the problem is that this thing's got us, we haven't got it. We're too busy ducking and dodging the press and the politicians and making excuses for why we haven't done this, that and the other thing." Shetland suddenly noticed that Harry had stopped listening; something was distracting him. He turned to see what it was: Jessica was waving to them as she pushed her way toward their table.

To Harry's surprise Shetland shoved over to make room for Jessica and when she slid in beside the lieutenant, greeting him with a warm kiss, Harry let out a puzzled grunt. Shetland started to introduce her, but Harry cut him short. "I know," he said, "Ms. Cummings. But do you know—"

"She works for Dority."

At that Harry wrinkled his forehead into furrows of bewilderment. "You're a bigger man than I thought," he said caustically. "Or a stupider one. In either case, Miss Cummings, you're a very attractive addition to this company."

Jessica smiled impatiently at Harry's patronizing remark. "I haven't got much time," she said. "I have to talk to you."

"If this is private, I'll leave," Harry interjected.

"That depends on Donald and how good a friend you are."

"You can stay anyway, Harry," Shetland smiled.

"There's a departmental investigation going on in your precinct," Jessica announced.

"I know," Shetland said, "Internal Affairs has been nosing around for the past week and so has your boss."

"Yes, and he's sharpening up his scalping knife, the one with your name on it."

Shetland's mood suddenly darkened. "Go on," he said, restraining his anger.

"I don't think Ray's been officially made privy to all the details," Jessica said. "He was raving about some departmental cover-up yesterday when he was on the phone with one of his political cronies. I think he went off this morning to meet with an informant."

"That's Dority's style," Harry said. "But what's the investigation about?"

"Who knows," Shetland blurted out angrily. "I've been running across a lot of funny irregularities myself the past few days."

"Okay," Harry said, shaking his head in bemusement, "but how do you figure this involves you?"

"That's a dumb question, Harry. The investigation obviously has something to do with my department. The captain laid it out plainly to me; he wants me to walk the straight and narrow."

"How involved do they think you are?" Harry asked.

"Apparently enough to get Dority licking his chops at the prospects," Shetland grumbled.

"So," Harry said, clasping his hands together, "what are you going to do?"

"Nothing," Shetland shouted. "If I go charging into the captain's office yelling that I'm innocent before any charges have been made, and I'm ignorant as to what I'm pleading innocent to, they're going to think I'm guilty of something—

If not of this, then of something else. I'm going to keep to my business and let them make the first move. If it comes in my direction then I'll deal with it."

"Sounds to me like a case of the lamb being led to slaughter," Harry commented.

After the unsettling lunch Shetland drove out to Crane's Neck for a second visit to the Sebastians. This time he was determined to speak with Aaron. Parking in the circular driveway, he was again met by the smiling Rudy and escorted to the stables where his mistress was choosing a horse for an afternoon ride. Renée Sebastian was openly hostile. "Absolutely not, Lieutenant," she shrieked, pacing the paddock as nervously as one of her highstrung mares. "I told you my brother sees no one outside the family and a few very close friends. Besides, he hardly knew Stephen and could be of no use to you in your investigation."

"Look, Miss Sebastian, I get paid to make that kind of judgment; your taxes help to pay me. Why don't you just let me help you get your money's worth," Shetland said.

"This is harassment, Lieutenant."

"Call it what you like, but I can get a court order if need be."

She whirled on him as if to attack him physically. "I doubt that," she shouted. "I'm aware of your situation, Lieutenant. I once told you I could buy you a lot of trouble. Well, it seems you purchased your own. But I can still afford all the luxurious options."

"And what would you get?" Shetland countered. "If it's not me it's going to be some other cop pounding at your door. I'm either particularly obnoxious to you or it's something else." For a moment Shetland thought she was going to go wild; blood rushed to her face and she glared murderously at him, then she coldly put it to him, right between the eyes. "Make no mistake about it, Lieutenant, our antagonism is purely personal." Wheeling about, she strode off to the stable, instructing Rudy, "Show that man out and never admit him to my presence again!"

Shetland's face flushed hot with anger at her humiliating

rebuff, an anger that in the next instant he knew would explode and blow the fragile structure of his better judgment to pieces. The urge to come down hard on Renée Sebastian, to shatter her arrogant illusion that he was just another one of her hirelings to dismiss at her own pleasure, grew almost overpowering but he regained control of himself and the flame of indignation sputtered out. Shetland merely shrugged his shoulders and began walking back to his car. Rudy reached for Shetland's elbow to escort him out, but Shetland pulled his arm away. "Put your hands on me, cowboy, and you'll spend the next calendar year humping the walls of a prison cell."

"Any way you want it, Lieutenant," he smiled, falling into step beside him.

Shetland hadn't noticed the bony ridges of calluses on Rudy's long thin hands before. "Karate?" he questioned.

Rudy turned his meat-cleaver hands over in a self-admiring gesture. "Black belt," he said with a threatening smirk. "It really blows men's minds," he said. "The thought, that is."

"What thought?"

"Getting the shit kicked out of them by a gay. They get all sorts of far-out ideas about what might happen."

"Can you blame them?"

Rudy laughed. "Well, with your looks, Lieutenant, you certainly wouldn't have to worry."

"I'm relieved."

Rudy was trying for a reaction. He didn't like the one he was getting from Shetland. "Why are all cops wise guys?"

"It's a defense mechanism," Shetland said. "Most of us are very sensitive underneath and we get hurt easily. Knowing karate must be a plus in your line of work."

"Like a degree in engineering when you're working for an aircraft manufacturer."

"I would imagine," Shetland nodded in agreement, but his next question wiped the smirk off Rudy's face. "Did you know Jules Arken?"

"Saw him around," he replied hesitantly, "when he visited Miss Sebastian."

"Did you ever pay him a visit yourself?"

"No; I told you where I saw him." Quickly he changed the subject. "You know, cop, I can take you. Someday I'll have a go at it."

"I forgot to mention," Shetland said, reaching for his car door, "I'm nonviolent. In fact, I deplore violence so much I always use my gun to end it as quickly as possible." He winked. "And besides, it's not nice to threaten a policeman. Remember those prison walls."

If Shetland could come up with a reason he'd peg Rudy as Arken's killer. Rudy was the kind who killed on command, but with enthusiasm once the order was given. His leash was in the hands of Renée. If Rudy was as professional as his record indicated, Shetland wasn't going to be able to prove his suspicions, anyway. On his drive to MacArthur Airport to say good-bye to Mrs. Weiss, Shetland recalled the file he had received from Interpol. He had learned that Rudy was born in a London slum, had a British passport and no juvenile record. He had joined the British army at seventeen, received commando training and served overseas; had been on security duty at Gibraltar and spent twelve months in Viet Nam. Exemplary record, according to British military files, then had a tour of duty in Northern Ireland. He was charged with brutality in questioning an I.R.A. suspect. Charges were dropped due to insufficient evidence. He was released from the service three months later for moral conduct unbecoming a soldier of the British Armed Forces; the specifics were not indicated. He'd joined a special mercenary unit connected with one of the white-ruled South African governments, became an officer and a full-blown psychopath. He came into the employ of Miss Sebastian after being acquitted of murdering half a dozen black nationalists. Rudy Carver's profile suggested a man whose cool-mannered exterior masked the viciousness of a rabid wolverine.

When Shetland got to the airport he met Carla in the coffee shop. He was happy to see her. Except for the bandages on her hands, she looked completely recovered.

"I'm glad you came to see me off; I wanted to talk to

you again before I left." She smiled warmly at him as he sat down next to her.

"Where's our lawyer friend?" Shetland asked.

"Mr. Bates is kindly checking to see that my flight reservations have been confirmed and that we can make the connection from here to Kennedy Airport in time. I think both he and you will be glad to see me go."

"I don't know about Bates, but I'll be happy to see a friend out of harm's way. And you don't look unhappy yourself about the prospect."

"I won't deny it: Holland will look very good to me after this. But I don't have the luxury of knowing that someone I care about is safe from danger. I have an old saying for you, Lieutenant: to be forewarned is to be forearmed. Do not disregard what the first sense tells you."

"Carla, I promise I'll keep my head down."

She looked at him as if she didn't quite understand.

"It means I'll be extra careful and observant," he said.

"Be both, Lieutenant, and I mean that very seriously. You are especially vulnerable to the forces at work on Crane's Neck."

The tone of Shetland's voice reflected the unsettling effect of her remark. "Why single me out?"

"I've prayed that I could help you know your enemy better—and I'm being precise when I say that it is your enemy—but I have not been successful except in learning that in some special way you seem to represent a threat to it, and like any life force it will try to survive. And that may be at your expense."

Their conversation ended when Bates showed up to inform Mrs. Weiss that if she was to catch her plane out of Kennedy they would have to leave now. Shetland walked them to the gate. "Carla, would you mind if I gave you a kiss good-bye?"

"I would mind otherwise," she said, offering her cheek to him, but he tilted her face up and kissed her on the lips. She looked up at him, pleased and surprised.

He smiled at her. "Just giving rein to my primitive vibes," he said.

She smiled approvingly, turned and walked through the gate.

Shetland watched her board a twin-engine Cessna sitting on the runway apron near the terminal; he waved but she did not look back. A few moments later the plane taxied out to the runway, lifted off and swung west toward Kennedy. Shetland stayed on the observation deck until the plane was out of sight.

On his way home Shetland stopped in a downtown liquor store to pick up a bottle of bourbon with the intention of drinking it until things started to make sense or stopped making sense altogether—or until he stopped caring. The owner was just closing up but suddenly became talkative. "Business stinks," he said, as if it were Shetland's fault. "Summer people cleared out." While Shetland looked over the shelves the store owner stood by the door. "I used to fill big orders for wealthy customers out on Crane's Neck five, six times a week and then again on weekends. They threw a lot of parties; now, nothing. You're a cop, aren't you?" he asked distastefully.

The last thing Shetland wanted was the wrath of the local citizenry. "Nope," he muttered disinterestedly, "fireman."

"What do you mean, fireman. I've seen you around the precinct lots of times."

"Not me, pal. Always wanted to be a cop but I flunked the entrance exam. Fireman's the next best thing, though. I'll take this." Shetland placed the bottle on the counter. Throwing him a suspicious glance, the owner went around to the other side to ring up the purchase. "You got a brother?"

Shetland shook his head. "Nope; I was an orphan."

Seemingly convinced, the man remarked that it was going to storm that night. "It's going to be lightning and thundering just like that other night," he grumbled, cursing under his breath. "Something bad's going to happen, can't you feel it?" The guy was jumpy and frightened.

"Look," Shetland said, "it's hot and gooey, that's all there is to feel. Don't psych yourself up. Besides, the wind's blowing the wrong way for a storm."

But it was raining before Shetland drove the couple of

blocks to his apartment. The lightning lashed and danced like a madly wielded bullwhip. The rain fell, heavily at times, pounding, driving. Shetland sat at the small table in the no-man's-land between the small kitchen and his postage-stamp of a living room, drinking bourbon. His thoughts, growing very cloudy, zeroed in on the washing-machine thrash of rain punctuated by the gun-shot report of the thunder. The wind whined and wailed outside but in the cramped apartment the air hung thick, warm and humid. He began to think about the air-conditioning unit he meant to buy but kept putting off because he was always intending to move and he'd just have to lug the thing to the new place where it might not fit the window; besides, the new places always had central air, he thought to himself. He had anticipated that move for five years; maybe, he thought, he should break down and buy that air conditioner. He shoved the bottle across the table. "Never could drink," he muttered to himself under his breath. He rummaged around in the refrigerator for something cool to drink. He found a half-empty can of Coke; it was flat and syrupy but he guzzled it with gusto.

He began to pace, like an animal in a cage, around the table into the living room, then back into the kitchen. He leaned over the sink to peer out the window through the parted curtains his landlady had put up. "Men would live with bare walls," she had said, "if you let them."

"Bull." He'd bought curtains but before he could get them up she arrived with the set she had made herself, insisting that she be allowed to hang them up so they'd be right. His curtains had been collecting dust in the closet ever since. "What difference do curtains make," he said aloud, but he knew he was trying not to think about what the store owner had said. "You're in great shape," he told himself sarcastically, "believing in omens and portents of doom from a peddler of cheap bourbon."

He flopped down on the convertible sofa bed, unmade for days, threw his forearm over his eyes and tried to sleep. He didn't even begin to feel sleepy; he tossed and turned, peering at the alarm clock, hoping the time would pass mercifully and it would be morning. But what seemed like hours, the clock hand mockingly ticked off as minutes. The liquor burned his stomach, the syrupy taste of the Coke coated the inside of his mouth, and the thick air filled his lungs like lead weights, until all he felt like was a stomach, a mouth and a set of lungs lying on a bed in a matchbox-sized room.

Shetland heard the sound of hurried footsteps climbing the outside stairway and rolled out of bed, his stomach sinking down a well and his head spinning in response to his impertinence in moving so suddenly. The anticipated knock came just as his hand reached the doorknob. He opened it and Jessica, drenched and looking wilted, dashed inside, leaving a trail of damp footprints on the paper-thin carpet. "Hello," he said, surprised to see her, following her with his eyes as she made straight for the bathroom to shed her wet clothes.

"How about something hot to drink for a lonely wayfarer," she said.

"Coffee?"

"Do you have any tea?"

"I'll check," he said and began looking around in the cabinets. He found a coffee can full of tea bags and set a kettle of water on the stove to boil, then went to the bathroom to tell her that the tea was a couple of years old. She was standing in front of the mirror, her discarded clothes in a heap around her ankles.

"That's okay," she said as he leaned in the doorway watching her naked body arch as she combed her hair and then wrapped it in a towel. "Do you have a robe?" she asked.

Shetland nodded, turned back into the living room and tore through the mangled bed covers. He retrieved the robe and presented it to her in a balled-up bundle. It hung on her like a tent, even after she wrapped it around twice and tied the cord in a big bow. When the kettle started to whistle she pushed him aside and hurried into the kitchen. Shetland sat on the edge of the bed while she rattled around in the kitchen getting cups and saucers. In a few minutes the table was set and she sat down. "I made you some coffee," she said.

He got up and joined her, waiting for her to say something, but she seemed perfectly content to sip her tea and look at him. Finally he broke the silence and asked the question, "What are you doing here?"

"Delivering aid and comfort to a man who looked like he'd been stabbed in the back this afternoon. Is that so unusual?"

Shetland glanced toward the door. "On a night like this," he said sarcastically, "my own mother wouldn't come out."

"I'm not your mother. I was hoping you'd come to me but I can see that like most wounded bears, you crawl off by yourself to lick your wounds."

"Look, I'm not wounded and I haven't crawled off anywhere. I happen to live here."

"Are you angry with me? Or is it that you still don't trust me."

"That's a laugh," Shetland countered; "I don't trust myself and you're talking about trusting others. I know what I want from you."

"You make it sound dirty."

"It is dirty, or it used to be, or it's only supposed to be fun when you think it is. Anyway, I just want to know where you're coming from. I'm as sociable as a pair of handcuffs, with a cuddle quotient of a snub-nosed .38."

"What difference does that make?"

"Crud," Shetland sighed in surrender, throwing his arms up and clasping his hands behind his neck, "nothing makes much sense, so why should you."

"You look horrible," Jessica said. "Isn't there some way you can politely bow out of this case?"

The suggestion startled Shetland. "Why," he asked, "would I want to do that?"

"Isn't it that plus the Internal Affairs probe that's got you so strung out?"

Shetland glared at her in astonishment. "I could just picture the detectives of the Seventh, and you might as well throw in Forensic and the coroner's office, calling a news conference to tell the public that we've decided to call a finish on this one, our reason being we can't figure it out and it's making us upset." Shetland laughed. "Besides, a lot of cases never get solved."

Jessica's eyes became searching. "But this one's different," she said, "isn't it?"

"Did I say it was?"

"You act like you know something the rest of us don't. Some people think you're spending an awful lot of time in areas that have no bearing on the investigation. Why, for instance, are you so interested in the Sebastian family?"

"This sounds like a rehash of my run-in with the captain."

"I told you," Jessica smiled slyly; "I've got connections."

"Let's just say I'm a masochist. The rougher the rebuff, the more interesting it gets. You can pass that on to your connections."

"Do you think because Renée Sebastian was cold to you she's trying to hide something?"

Shetland stroked his chin thoughtfully. "It had occurred to me."

Jessica looked amused. "People like Renée," she said, "wealthy people, especially those who've had wealth for generations and have known and lived nothing but an existence created by wealth, have a tendency to see the world from a medieval point of view. There are the rulers and the ruled, and rules are for the ruled. Nothing is denied to the rich and that translates into the right to have everything and do what they like. They don't have to achieve because achievement, like everything else, can be bought. Worries about paying the rent, keeping a job, simple everyday survival mean nothing to them. Fear, poverty, human degradation are empty phrases. Some of them make a pretense of understanding but it's just that, a pretense. It's the old adage that you don't know what hunger is unless you've starved. The point to this lecture, my darling policeman, is to warn you that the wealthy are above human pettiness. They have their own brand of ruthless cruelty, a birthright engendered in arrogant ignorance. In short, they have no qualms about tossing a threatening peasant into a pit of wolves."

Shetland was furious. He had already agreed with the

captain to back off but now Jessica's words, intentional or not, had goaded him in the opposite direction. He shouted, "That rich bitch can kiss my ass." His righteous wrath quickly sputtered into an impudent whimper. Indignation aside, he knew he'd been put in his place and there wasn't anything he could do about it. He got up from the table feeling cooped up and anxious. It was the damn storm, he told himself. He turned into a cringing ninny in thunderstorms: he had a phobia about getting hit by lightning.

Jessica came over and put her arms around him. "Let's forget everything," she said; "make love to me."

Beyond the passion and the need, Shetland detected the chess player, the manipulator. It was an unpleasant aspect of her personality that exposed some of the characteristics of the aloof, insensitive, moneyed aristocrat she had disdainfully lectured him about. Like the storm, there was a violence to their lovemaking. Afterward came exhaustion. Shetland fell into a dead sleep with Jessica curled up in his arms. He awoke with a start. He heard himself moan and cry out. He was brushing his head and face and body with his hand, brushing away crawling spiderwebs. He sat up in bed trembling and whimpering; electricity seemed to be dancing on his flesh and then the frightening sensation stopped. He had been dreaming of Peel again, or of himself; that was the only part that wasn't clear. Peel's house cowered and drew into the earth against the storm. Peel sat alone, submerged inside the house, feeling frightened and constrained. Something urged him up from his chair in the study toward the window. He stood before the drawn drapes, feeling at once repelled and driven, for the caller that lay beyond was not altogether unknown to him. Could the fraternal twin of one's soul be a stranger? It was out there, waiting, watching, perhaps recoiling from the dark foreboding house, sensing that within lay a terrible truth. Apprehension and dread disappeared as, in a fever of excitement, he took hold of the drape and tore it from the window. A bolt of lightning sizzled across the heavens and the room blazed with an eerie brilliance; a thunderclap followed shortly and the house shook and trembled. Though blinded, he forced himself to look and there, beyond the rain that came in shimmering curtains against the window, turning the panes into molten cataracts of glass, beyond the distortion, in the very midst of the cold radiance, blinking like a hungry eye, fragments of shadow and dazzling light gathered and coalesced into a specific form for an instant. Near the spot at which he stared with gaping horror a limb broke off a tree with a whining creak and flew, like a severed claw, toward the window. Reflexively he jumped back as the branch harmlessly brushed the side of the house. The specter vanished in the concealing folds of the storm. Pressing closer to the window, he kept watch, but nothing appeared in the night storm and finally he drew back into the room. Unmindfully he took up the pen and tapped it slowly on the blotter. He seemed more at peace and became less afraid to think. He wondered if madness came over the mind with such swift imperceptible stealth that its victim knew not of its approach and then afterward cared not. Or, he wondered, did it creep over the intellect with the prolonged corrosiveness of leprosy, ravaging bits and pieces of reason until, one day, the afflicted realized his loss? Had he gone mad at some point; was there hope for salvation in oblivion? If that were so he surely would pray for the merciful deliverance.

As he contemplated the method of his destruction he sensed the presence just outside the door of his study. "You're afraid too, aren't you," he said mockingly. "Afraid to come through the door and confront the truth." Peel snatched up a book and flung it; it bounced off the door and fell open on the floor.

He stood before the fireplace, the red journal in his hands. He put it into the fire and returned to his desk, where he spied the letter opener. Without hesitation he picked it up in his right hand; with his left he searched his throat for the sensuous, throbbing line of the jugular vein. Finding it, he placed the point of the letter opener on the position his finger marked, held it there for a moment, then plunged the blade in. His jaw clenched shut at the pain, and blood shot across the room. Peel quickly weakened, his hand released its grip on the handle of the letter opener, which remained lodged in his neck, and he fell listlessly on his side. Blood continued to pump from the wound, soaking his clothes and forming a pool on the floor around his feet. His frame sagged, then slowly he slumped forward onto the desk. His breath ceased to gurgle in his throat, his eyes became cold, sightless orbs of glass. Peel was dead.

The dream was so real—too real. Shetland sat with shoulders hunched, breathing laboriously, slowly gaining his bearings in the darkened room. The panic faded and he realized the phone was ringing. He looked down at Jessica. She was still asleep. Just as he started to get out of bed, her eyes opened; they were sightless amber fires transfixed on the ceiling. For an instant he was overcome with the sensation that he was tumbling into them; then they focused on him and the spell vanished. Shaken and still groggy with sleep, he stumbled across the room, picked up the receiver and waited dumbly for the caller to speak.

"Hello, Lieutenant? Lieutenant Shetland?" a woman's disturbed voice said.

He slurred a yes.

"Thank God," she said. "This is Mrs. Peel. I know this sounds like madness, but can you come right away? It's urgent."

He had to stop to think. "Where are you and what's the matter?"

"I'm at the house," she answered, her voice filled with alarm; "I can't explain over the phone."

The last thing he wanted to do was drag himself out on a miserable night in a miserable storm. He asked, "Could you just give me an idea of what the problem is?"

She shouted back hysterically, "No. If I do I'm afraid you won't come."

"Okay, okay," he said reassuringly, "I'm on my way. But at least tell me if you're in any immediate danger because if you are, a patrol car can get to you a lot faster than I can."

"No, I don't think so, but hurry," she said.

"Give me ten—no, fifteen minutes, all right?"

She hung up without answering.

When he put the receiver down he mumbled as an afterthought, "I'm off duty."

"This is crazy," Shetland said, turning to face Jessica, "but I have to go out." He didn't mention the dream or his sense of uneasiness.

"You said it," she retorted coolly; "it's crazy." And that was all she said on the subject. She kept silent while he dressed like someone holding his breath the moment before undertaking a daredevil stunt. Shetland paused at the door before hurtling himself into the furious night. "Look," he said, "I should be back before daylight. Will you be here?"

"Don't go," she said. It was a warning, not a plea.

"You know us chivalrous types; we're suckers for damsels in distress," Shetland said, pulling up the collar of his raincoat. He bent his head and went out the door. Hunching over as he walked into the flat, colorless gloom, he was buffeted by blustery winds and intermittent rain squalls. He reached his car just as a new downpour struck. The hood of his car was a seething cauldron of water as he turned out of the driveway. In the quarter of an hour it took to reach the beginning of Crane's Neck Road two rain squalls had come and gone. He was thankful that it wasn't raining as he hit the long open causeway, which melted into the gray, overcast darkness ahead of him. His headlights were soaked up by the shimmering pavement; as it was he was nearly driving blind. He clenched his teeth in horror when a maniac huddled against the weather in a hooded rain slicker roared past him in an open jeep.

The road climbed and then forked. The route to the left had been closed off with barricades and flashing signal lights because of the extensive work being done to move the old rim road back from the edge of the bluffs, which were threatening to cave in as a result of erosion. The taillights of the jeep were no longer in sight and Shetland began to wonder if the driver had disregarded the detour.

A few moments later Shetland stopped the car as a pair of unsavory-looking dogs came out of the woods and weaved across the road ahead of him, their muzzles to the ground. They were too far away for him to get a good look, but something about their behavior did not sit well with him. In a moment they were gone and he crept up to the approximate spot where they had crossed, stopped and peered into the blackness of the woods. He was startled to discover a pair of red, dimly-lit eyes staring back. He got the chilling feeling that the canine mentality directing those mesmerizing eyes was dangerous. He blinked, and when he looked again the glowing coals had disappeared.

Several hundred yards past the point where the pair of stealthily loping shadows had turned into the woods, George Coleman, assistant county road engineer, sped along the condemned portion of the Cliff Road, cursing himself and the war surplus jeep that squeaked like an old mattress full of rusty springs. "Eight miles," he groaned to himself, "through this shit." Because of a clever decision on his part to leave the heavy equipment on the worksite, in the middle of dinner with his wife it had suddenly occurred to him that with all this rain the whole damn area might slide down onto the beach. To reassure himself he had come out here to examine the ground to see if it was safe; if it wasn't, he'd have to move the flatbed truck and the tarpaulin-covered bulldozer himself. His frustration turned to anger when the gear shift wouldn't catch. "God damn," he hissed as the stick shift suddenly flopped around like a useless piece of junk. Vengefully he shoved and jerked with his arm until finally the archaic device settled into its well-worn niche. The vehicle shuddered and buffeted, grinding into first gear at the same instant that Coleman hit the brakes and clutch. The front end dipped low on its worn-out suspension and the rear fishtailed. The jeep stopped. Putting the car in neutral and leaving the motor running like a percolating coffee pot, Coleman seized the flashlight on the seat next to him, jumped out and immediately began to look over the site. He examined the ground thoroughly from the edge of the bluff back to the flatbed. Except for some new slippage near the old roadbed it looked hard as a rock. Reassured but disgruntled that the unpleasant trip had been made for nothing, he got back in the jeep and, using a clipboard for a writing surface, wrote out and dated a notification that he had made the inspection. Just in case something did happen, he was covered.

THE SUMMONING

A pair of menacing red eyes watched him from the underbrush. The German shepherd raised its aquiline muzzle to sniff the air; most of the fur on its face had been burned away, leaving a mask of raw flesh on one side of its brutish snout and around the eyes. The dog's nostrils flared, drawing in the full scent of the man, the gasoline and the oil, then the shepherd exhaled with a rough snort. Another form moved in the lurid darkness, ears flattened against its shaggy head. The beast pressed forward a few steps, then bent its head down close to the ground. A growl rose from deep within its chest and gathered in its muscular throat. Padding silently through the underbrush, the two huge shapes passed out of the woods to the edge of the road. They halted for a moment, glancing back, as if for reassurance, towards some unseen presence in the woods. Then they ran low to the ground until the last moment.

From the corner of his eye George caught the massive blur of one of the dogs, which swung wide to draw his attention. As the ancient ploy worked, the other dog launched its attack. Silent as a thrown javelin the German shepherd leaped through the darkness to sink his fangs deep into George Coleman's neck. The white daggers pierced the rubberized material of the slicker, warm flesh and muscle; and then, driven by powerful jaws, crunched down on bone. Coleman's body shuddered in convulsions, and before he could cry out his dreadful amazement, the decoy too was upon his helpless victim, tearing out Coleman's windpipe with a quick jerk. Blood jumped from the severed arteries onto the heaving chest. The pair of elated attackers rubbed their muzzles in the blood which was gushing forth, their tails wagging in murderous fanaticism. Both animals delighted in the successful kill by nipping at the cooling flesh. No longer able to restrain the delirious joy of killing lust, the German shepherd jumped to the hood of the jeep, grunted, and then howled. The demented cry could be heard even in the midst of the deluge; they had pleased their master.

During the minutes of Coleman's savage death Shetland arrived at the Peel house. Mrs. Peel opened the door as he was walking up the driveway; he hurried at her insistence and followed her into the living room. Dressed in a nightgown, with a sweater thrown over her shoulders, she was nervous and frightened. "I was busy all morning making the final arrangements for my husband's funeral tomorrow," she said. He started to speak but she lifted her hand. "Please let me tell it through. When I got home I was tired. I took a shower, got into my nightgown and came downstairs to make myself a drink to be sure I'd sleep instead of tossing and turning all night." Shetland thought he heard something being knocked over somewhere in the house. Mrs. Peel noticed his alarm and begged him to let her finish. "I was more tired than I realized because after the drink I got very sleepy, so I lay down on the sofa and I guess I just nodded off." She sighed breathlessly and said, biting on her lower lip, "Dear God, I was awakened because something was touching me." She began to tremble, her voice faltering. "Here and here," she said, indicating her breasts and her crotch. "I opened my eyes. The room was dark but I saw them standing over me." She began to cry. "I could feel my nightgown had been pulled up and I was exposed and they were touching me." She covered her face with her hands. "I don't remember much after I started to scream except that I must have gotten up and turned on the lights because the next thing I remember I was standing alone in the room. It wasn't a dream; it wasn't."

"What happened then?" Shetland asked.

"I called you."

"No one else?"

"No, just you. I didn't know who else to turn to!"

Shetland got that sinking feeling again; he had an unlisted phone number and he hadn't given it to her. The only way she could have gotten it was from the precinct. The strange, intangible sense he had that someone or something was moving about in the house became stronger. Mrs. Peel poured herself a shot of straight scotch. "Let me start from the beginning," she said, "but first, do you believe in ghosts or hauntings?"

Shetland looked puzzled and unsure.

"Can you at least accept the possibility?" she asked insistently.

He could hardly believe his own words: "Yes, I can."

That seemed to relieve her. "I understand now," she said, "that the first day I arrived here you were trying to warn me. It was something you felt about the house. It affected me almost immediately and I was all set to turn right around and walk out the door and follow your suggestion that I stay in town. But I didn't because I began to feel that this thing I sensed was Stephen's presence." She wrung her hands nervously. "I was so sure at first—don't ask me to explain why or how or my reasons for wanting to stay. Perhaps I felt sorry for it and hoped once Stephen was buried, that part of him that still remained would depart. This is madness, isn't it?"

"I'm not calling the men in the white coats, am I?"

"I think I almost hoped you would."

"You indicated that you had doubts about it being your husband?"

"Yes. I thought it was Stephen but I'm still not sure. The presence is like a mimic, very convincing at times and then, and then . . ." she groped for the right words, "it reveals itself not as Stephen but as a reflection, like in a mirror, identical and yet reversed. I can't explain it any better than that. And now, tonight, those creatures were real," she said, slipping her nightgown over her shoulder to reveal thin, red lacerations like paper cuts on her upper arm and chest. Suddenly she reached the end of her emotional tether. "I couldn't block out the thought that Stephen's spirit was in the company of those things and that his soul was lost in hell. It's strange," she said; "a lot of religious people I know believe in heaven but can't accept the possibility of hell; it's too monstrous, I guess. But if there is a heaven, then there must be a hell." Shetland had no answer to the pleading look in her eyes. "I don't think I could stand knowing that someone I loved was doomed in that place."

"Look, Mrs. Peel, we don't know what we're dealing with here: imagination gone berserk or a crack in the universe. In either case it's dangerous. I want you to come with me now."

She recoiled at the suggestion. "I have to know," she said. "Maybe there's some way I can help."

"Mrs. Peel, stop and think for a moment. If your worst fears are true, how can there be any help? That's a steely barb, I know, but if that doesn't convince you that we're totally unequipped to deal with this situation at the moment then just remember what those things were doing to you when you woke up."

She closed her eyes and drew in a deep breath, then slowly exhaled. "All right," she said. She glared bitterly at the glass in her hand. "God," she said, "this stuff's not helping," and set it down on the lamp table.

Shetland took her by the arm. "I think we'll leave right now," he said.

"My clothes," she protested.

"We'll come back for them," he retorted, shoving her toward the front door. He suddenly got the feeling that something bad was about to come down hard. It was the same kind of feeling he had experienced as a G.I. in Viet Nam when Charley was about to spring an ambush. It was like religion: you followed its tenets on faith; those who did, lived. The lights began to flicker, then to dim, and it sounded as if there were some disturbance coming from the study, with books being knocked off the shelves and spilling onto the floor. Mrs. Peel froze in her tracks and her eyes darted about wildly as if she were trying to decide.

"No," she shouted and twisted free from his grasp. Shetland bolted after her as she ran toward the study. He caught up with her just before she reached the door and pulled her back, forcing her against the wall. She was stammering, on the verge of hysteria. "Please, I must know," she cried. The rest of the house suddenly went dark except for the dimming hall light overhead and the bar of light shining underneath the study door. The front door was no more than twenty feet from them, invisible in the gloom, but something told him not to go that way, to stay out of the darkness. You're being stampeded by a child's fear, he told himself, but he couldn't get rid of the notion.

"We could go through that door," Mrs. Peel said, sensing his fear.

Confused, Shetland glared at her. "What the hell are you talking about? Do you have any idea what might be on the other side?"

"Then why else were we lured here and then trapped?"

"We weren't lured anywhere; we got here on our own steam. And who says we're trapped?"

"Your expression, Lieutenant."

"Hold the phone. We're both psyching each other up and we're tossing away all the obvious explanations."

"All right, Lieutenant, perhaps you're right. Then the rational answer is inside that room; maybe we can end this nightmare right now."

Her argument made a crazy kind of sense. If he didn't go into the study he would be admitting to the fantastic and that he was indeed trapped. "Okay, Mrs. Peel," he said; "we go for broke." He handed her the keys to his car. "If anything happens to me you get out of here; run like the devil is chasing you and don't look back."

He felt like someone afraid of heights rushing toward the edge of a steep cliff and unable to stop himself. His hand reached out for the doorknob; his guts were turning to jelly. He twisted around, then hesitated. "Go back, Mrs. Peel!" She stood frozen, looking bewildered about what to do. He started to back off, his courage faltering. The lights went out and the door, its handle firmly in his grasp, flung open, catapulting him into the room. His head struck something hard in the dark. The blow stunned him. He staggered, then dropped to his hands and knees and finally collapsed. Multi-colored lights flashed before his eyes and his ears were assaulted with an unearthly roar that seemed like a combination of jet engines and human screams. He felt himself slipping into unconsciousness and he tried to fight it. He could hear his own voice, groggy and slurred, crying, "Get up, get up!" Though his right arm was twisted under his body, he managed to free it and grab for something he could use to pull himself up off the floor. He found the desk and with his left arm pushing from underneath he got to his knees. The movement very nearly caused him to pass out but Mrs. Peel's wretched cries for help spurred him on. He faltered, his head bursting with pain, then struggled to his feet and blundered in the direction of her tortured voice. He got to the door and peered down the hall; he saw nothing. Then Mrs. Peel came running toward him out of the dark, her clothes torn and bloody, her bruised lips quivering in silent cries for help. Her arms reached out pleadingly to him. Before he could react she was seized from behind and thrown against the wall. He saw her gasp for breath, then fall to the floor. His mind blanked out and he lurched forward, fumbling for his gun; then something rigid and burning cold clamped around his neck like a vise. The vertebrae in his neck immediately buckled under the pressure; his windpipe was being crushed. He fought back, flailing his arms, but without air he quickly weakened and in a matter of seconds he was as helpless as a rag doll. Everything began to spin, and just before he blacked out he saw, through a dizzying fog, Mrs. Peel being set upon by glistening bestial monstrosities. The nightmarish mutations dragged their victim up off her hands and knees as she wept in vain for a swift deliverance into death. They ripped off the tattered shreds of her gown and tore licentiously at her flesh. He prayed for his last breath to be choked out of him but to his horror, realized he was meant to witness her torment. Tears of helplessness filled his eyes but still he could see. He squeezed his eyes shut but the image was still there. The last sight he remembered before his head exploded in numbing pain and he blacked out was Mrs. Peel, her arms pulled straight up over her head, her face expressionless, her body slithering serpentlike, her breasts ripped open and bleeding, legs red with blood from her buttocks and womb and her eyes made vacant by madness.

CHAPTER NINE

THREE DAYS LATER, unable to remember anything of the last seventy-two hours, Shetland woke up to the gray calm of a private hospital room. All the doctors would tell him in their detached professional way was that he was in pretty bad shape when they brought him in; a self-examination confirmed the assessment. He had stitches running from his lower lip down to his chin, and he was wearing a neck brace. The doctors said that although nothing was broken, some of the ligaments and muscles were torn. When he was able to get out of bed and take a good look in the mirror he saw that his face was swollen and puffy, both his eyes were blackened and a lower front tooth was missing. To Shetland it looked like he had gone fifteen rounds with a gorilla wearing steel boxing gloves. The rest of his body was stiff as a board. He was given pain killers; otherwise the pain would have been excruciating. The doctors were primarily concerned about possible damage to his back, which they X-rayed several times. But what worried Shetland most were his sudden, nervous seizures. For no apparent reason he would break out in a cold sweat, shaking like a leaf. The seizures were always accompanied by head-spinning rushes that left him dizzy and exhausted. The doctors told him the attacks were the residual effects of shock and gave him more drugs—tranquilizers, he guessed. But the drugs and solicitous care didn't help his depression or the bad dreams. Day or night, whenever he slept, the dreams would come, agonizingly incoherent and filled with frenzied horror. When he awoke the depression came.

As Shetland began to feel better, at least physically, his small hospital room appeared less drab. He began to notice the potted plants on the windowsills and bouquets of flowers on the bedside table, all accompanied by get-well cards from the department personnel and their families. The activity in the hospital corridor outside made him feel less detached, and even the doctors and nurses who came to check on him seemed less like automatons and more human: they even smiled. He was not allowed visitors on his first day back among the living. His doctor would not even allow him to be questioned about what had happened. Not that it would have done any good—to Shetland it was all a blank. The next day a psychiatrist from the hospital staff talked with him and explained that he was suffering from amnesia brought on by the trauma of what had happened.

"Which was . . . ?" Shetland asked, hoping to trick the doctor into revealing what no one else would.

"Not yet," the psychiatrist answered. "I think it's best that we let it come back to you slowly."

"And if it doesn't?"

"In cases like this it usually does. And I must warn you that it can be quite disturbing to have your memory come back in disconnected snatches, but we'll be keeping close tabs on you."

After the session with the psychiatrist Shetland was allowed visitors. Jessica came for a short while. She was curiously uncomfortable and somewhat withdrawn. Harry dropped in just as she was leaving and stayed for perhaps ten minutes, talking about everything except what had happened. He let slip that the reporters were all over the hospital trying to find out about Shetland's condition.

That night Shetland began to remember. It was perhaps

the worst night of his life. The horrible scene of Mrs. Peel's death came back just as the doctor had predicted, in dissociated flashes which shuffled and reshuffled themselves. His mind recoiled as if from electrical shocks until the whole ghastly nightmare worked itself into proper order. Early Saturday morning Scalley and Casey came by on an official visit to take down his deposition; a police stenographer was with them. They were friendly and took it easy, but it was obvious to Shetland that they had been under a lot of pressure in the past few days. He asked them what was going on but they were reluctant to discuss it. There was no way he could tell them what had really happened, not unless he was prepared to be committed to a mental hospital. He told them everything straight: the phone call, the fact that Jessica was with him when he received it, and gave them the conversation almost verbatim. He even mentioned the dogs, and they went over that part several times. It was after he got to Mrs. Peel that he began to lie. He said that she had called him to the house because she thought someone had broken in. They heard something in the study, he went to investigate, the lights went out and somebody hit him from behind. He didn't see who it was. "That's all there is to it," he said. Then he asked, already knowing the answer, "What happened to Mrs. Peel?"

Casey and Scalley looked at each other. Then Casey turned to him and said, "She died, Lieutenant. We found her body in a shallow depression in the woods behind the house."

He didn't ask any further questions, which obviously relieved them. That evening Scalley returned for the eight o'clock visiting hour. Shetland wasn't surprised to see him. "Pull up some bed and sit down," he said.

Scalley was not the sort of man to let his job get to him, but as he sat uncomfortably at the foot of the bed trying to act the part of the dutiful friend, his worry showed through. "Looks like you've got it made here, Lieutenant."

"Yeah, sure, good food, great service, and pretty nurses. Of course the price of admission is a little steep . . ."

Scalley looked around, paying an inordinate amount of attention to the view of the parking lot from the window, the flowers in the room, and the tray on the bedside table loaded with Shetland's medication; he was stalling. Then he blurted out, "I got that information on the Sebastians you asked for. It's not much and it's not fully corroborated."

"You were told to drop that line of investigation."

Scalley hesitated at the mild rebuke but then continued, "You might as well hear it since I've got it. I found out that the boy was on the plane because his father was personally escorting him to Europe to enroll him in a special school for gifted children. That was the statement made to the press by the family's attorney. But actually the kid was being taken out of the country because he was involved in a family scandal. That's where I ran into a stone wall. A lot of the papers alluded to some unseemly goings-on but it was mostly vague; no direct accusations were made. They were afraid of lawsuits, I suppose. Apparently at that time the old man was considering the possibility of entering state politics. In either case, the whole affair was quietly shoved into the background."

"Back up a bit. Did you happen to find out what the naughty secret was?"

"Incest, Lieutenant, between Aaron and his sister Renée. The rumors have it that Renée was three months pregnant by her brother when he was shuttled out of the country. When her brother had the accident she fell ill. There were several versions to the story, one being that she simply collapsed into a coma at the same moment the airplane crash took place. You've heard about that kind of thing, where twins are supposed to have this bond so that when one of them feels pain and gets sick, the other does too. Whatever the truth is, her illness supposedly caused her to have a miscarriage."

"Supposedly?"

"I don't know, Lieutenant: There was no reliable way to check. I couldn't find any records of an infant's death but she could have been attended by a private physician paid to keep quiet." Scalley was visibly disappointed at Shetland's seeming disinterest in what he said. "Well? Say something, Lieutenant!"

"What do you want me to say?" Shetland questioned. "The captain was right: all we came up with was some dirty laundry that has nothing to do with now."

Scalley became angry. "Lieutenant," he said sharply, "you must have had some reason for wanting to check into Aaron Sebastian's past."

"I had a vague hunch that didn't work out, that's all, so leave it at that."

To his surprise Scalley had no such intention. "We can't," he said, then suddenly fell silent.

"And why not?"

Scalley looked like he had something he wanted to get out but was holding it back. Shetland sat up in bed and looked him straight in the eye. "Give with it," he said. "What's going on?"

"I'm not supposed to bring this up," Scalley said, "because of your condition."

"Screw my condition."

"Lieutenant, two other people were savagely murdered that night. That man you saw in the jeep was a county engineer. He was one of the victims. The other was a man who worked a small truck farm on Crane's Neck, the same guy who owns that vegetable stand on the state road."

"How were they killed?" Shetland asked.

"Maybe I shouldn't . . ."

"Maybe you should have thought of that before. Go on."

"We're not sure of the method yet but they're bad, like the others."

Shetland threw up his hands. "I don't want to hear any more. I'm out of it."

Scalley was puzzled. "What do you mean, out of it?"

"I'm applying for medical leave, and after I hand in my official report there won't be any problem getting it."

Scalley had half expected something like this; he knew the lieutenant had been lying about what happened that night at the Peel house but he was determined to convince Shetland not to take himself off the case. "Look, Lieutenant," he began calmly, "we're all up the wall trying to deal with this thing by the book. It's not working because we're all stuck using police procedure."

"What the hell do you think I am," Shetland said, "a

free agent? If I got back into it my hands would be tied like everybody else's."

"It's different," Scalley insisted; "you've come face to face with it."

"Believe me, it doesn't make any difference. You're right, I've come face to face with it and look what it's done to me. I'd be trembling like a scared rabbit except the doctors here have got me so sedated that I can barely wiggle. My nerves are shot and so are my guts."

"Lieutenant, at least you're better equipped than the rest of us, if only in the fact that you've survived."

"Survived," Shetland laughed. "I was got to, pal, turned inside out. Don't think I haven't been asking myself why I'm still alive, and the answer is, it was toying with me. The next time it might get tired of the game. Round one was theirs by points; they can have round two by default. There are no heroes in this bed, just us whimps. I'm scared and that's the living truth."

The argument ended with an abrupt silence. Getting up to leave, Scalley apologized for having upset him. "Don't sweat it," Shetland said as Scalley walked out the door; "it's called the million-dollar wound."

Shetland felt angry at Scalley for trying to lay a guilt trip on him about his duty. "What the hell does he know about it," he muttered to himself. He figured nearly getting his head torn off in the line of duty was all anyone could ask; any more would be stepping over the line. But his anger was not aimed just at Scalley; he also turned it upon himself. Shetland always thought that surviving a harrowing experience was supposed to make you stronger, but he could neither deny his fear nor overcome it.

Just before noon the next day the doctor came in to give him the final once-over before he was released. "You're fortunate, Lieutenant, that your condition wasn't quite as bad as we originally thought or you could have been flat on your back for months. In any case, your neck muscles took quite a strain. They're still weak and will need to recuperate." The doctor handed him a prescription. "This is for a neck brace," he said; "you can fill it at any medical supply house. It won't be very comfortable but I strongly suggest you wear it at all times." Just before they shook hands and said good-bye the doctor mentioned that the wife of the farmer who had been murdered was on the same ward. Needing confirmation of his own nightmare, Shetland said he wanted to talk to the woman. The chief resident wasn't too keen on the idea but Shetland argued that perhaps there was a connection between what had happened to him and the farmer's death, and said that a talk with the wife might help him to remember more. Finally the doctor relented, on the condition that Shetland not upset her—or, for that matter, himself. Another stipulation was that the staff psychiatrist be present. Shetland agreed and was taken to her room. Before they entered the psychiatrist explained that Mrs. Whitiker was irrational and they were holding her until room could be found in a state mental institution. "She might not respond at all," he said, "but if she does and she shows the slightest sign of distress we have to leave immediately."

When Shetland assured the psychiatrist that he understood the ground rules they entered Mrs. Whitiker's room. Sitting rigidly erect in a leatherette chair near the bed, her weathered hands folded carefully in her lap, the woman did not acknowledge their presence as they entered the room. Shetland pulled up a chair in front of her, introduced himself and explained why he and the psychiatrist were there.

She didn't react except to turn her gaze for an instant in his direction. "Mrs. Whitiker, do you feel up to telling us what happened?"

She turned her vacant eyes to him again. "I must go to church," she said, "to pray for Charley. He committed a mortal sin. I tried to explain to the others but they said I had to wait for someone. I suppose they were talking about you."

"I don't understand, Mrs. Whitiker."

"It's like I told the others, Charley saw the face of God and was punished like the Bible says. I'm afraid for his soul."

"Please, Mrs. Whitiker, where did Charley see the face of God?"

167

She turned away. "In our yard between the house and the barn. I tried to warn Charley when he grabbed his shotgun and ran outside, but he wouldn't listen. It was the Son and with Him was the warrior angel, Michael the Archangel holding a flaming sword. It was Michael's sword that struck down my Charley." Suddenly she began to cry.

The psychiatrist told Shetland they had to leave.

Harry Simpson was waiting at the reception desk swigging a cup of hot chocolate. "Hey, listen," Harry said. "Scalley told me about the conversation you two had last night, about having yourself put on sick leave."

"You don't think it's warranted?"

"On the contrary, Donald, my boy, I think it's a smart move. You see, I know why you took that vacation. It wasn't to sail, was it?"

"You're doing the talking," Shetland said.

"Your life just turned rancid; you had to get away."

"If that's what you think is true about me then I'm right in getting clear of this."

"Oh it's true all right, and yes, as a friend, I think you should get clear of it. But Scalley thinks it's important that you don't."

"Scalley's got crazy notions."

"Crazy or not, he asked me to convince you to stay on this case."

"Is that what you're doing?"

"That depends," Harry said.

"On what?"

"Nobody's kidding himself anymore about what's happening. We've got some devil of a something by the tail, we can't let go, and we can't do anything with it. This isn't something we can throw handcuffs on."

"You asking me or telling me?"

"I'll tell you this: we have one dead man hacked up in pieces like he was thrown through a giant fan and another killed and half eaten by dogs and a woman who died in a manner impossible to accept even in this corrupt insane world, all in one savage night. And then you can't tell me what really happened. If it's even half of what I imagine, then explain why you're still alive, with your mental faculties intact, if it isn't because you were meant to confront this thing."

"Do you know what the hell you're saying? That's voodoo bullshit," Shetland laughed sarcastically. "Appointed champions, comic book heroes—they don't issue silver bullets in the police department, old chum. Half of what you imagine?" Shetland sneered. "You don't have that kind of imagination, Harry."

Their conversation started drawing attention from several people in the waiting room and Harry suggested they move on. "I'm here to give you a lift home," he said; "if you need one, that is."

"I need one," Shetland said, "but not home. Crane's Neck, the place where this engineer was killed."

Shetland filled out the forms and signed the releases at the hospital desk, then met Harry in front of the building.

"You sure about this?" Harry asked gently, as Shetland climbed into the front seat of his car.

"What's the matter, Harry?"

"Nothing; I just don't want to be responsible for talking you into something against your will."

"Relax; you haven't. I'm just curious."

Harry was at once relieved and disappointed. Shetland looked at him intently. "Suppose," he said, "I told you what happened to me. I would be doing so knowing that I was putting you in danger. Would you still want to hear it?"

"Is that the case?"

Shetland stretched back with a sigh. "I can't be sure, but I think so."

"I'd like to say that doesn't make sense; but then, what about this business does?"

"What's possible, Harry?"

"That sounds like it should be addressed to a philosopher, old buddy."

"Give it your best shot, Harry."

"Okay. Anything's possible—how's that for a cop-out—except I think I believe it," Harry said, grinning sheepishly.

"Do you believe in a hereafter?"

Harry thought for a moment, then nodded. "Yeah."

"Do you see a God and a devil in your afterlife? What I'm trying to say is, is there good and evil?"

"That's all very religious," Harry said. "I don't have all that paraphernalia, I just picture it as sort of a spiritual existence."

"Because you haven't thought about it much?"

"I wouldn't say that exactly. I haven't thought about it up front, but there is this kind of intuitive understanding, a priori knowledge."

"Run that past me again."

"Hey, listen, Donald, if you're saying we're dealing with the supernatural, then spit it out. I'll believe anything at this stage of the game." Harry became vehement. "Go ahead; if that's what we're dealing with, say so, goddammit."

Shetland didn't oblige.

It was warm, humid and windless on the bluffs. The Sound spread from the beach below as still as pale gray marble, away into a colorless haze. The air hung thick and lifeless; to Shetland breathing it was like chewing. Sound was absorbed like water into a sponge. "Here we are," Harry said; "there's not much to see. The jeep was in the middle of the road, approximately where we're parked now. There were some paw marks in the soft sand over there and up there, about fifteen yards farther along the road. According to the animal experts your department called in, the attack was, in a manner of speaking, very professional. The decoy distracted the victim while the other animal laid in wait to launch the attack. Quite wolflike, except they weren't wolves."

"Does that mean something, Harry?"

"They seem to think so; the experts, that is. Dogs, even feral dogs, are pretty amateurish when it comes to hunting. A pack will gang up on their victim with no coordination or pattern, like a mugging. The experts said all wild carnivores not only have a method of attack, but also what they called a killing bite. Some of the big cats bite through their prey's skull or break their backs; others actually suffocate their victim by covering his nose and mouth with their own mouths. The exceptions to that are animals raised in zoos and domestic dogs, because it's a learned behavior, passed on from parent to offspring." Harry shook his head. "Damn interesting stuff."

"So where'd our hairy killers pick up this trick?" Shetland asked.

Harry shrugged in silence.

"Where was the body?"

"This way," Harry said, trotting off the road into the brush. "It's not much of a path," he said; "thank God the poor bastard was dead when they dragged the body through here. Even with the rain there was blood all over the place."

Shetland followed closely behind Harry and soon they came to a clearing overhung with tree branches. A circle of paw marks was still visible. "Was that where the body was?" Shetland asked, pointing to an untrodden patch of ground.

"No," Harry said; "they found it over there underneath those bushes."

"Then what was in that spot?"

"Nothing. Why?" Harry was puzzled.

"Oh, but there was something. Look closely."

Harry stepped into the clearing and crouched down. "I don't see anything," he said; "no track, certainly."

"No," Shetland agreed, "but the ground has been disturbed."

Harry shook his head. "I still don't see it, but maybe if there was something it was just more tracks that got washed out by the rain."

"In this thick cover, Harry?"

"Okay," Harry raised his voice in frustration, "what are you intimating—that something was there? I'll buy it, but what was it?"

"Some devilish thing, Harry, that sent those dogs out here to kill Coleman."

Harry jumped to his feet. "You're serious, aren't you?"

"Just a few minutes ago, in the car, you said anything was possible."

"Yeah, I know what I said."

"Harry, for God's sake, Arken's cottage wasn't a Halloween holdover."

"Oh, for crying out loud. The supernatural? The devil? Donald, how do you expect me to accept that?"

"My point precisely, Harry. It's staring us right in the face—something screwy, demented—and there ain't no way we can handle it because we can't accept it. The department, the D.A.'s office, the courts and every little bureaucratic department high and low and in between can't accept it—God, it would come unglued if it tried. Whichever way I try to pursue what I know is true, I become the sacrificial goat. I get a straitjacket and a rubber spoon or I get eaten up by a nightmare. That's why this kid is getting his beloved ass out of harm's way."

Harry was alarmed. "Okay, okay, maybe my imagination is too sanitized to believe in what you're saying, but if by some freak turn of events you're right, then that's all the more reason for you to hang in there. Forewarned is forearmed, isn't it?"

Shetland remembered Carla Weiss telling him the same thing, but now his only thoughts were of getting out and forgetting what had happened.

When he got back to his apartment he tried to call Jessica at her job and then at home. but she wasn't at either place. He couldn't face the prospect of being alone with himself. He took a sleeping pill prescribed by his doctor and curled up on the couch to sleep.

When Shetland awoke it was to an extraordinary feeling of well-being; it seemed to pervade the apartment like some tangible entity. He had dreamed of Jessica and her name was on his lips when his eyes opened. He remembered being afraid for her, or of her, it wasn't clear which. It didn't seem important now. He sat up, planting both feet firmly on the floor. The sense of well-being grew more intense, and the fear and depression were gone completely, as if they had never existed. So overpowering was this strange euphoria that he felt weak and giddy. There was a flutter in his stomach and blood seemed to be rushing to his head. The sublime sense of warmth and peace that infected him was so overwhelming that he wept. He tried to tell himself it was the residual effect of the sleeping pill or, worse, that he was cracking up, but such thoughts seemed ludicrous. The feeling was almost unbearable. He threw his arms around himself as if to keep from flying away. There were no more shadows. His senses were numbed to ugliness; all was joyous rapture. Tears ran down his cheeks, he was like a child overcome with the happiness of the instant. When he stood up he was lightheaded. It was as if the laws of gravity had suddenly been rescinded. "Jessica," he cried in bewilderment. She was coming to him; he could almost see her hurrying up the drive; she was on the stairs.

He started across the room to let her in; he knew she was out there, raising her hand to knock on the door. He wanted her, he needed her; his joy would be complete then. His skin crawled and tingled and he reached out for the doorknob. Suddenly his hand recoiled as if he had touched something cold and slimy. A death that was not death was on the other side of the door, a hydra with heads of good and evil tearing at one another. Dread filled him like water pouring into the lungs of a drowning man. He stepped back slowly, the sense of evil growing stronger. The air pressed in around him, squeezing sweat out of his pores. He could feel his heart crashing against his rib cage, his brain constricting into a smothering unconsciousness. His life was being hemmed in on all sides, confined until it had no place to exist. He was blinded by sweat, and panic pricked at his flesh.

He was acutely aware that he would go under if for one instant he gave himself up to fear, if he lost control and cried out. He rubbed the sweat and tears from his face with his bare forearm. The knocking became more urgent, like the frenzied booming of a hollow drum. He stumbled backward, a guttural squeal wrenching from his throat. "No, no, I'm through with you; leave me alone." He grabbed the revolver on the lamp table, undid the holster snap and pulled the gun free. His whole body trembled uncontrollably but a voice from within cried that he must not panic, he must not let it invade his mind; it mustn't come through the door and into his mind. The phone rang and suddenly it was gone.

CHAPTER TEN

J ESSICA TRIED TO STAY AWAY. Her reasons were strong: there was Donald. She felt something new with him, and there was the danger to them all, but the lure of the sin of abomination was stronger. It appealed to the dark creature within Jessica who saw her soul as the twisted thing that it was and who belied her pretense. She had always struggled but always in vain. The voices on the terrace flared heatedly. Careful not to be observed, she stepped to the window and looked down. Renée's alabaster skin was flushed with anger as she ranted at the man.

"Why did you come here?" she demanded. "It was a stupid, irresponsible move that puts us all in unnecessary jeopardy."

The man twisted his hands nervously and followed Renée into the house. A few moments later Jessica heard them in the hall, then again as they resumed their argument in Aaron's room. Jessica waited impatiently as the dispute went on and heard them as they came out and went into Renée's private chambers, which adjoined the room Jessica occupied. No one was aware that she was in the house. Quietly she slipped to the partially opened door that connected the rooms. They were in Renée's dressing room, and in the mirror Jessica could see the reflection of the man, who was sitting in an absurdly small chair. His head hung down and he was sweating profusely.

Renée paced the room.

"Can't you get it through your head?" the man said weakly. "They know—I mean, it's only a matter of time before they figure it was me, and then . . ."

"And then what, Sergeant," Renée said threateningly.

"Look, I've got to protect myself. I want the truth about what happened to the girl. What you told me doesn't wash anymore."

Renée laughed savagely. "Doesn't wash anymore," she hissed.

The man broke down. "Jesus, how did I let myself get talked into this damn mess—why, why?"

"You have a short memory, Sergeant," Renée said scornfully. "Greed—twenty-five thousand dollars' worth—was your motivation. Do what you've been told and I'll reward you well. We can still stave off disaster."

"No," he shouted, slamming his fist against his thigh, "it makes no sense at all. Even your brother agrees with me."

"Aaron's sickly and weak; he doesn't comprehend."

"Jesus, lady, what good would it do to kill Shetland? It's not going to stop anything; in fact, it'll make it ten times worse."

"Not if you make it look like an accident or suicide."

"You're talking crazy. I'm not killing a cop—I'm not killing anybody."

"You don't have a choice," Renée said calmly. "I promise you won't get free of this with a simple charge of covering up a missing person. No, Sergeant, I'll make sure you're charged with concealing a murder. They'll believe me because they won't have any reason not to, when I confess that I killed the girl with my own hands. Only I can help you. Do this for me and I will say that you knew nothing about the girl if it comes to that."

The sergeant seemed defeated and won over but he left

without saying anything. The moment Renée departed Jessica slipped out of the room and down the back staircase that led to the service area. She waited several minutes, until Renée had resumed her afternoon tea, which had been interrupted by the sergeant's visit, and then made her appearance. Despite her cool exterior Renée was obviously pleased to see Jessica; her mood softened and it seemed to Jessica that she was forgiven her past transgressions. There was no trace of the shrill harlot who less than a quarter hour ago had bullied, cajoled and commanded that a man be killed. Jessica had always admired Renée's strength; her will was almost irresistible, her beauty and youth impervious to the ravages of time. Once she had perceived Renée as a goddess of mortal flesh; that image still lingered but now there was a visible flaw, the indomitable force of will applied with delicate subterfuge was giving way to the churling outbursts that had cowed the police sergeant.

"Will you see Aaron?" Renée asked.

"No. I came to be with you."

"That's not fair. He cares for you; he has a right."

"He despises me and I him. There has never been affection between us, not from the first. How could you expect there to be? To him I'm just one more plague upon his house for the unredeemable sins he has committed." Jessica's voice was shot through with hatred. "If you insist on harping on this subject perhaps it is better that I leave."

"No," Renée said, imploringly placing her hand upon Jessica's. "Of late you come so rarely. I will say no more about it."

Jessica relented. "Perhaps," she said, "I will see him later."

That evening they had a light meal together. Afterward they strolled in the garden, and then retired to Renée's apartment, where Jessica had overheard the assassination being plotted. Jessica was delirious in the mere anticipation of their lovemaking, of the forbidden taste of a woman's flesh. It was the essence; the meaning of her existence. Renée knelt on the bed, her back arched like a cat's, hair spilling like a shadow upon the snow of her shoulders, the fragrance of her skin hypnotically intoxicating. She pressed cold fruit to Jessica's mouth and then kissed the tart juices from her lips. She moved fluidly, catlike. As if taunting her prey, she placed electrifying kisses on her cheek and the smooth contour of her throat, her actions becoming more urgent as she drew from Jessica the first breathy moan of arousal. Her warm moist mouth and tongue licked and suckled on Jessica's nipples until they stood hard and erect and aching with the pain of desire.

Cradled in each other's arms, they lay touching, searching. But the tender moment dissolved in the light flooding into the room from the open door. Rudy pushed Aaron's wheelchair to the foot of the bed. Jessica covered her nakedness against the cold reptilian gaze of the broken creature captive in the wheelchair. Renée got out of bed, put on a dressing gown and wheeled her brother out of the room, closing the door behind her.

When she did not return Jessica dressed and went looking for her. She went to Aaron's room and listened but heard nothing. She went downstairs and found Rudy alone in the small library off the main dining room. "Where is Renée?" Jessica asked.

"Where do you think?" He nodded toward the French doors that opened onto the terrace. "She's gone up to the grove."

She detested this smug, vicious man; he was too clever, too calculating. "Be careful," she warned, "that you don't become too sure of yourself. There are things that even you would cringe at."

Rudy smiled. "Threats," he said, "sometimes have a way of coming back at the one who makes them. You know what I mean; like, cast thy bread upon the waters."

There was no time to banter with Rudy; she turned and hurried to the grove. She caught up with Renée near the pool. Renée walked as if she were in a trance; her gaze was fixed on the dark, looming hill beyond. Jessica suggested they return to the house but Renée merely answered, "Go back if you want," and continued on.

Jessica placed a restraining hand on her arm. "It's not safe out here."

Still Renée ignored her warning.

For nearly a century the grove had looked down upon the Sebastian house and the fortunes of its occupants. The family had tended the trees, clearing away the brush and thinning out the saplings until the surviving trees had grown monstrously large and spread their crowns over the earth so that nothing else could survive in that place. It was like being in an underground catacomb, and was blacker than night. Renée knew the passageways through the trees by heart, and without hesitation she and Jessica made their way over the serpent roots that spiderwebbed the mossy ground. "She lies over there," Renée whispered, pulling away from Jessica. She was immediately swallowed up in the darkness.

Jessica called to her. "Please don't leave me alone here."

"I'm not far; I'm over here by the grave," Renée called.

Jessica did not approach, for there was something in Renée's voice that alarmed her. She pleaded with Renée to come back down to the house. It was terrifyingly plain to Jessica that Renée was going mad.

"It was a lie," Renée said, moving further away and to the right as if to circle around and come behind Jessica. "Shall I tell you the truth? But of course, you already know it, my darling Jessica."

Jessica cupped her hands over her ears and screamed, "I don't want to hear." There was no telling what Renée was capable of doing. "What were you and the man planning?"

Renée didn't answer.

"I saw him on the terrace; I heard you."

There was movement on one side and Jessica wheeled around. Suddenly Renée appeared, her face expressionless and a strange fire burning in her eyes. Jessica had an overwhelming impulse to run, but just then Rudy called to them from the edge of the grove.

"Miss Sebastian, your brother sent me to fetch you back to the house. The police are there."

Renée took Jessica's hand and said, in a very calm voice, "We'd better go."

Jessica stayed in the library, out of sight. From there she could overhear the conversation in the foyer between

Renée and the uniformed officer. The officer told Renée that there would be men from the police and sheriff's departments moving about in the woods near the house and that she was not to be alarmed. He also insisted that everyone stay indoors for the rest of the evening as a precautionary measure, for the police were hunting for the animals that had killed the man on the bluffs. Jessica heard the door shut and went to the window to look out through the parted curtains. The officer walked to an unmarked car and there, sitting in the driver's seat, was Sergeant Tedeschevich.

When Renée returned to the study Jessica was gone. Rudy appeared in the doorway. "Where is she?" Renée demanded.

Rudy had a chilling smirk on his face. "I'm sorry, Miss Sebastian, I thought she was with you."

In a sudden movement Renée seized a crystal vase and threw it at Rudy. It shattered on the floor at his feet. "Don't ever let me see that contemptuous look on your face again," she raged. When Rudy's expression didn't change she grabbed a book from the shelf and threw it at him. He didn't move and it struck him hard in the face, leaving a red mark on his cheek. "I won't tolerate contempt from an unnatural little weed like you; I'll tear you out of the ground first!" she said, advancing upon him. "Find her," she hissed. "Go to the beach house and find her."

Rudy returned a short while later. "She's not there, Miss Sebastian," he said, keeping tight control on his tone of voice.

Renée wrapped her arms about herself as if she were suddenly chilled, then she placed her icy hand on his cheek. "Does it hurt?" she asked. Then, without waiting for his reply, she withdrew her hand and said, "Jessica's such a vexing child." Rudy watched silently as she walked out of the study and went upstairs to her suite.

It was the captain's voice that Shetland heard when he picked up the phone. "Are you up to a meeting tonight?" Rutledge asked.

"Sure," Shetland said in a shaky voice. "What's it about?"

"I'd like you to come in to talk with Jackson from Internal Affairs and myself, but the way you sound, maybe we should put it off."

"No, no, I'm okay," Shetland said. "I'm just a little groggy from the sleeping pills the doctors gave me, but I can make it."

"Maybe we should come by your place," the captain suggested.

"It's all right," Shetland said. "I prefer to come to your office." Reluctantly the captain agreed.

When Shetland arrived shortly after six P.M. he found the station in turmoil. A large topographical map of Crane's Neck with different-colored pins stuck in it was set up in the squad room. Men from the sheriff's department, surrounding precincts and auxiliary police units were gathered around the map while Casey gave out a spiel that sounded like battle orders. On his way up to the captain's office Shetland managed to latch onto Scalley as he came out of the washroom. "What the hell's going on?" he demanded.

Scalley, surprised to see him there, just stared for a moment.

"Why wasn't I told this was in the works? I know—orders," Shetland muttered, answering his own question. Pulling Scalley back into the washroom to get out of the flow of traffic in the hall, he said, "Okay, give with the details."

"The thing about the dogs got out to the newspapers and all hell broke loose. They couldn't do anything else," Scalley said defensively.

"Maybe not," Shetland retorted. "How many men are on it?"

"The ones you see here and over a hundred already out there. In some sectors they've already started."

"At night? God!" Shetland shook his head in bewilderment.

"They couldn't wait till daylight."

"If we get through the night without somebody getting his head blown off it will be a miracle."

"You can't blame them for going out now."

181

"I don't. I'd do the same thing if I were pressed to the wall. You on your way out there?"

"Yeah. I'm coordinating a bunch working from Grist Mill Road down to the Whitiker farm."

"Good luck, and keep your head down," Shetland said.

He knocked and entered the captain's office. Jackson was standing in front of the desk, hands clasped behind his back. He smiled a greeting but said nothing, looking over his shoulder for the captain to begin.

As Rutledge pulled himself up from his chair to shake hands, Shetland could see that the captain was tired and the strain was wearing on him. "I want to thank you," he said, gravel-voiced, "for coming down here. I'll come right to the point. As you have undoubtedly already guessed, Internal Affairs has been conducting an investigation into the activities of your squad." As the captain spoke his thoughts seemed to be elsewhere. "The inquiry was brought about by the diligent efforts of a fellow officer from the New Rochelle police department. We're caught up in the unpleasant and distasteful circumstance of an outsider having to point out the ring around our collar, which I intend to see never happens again. That, however, is neither here nor there for the moment. I.A. is now in a position to call for an official departmental trial by the police review board while at the same time a grand jury will be summoned to conduct hearings on criminal charges to be lodged against this individual." Just like that, Shetland was off the hook, but instead of being relieved he was angry.

"Why the hell was I kept on the roasting spit for so long?" he shouted.

"The plain truth, Lieutenant," Jackson cut in, "was that at first we weren't sure if you or Sergeant Tedeschevich was the culprit. His careful fudging of the records threw us for a while."

"It couldn't have been for that long. Why didn't you inform me sooner?"

Jackson tried to be delicate. "I apologize, Lieutenant. I know what you must have felt."

"Bullshit," Shetland snapped. "I nearly got the axe once

before because of that bastard. Since you boys weren't very smart then, how was I to know you picked up a couple of I.Q. points."

The captain suddenly and decisively intervened on I.A.'s behalf. "Lieutenant, cut the whining. You know the rules. Immediate superiors of a suspect under I.A. investigation are not to be informed of details of said investigation until such a time as sufficient information has been compiled to recommend specific charges for prosecution or further inquiry. And that's what this is all about. So if you can unruffle your feathers we can proceed."

Shetland cooled off and Jackson explained what they had come up with. "Apparently Tedeschevich started out routinely on this missing-persons investigation but then somebody bought him off because he quietly dropped the whole business in midstream, using stalling tactics and file-shuffling to cover this girl's trail."

"Greedy crooks are usually fools," Shetland interrupted. "But Tedeschevich never struck me as stupid. There must have been a lot of money involved for him to put it on the line for something like this."

"Yes," the captain said, "more than the girl had—a lot more. We suspect this woman she was involved with had a part in it."

"Any ideas?"

"Yes; your Miss Sebastian."

This was a new wrinkle, a possibility Shetland hadn't considered, and he found himself at a loss for words.

"We've done some checking ourselves," Jackson said. "Miss Sebastian has never made a secret of her bisexuality. She had similar love affairs with young girls before, often at the same time that she was involved with a male admirer."

"Okay," Shetland said, "that points the finger. How do we pin the tail on the donkey?"

"That New Rochelle cop discovered that Savien's paramour was a dark-haired, exceptionally attractive woman in her mid-thirties. The motel manager remembers seeing a silver Mercedes limousine parked near the place on one occasion and he thought he saw the girl sitting in it with another woman."

"Okay, I'm convinced. So what happened to the girl and why would the rich Miss Sebastian get involved with an unsophisticated chippy when she could probably have the pick of the chic dames who run in her own circles?"

"Good questions, Lieutenant, for which we have no answers. Perhaps we'll get the answers in the hearings," the captain said, "but we're holding off on this thing until we can get clear of these killings on Crane's Neck. Do I have your cooperation on that?" The captain wasn't asking, he was telling, but Shetland hesitated anyway.

"On one condition," he said. "When the times comes, Tedeschevich is mine."

The captain gave him a warning glare. "No vendettas," he said; "strictly business."

"I wouldn't have it any other way."

When Shetland thought the meeting had ended the captain asked him to remain a few minutes longer. When Jackson left he shut the door behind him. "I know," Rutledge said, "this must be very fatiguing to you, Lieutenant, but I've got to know what really happened that night."

Shetland found himself in a paradoxical situation. A few hours ago he would gladly have told him the unvarnished truth because he would have thought it was the way out. The strange visitation in his apartment had unraveled another one of the passages in Peel's journal: "To know is to be corrupted." Unwittingly he had planted both feet into a quicksandlike nightmare, and he was too far from shore to pull himself out. The only other alternative was to sink until he could swim. "I stand by my deposition, Captain," he said.

The captain wasn't buying it. "Listen," he said, searching Shetland's face for some indication of the truth, "I don't know you that well, but I know what it says on your record— your war record, your psychological profile at the police academy, and your performance after nine years on the force, you're not the bravest guy in the world, but when we carried you out of that house your mind had been bashed up more than your body and that wasn't caused by a blow on the head. If you're afraid of what might be said, forget it; we all know this is a strange one."

At that moment Shetland was almost tempted to tell him everything, but if he couldn't accept it, he thought, how could someone who hadn't seen it. It was too much to ask, no matter what anyone thought himself capable of believing. "Listen, Captain, I think I want to go out to Crane's Neck and join the hunting parties."

"Do you feel up to it?"

"Let's just say I'll feel better when we get this over with, and I think everybody else will too."

"Okay, Lieutenant; I won't presume to know your condition better than you do. We can sure use all the help we can get out there. I'll let them know to expect you."

Shetland didn't return immediately to his apartment to get ready for the hunt but instead drove around for a while. He was acutely afraid to think about what had happened; he felt the need to keep moving. There were so many questions. The profound sense of good, of love, had been as tangible as the sense of evil. At first he thought it was a trick to lower his defenses, but he knew now that his apartment had been invaded by opposite visitations, fundamental and diametrical opposites, yet connected by some twisted universality that seemed to be two faces of one reality. He thought about the old farm woman who had seen Christ and Michael the Archangel; good wielding a sword of evil? It was all crazy. If it wasn't crazy, then light and dark were one and the same. His head was spinning on that damn merry-go-round. "You started and ended from where you began." The rhythmical phrase popped into his head and began to repeat itself like a skipping record or a maddening chant. It went on and on, never changing tempo. Finally he drove back to his apartment, too fatigued mentally to think any more; all he wanted to do now was act.

He trudged up the stairs and found the door ajar. There was no feeling of dread or terror as he reached inside and switched on the light. Pushing the door open, he saw Jessica curled up in a chair. She looked up at him, bleary-eyed. "I've been waiting," she said, "to warn you. She wants you dead."

Shetland stepped inside, closing the door behind him. Somehow he knew what she meant. To his surprise he casually asked, "Why?"

"Because of me, I think." Jessica got up and went into the bathroom to wash her face with cold water. When she came back she said, "I know this is difficult to understand."

"Try me," Shetland said.

"I was just with her; she's insane. I love her but she's insane." Jessica placed her hands over her face as if to cry, but she didn't. "It's all been a nightmare," she said. "She's forcing one of your own men into doing it, into killing you. I was there. He refused at first but he'll eventually do it; he's weak and frightened. I had to warn you."

Something snapped inside of him. He wanted to kill her, to smash her face into unrecognizable pulp. He lunged at her. She stood frozen. He raised his clenched fist but when he struck her it was with his open palm. She cried out and reeled under the blow and he struck her again, back handed. Blood trickled from the corner of her mouth. To stop him she threw herself at him, putting her arms around him and clinging tightly. "No, no, no," she cried. His murderous rage suddenly exhausted itself. He held on to her, then coldly pushed her back at arm's length. "You're a filthy woman's whore," he shouted, shaking her violently. Then he released her, drained of emotion.

"You must listen," she cried. There was a moment of tense silence and then Jessica said, "Renée said she killed a girl in some monstrous ceremony. God, it was horrible listening to her talk so callously about the instrument she used to murder the girl, some sort of long, thin, needle. She said she buried the body in the oak grove, near Azareal Sebastian's grave. I'm not sure why I do, but I believe her. She's holding it over Sergeant Tedeschevich's head to make him kill you. That's the man she was talking to today. Renée and her brother, Aaron, have powers of the mind that are beyond imagination. I'm sure they've brought this calamity down upon all our heads because of this power."

Shetland began to listen intently, wanting to despise Jessica but somehow unable to.

"They formed a group: Aaron, Renée, Jules Arken and Stephen Peel. Their intent was to break the barrier of death through psychic powers. Each of the members had had an afterlife experience except Jules, who had been drawn into the group because of certain experiments he was conducting. You see, Aaron and, to a lesser degree, Renée, were the instigators. Years ago Aaron suffered a terrible accident. For a short while the curtain was pulled back for him and he saw what lay on the other side. Even more extraordinary was that Renée, a thousand miles away, experienced the same vision. It's incredible to believe that the twisted monster imprisoned in that wheelchair is Renée's twin." Suddenly a strange, look came over Jessica's face; savage, vindictive. "Surely such a maiming affliction was retribution for a terrible debt. Their experiences profoundly changed their lives. They spent fortunes in time and money trying to find their way back, perhaps because Aaron has lingered so near death all these years or for some other reason, I don't know. But it was an obsession that they never let go of. When Stephen, the most rational of them all, killed himself, I knew it was because of some terrifying discovery they made. I knew Renée was in trouble and needed my help but she wouldn't let me help; she shut me out. And then I came upon the idea that perhaps through you I might discover something that could help me help her. Then it got all turned upside down. Jules died and I knew it had to be murder because he was too much of a coward to take his own life. And then I fell in love with you." Jessica finally began to cry. She wiped away her tears and went on, as if to get it out before her courage failed, "I'm not sure how your sergeant got involved but I know he'll try to kill you and he must be stopped. And this thing that's come among us must be stopped but I don't know how."

Shetland waited a few moments for her to regain control, for she was breathless and trembling. He needed the time himself to block out his personal feelings. "This mental power, can you tell me some more about it? Does it come from some sort of self-discipline? How does it manifest itself? Can they turn it on and off?"

"I don't understand it completely and I don't think they do either. Renée told me that the power had manifested itself in certain members of her family in the past, to a greater or lesser degree. Sometimes it skipped a generation or even a few generations, but it always showed up again. Her father didn't possess it but her grandfather, Azareal Sebastian, the man buried under the stone slab in the grove, had extraordinary mental powers. Renée described the power as being similar to extrasensory perception. I'm sure the power in itself is not dangerous. Renée never talked of it in that vein; it was like a gift that in a special way put them more deeply in touch with the rhythm of the universe."

"Well, something must have changed all that, mustn't it?" Shetland's voice cracked fiercely. "The thing I met wasn't no messenger of rhythms. What about Arken—did Renée have him killed?"

Jessica looked at him in confusion. "I thought . . ."

"No, Arken was murdered by a pair of good, old-fashioned human hands. Why would she have Arken killed?"

"Maybe he knew about the girl," Jessica said.

"Did you ever meet the girl? Did Renée say why she had killed her?"

"I broke away from Renée before she came into the picture. I saw them together once or twice but we never met."

Shetland could tell she was still holding back and he began to throw questions at her. "You must have some idea why she killed the girl."

"Renée said she did but I don't know if she did," Jessica said.

"What the hell does that mean?"

She reacted as if he had struck her again. "I told you; she's not responsible; she may have made it up."

"How much does the sergeant know about the power and what this group was doing?"

"I imagine," Jessica said, "not much. He may not have even connected them with what's been happening." Suddenly Jessica turned on him, her eyes filled with tears. "Why are you doing this," she shouted, "firing questions at me, not giving me time to think. Because you hate me for deceiving you, you despise me because I could love a woman?"

Shetland came toward her, unsure of his own intentions. She backed away. "Don't hit me again," she shouted. He put his hands on her shoulders. She stiffened and then, sensing no threat in his touch, relaxed. His voice still had a harsh edge but it was because of emotional confusion. The hatred was gone. "You've told me everything?" he asked gently.

She nodded.

"Don't go back to your house and don't see Renée again."

"Can I stay here?" she asked.

"Yes." Shetland knew that once he was gone she would be safe. He understood, by what manner he wasn't sure, that the thing had been with him from the night he walked out of Peel's study with the journal. In some odd way it was like being infected with a disease; he carried the baccilla in some dark passage of his mind and it grew, spreading its contagion until it seemed almost free of its host. The final revenge would come in his destruction. It was there with them now, watching, waiting, hesitant, perhaps even fearful. When he left Jessica he took with him the journal he kept under the mattress to destroy it.

He had no way of knowing Sergeant Tedeschevich's state of mind. He knew the sergeant must be running scared; that in itself made him dangerous, whether he had decided to throw in his lot with Renée or not. In either case Shetland thought it worthwhile to try and get him before he made his next move. Tedeschevich was the sort who looked after number one, so all Shetland had to do was convince him that the jig was up before the sergeant let daylight through him with his .38 revolver. It wasn't heroics or concern for the cop's welfare that sent Shetland in pursuit of him; it was a simple matter of survival: the sergeant might have answers.

CHAPTER ELEVEN

THE SERGEANT, like every other able-bodied officer with the exception of a few patrol units, was combing Crane's Neck for the pack of dogs described by Shetland. The hunting parties were working the northwest sector near the farm where the old man had been murdered. The command post on Willet's Path to which Shetland drove consisted of a special radio-equipped police van manned by three uniformed officers. There was a lot of radio chatter going on between field units and they were having a devil of a time keeping tabs on it. "They're talking so much," one of the officers said, "I'm beginning to think they're afraid of the dark." The officers turned around and spotted Shetland sitting on the lowered tailgate. "Hey, good seeing you, Lieutenant. We were all glad to hear that you're all right. When we got the news from dispatch that you would be joining us out here we let everyone know over the radio."

"I really appreciate the nice reception, fellas," Shetland said.

"Our pleasure," the officer said. "What can we do for you?"

"I'm looking for Sergeant Tedeschevich."

"You missed him. He was here about thirty minutes ago, when we got the news about you. In fact, he asked which hunting party you were with. We didn't know but we said we'd try to contact the field radio units to find out, but we told him there was a lot of chatter and it would take some time. The offer holds for you, Lieutenant."

"You've got your hands full and I'm sure I'll run into him. Did he mention where he was heading?" Shetland asked.

The officer thought for a moment. "Not exactly," he said. "The sergeant mumbled something about checking with the forensic team that was still working at the Whitiker farm."

"Thanks," Shetland said, "I'll take a look over there."

"Before you go, Lieutenant, you wouldn't happen to have a couple of extra cigarettes? I'm all smoked out."

"Here," he said, tossing him his pack, "I'm giving them up."

"At a time like this?" the officer quipped. "We've been sitting on pins and needles waiting for something to break over that radio. This is going to be a night for taking up nervous habits, not giving them up. More power to you, though."

The Whitiker farm was at the end of a winding dirt road that slipped between two pastures. Shetland figured there was little chance of approaching the farm house unobserved, but he turned off his headlights and cut the engine, coasting the last hundred feet into the front yard. He didn't imagine that Tedeschevich would start blasting the moment he showed his face; if he was planning murder it could not be witnessed. It would have to look like an accident. Nevertheless Shetland wasn't taking any chances. He got out of his car and moved cautiously along the side of the house, his gun drawn. There didn't seem to be anybody around. He started out into the open, then stepped back when he saw a light and heard voices coming from the barn. A moment later a man carrying a suitcase came out and headed for the parked police cars. Shetland waited a moment longer to see if anyone else followed, then crept up behind him as he was slipping the suitcase into the back seat of one of the cars.

When he called out Casey's name in a whisper the man turned around with a start, dropping the suitcase. "Jesus, Lieutenant, you just pushed me five years closer to retirement," he said when he saw who it was.

Shetland gestured at him to keep his voice down. "Who's in the barn?"

"Riker," he whispered, still shaken. "You won't believe how it's been, Lieutenant. It's bad enough just me and Riker working on this thing alone out here. I mean, it's spooky. They found the old man lying over there among a pile of spent shells. The guy unloaded a twelve-gauge pump shotgun on his assailant with a staggered-load magazine—buckshot, slugs. He was shooting toward the barn, like to blow the whole damn side in. So how did he miss, and if he didn't," Casey slapped the side of his holstered service revolver, "what damn good are these things going to be if we meet up with whatever it was he was shooting at. No damn good, that's what."

"Calm down, Casey. Why are you still hanging around here?"

"Trying to find some of the slugs. Maybe there'll be a piece of whatever killed the guy on one of them. I wouldn't bet on it, though."

"You can take off," Shetland said, "on my authority. Try again in the morning."

Casey started back to the barn to get his partner when Shetland called after him, "Was Sergeant Tedeschevich here?"

"Yes, he was Lieutenant," Casey said, continuing toward the barn.

"Damn it, Casey," Shetland said, "will you hold on a minute and tell me what happened with the sergeant? Was he asking for me?"

"No, Lieutenant. He wanted to know where the nearest hunting party was. I told him that the closest group was in the woods straight across that potato field, but if he didn't want to get his head shot off he'd have to take the road to get in behind them."

Shetland said, "Thanks, Casey," wheeled about and started for his car.

"Hold on, Lieutenant; he didn't go that way."

Shetland turned around. "What do you mean?"

"I mean," Casey said, "the guy's crazy—he was in such a damn big hurry that he went across the field."

This new information disturbed Shetland. He sat down on the car hood and thought out loud. "He's gunning for me, that s.o.b.," he muttered. "Since he's apparently decided to kill me he sure as hell can't go around asking for me, then have me turn up with a bullet hole in the back of my head. So he's taking the chance of methodically going from group to group. He's hunting me down like we're hunting those dogs. Casey's right; Tedeschevich can't be thinking rationally. Crazy or not, I should let the bastard get his head blown off." Shetland knew even before he finished saying it that he wasn't going to be able to. "He's crazy, I'm crazy, we're all crazy but somebody should tell him killing me would be a waste of time." Shetland got up with a grunt. "I guess," he said to himself, "I'm elected to do the telling." He turned and trotted off across the field.

The sergeant's footprints were easy to follow in the newly tilled earth but Shetland lost them in the woods. Luckily he didn't have to rely on his tracking ability; he had a pretty good idea where his quarry was heading. There had been a great deal of controversy when the hunt got under way about continuing it after dark because it increased the chances of a shooting accident. Tedeschevich was planning to provide that unfortunate accident. The hunters were working in a driving line about five hundred yards long, starting out from Foxberry Road and swinging toward standers on the Willet's Path. To be between those two converging lines was about as unhealthy as Shetland could imagine; but that was where Tedeschevich was heading and so, reluctantly, was he. He had no intention of giving Tedeschevich an easy out by letting him get shot by one of the hunters, so he moved as quietly as he could and, though he made a better target for Tedeschevich, walked erect. The moment he caught sight or sound of the hunters he planned to yell his head off. It was a tricky damn business and a good indication of how desperate Tedeschevich was, putting himself in danger of getting shot on the unlikely chance that he would be able to find his man in the darkness—a darkness so impenetrable that Shetland found himself getting turned around every dozen paces. Shetland began to have serious doubts about whether he could deal with such a man. It was beginning to look like one of them out there was a fool, and Shetland had a good idea of who it was.

He guessed he was pretty close to the left flank of the driving line when he stopped to rest against a tree trunk, legs lead-weary from dragging them through half a mile of entangling brush. His nerve endings were beginning to pop like eight spark plugs kicking out 6000 rpms. Any second he expected a bullet or a hail of buckshot to come winging out of the darkness and Tedeschevich's job would be done for him. With growing hesitation he forced himself up. A slight breeze blew the clouds away from the moon, but the wind didn't help; it merely played tricks and covered over sounds. Nor did the moonlight, which made shadows as hard to see into as a solid stone wall. Several times Shetland thought he heard the hunters and started to cry out, only to hesitate for fear that Tedeschevich was just up ahead. He was about to call it quits when he stumbled upon a dry streambed that ran in the approximate direction he wanted to go. He jumped down into it, exhaling with relief; at least he was protected on two sides by the five-foot-high embankment. He moved with more assurance now but continued to peer over the rim at measured intervals and to look behind him.

By ten o'clock Shetland was beginning to grow curious as to where the driving line was. At that moment a rapid, echoing report of gunshots roared through the woods. Clambering up the steep side of the ditch, he stuck his head up just far enough to see out. To his right and left, about a hundred yards away, were the searchlights of the hunters. They were coming fast toward him, and he heard another shot that was even closer. Something was up; he slid back down to the bottom of the ditch and started yelling, "It's Lieutenant Shetland; I'm in front of you; hold your fire." Then he got a jolt, as if somebody had stuck an icicle down his back. Something was approaching from the far end of the trench in the direction he was heading; it was ripping through the brush on four legs. He could hear the deep, quick pants and the low, guttural growls. Whatever it was, was coming on like a freight train down a mountain. He knew he couldn't outrun it and he wasn't about to face it without magnum cartridges in his revolver. He could either get torn to pieces or shot to pieces. When he saw the pale glint of white canines and the glow of burning red eyes coming at him like an onrushing torpedo, he chose the latter. Screaming, "Don't shoot!" he clawed his way up the side of the ditch on his hands and knees. When his body was halfway over the top, the dog passed underneath him. He felt its jaws clamp shut over his shoe and he let out a shrill howl as he urinated in his pants. His shoe came off without his foot and the monster kept on going.

Shielding his eyes, Shetland stumbled into the search-lights, happy to be alive, even if only for a few moments longer. He began to wave his arms high over his head and shouted, "I'm over here. Hold your fire! For God's sake, nobody fire; it's me, Lieutenant Shetland!"

More searchlights were turned on him from the front and the sides and he could hear men coming toward him, breaking through the brush. Still more searchlights turned on him from behind until he was standing in a crossfire of light. Continuing to wave his arms Shetland began to jump up and down until he heard voices. "Lieutenant, what the hell are you doing here?"

For some reason that made Shetland laugh. "Trying not to get killed," he said.

"You sure picked a heck of a place to do it," someone else said, and then the woods came alive with men's voices and their forms, moving awkwardly through the underbrush.

"You're damn lucky," said a sheriff's deputy with a two-way radio strung over his shoulder. "We just got word from the standers over the field phones that we were approaching the no-fire zone. What the heck were you doing here anyway?"

"It's a long story," Shetland said, "but one of your dogs just ran down that creek bed."

"That's what we figured when the dogs didn't try to break through the line of standers or come back toward the driving line."

"You can move some of the standers by car along the road to the end of this ditch," Shetland said. "Start the driving line from here and maybe you can still catch them."

The sheriff gave him a sarcastic look. "The idea of continuing this hunt isn't going to sit well with anyone, but as soon as we can get these men untangled we can start again."

Shetland's foot felt like it had been caught in a vise; it was swelling up so severely that he had to be helped back to the command unit. There he rested and managed to procure a change of clothes. Shoes were a little harder to come by but he finally found someone who kept an extra pair of work shoes in the trunk of his car. They were a perfect fit, at least on the swollen foot. He also changed the .38 special cartridges in his revolver for some .357 magnums; the Smith and Wesson he owned had that capability but up until now he had never felt the necessity for the extra punch.

Two hours passed without incident. At midnight Shetland was preparing to go out and hunt Tedeschevich again when the radio started crackling with messages; they had the dogs cornered in an abandoned shack in the field less than a mile away. He made the short dusty ride with the command unit, figuring it would be the most likely place to find Tedeschevich. Police cars, sheriff's cars and pickup trucks lined the road alongside the field; armed men were already stationed in the woods on the other three sides. The scene had the appearance of a major military operation. The captain was standing in the back of one of the trucks shouting commands over a bullhorn; mostly he was calling for everyone to keep back and hold his fire. A dozen men carrying shotguns and rifles with telescopic sights tromped along the road in ragtag file. The command unit pulled up alongside, just as they peeled off to take up position in front of the vehicles. Shetland suddenly forgot Tedeschevich when he realized that they had a potential disaster on their hands. He jumped out of the van and limped over to the captain. Rutledge was conferring with several officers. Shetland barged right in and loudly announced, "Somebody's going to get killed out here."

Rutledge turned to him, his face twisted with strain.

"Give me three men and keep the rest back." Shetland could hardly believe he was speaking. After his earlier brush with those monsters he thought he had used up the last of his nerve. Now he was asking for a head-on crack at them.

Rutledge didn't hesitate. "You've got it," he said.

Suddenly Shetland was at center stage, an honor he could have lived without; an honor, he realized, he might not be able to live with. He chose quickly, the first man at random, the second a black patrolman named Farrell whom he had observed on the police shooting range; he was a virtuoso with a scatter gun. The third was a volunteer from the sheriff's department. In the commotion of giving orders someone tossed him a machine gun. He returned it, commenting, "I'd hit everything but what I was aiming at," which produced a nervous ripple of laughter among the men.

Illuminated by the moonlight, the crumbling, swayback wooden building was waist high in weeds. Its doors and windows were securely boarded up. Finding the entrance was the first order of business. The men approached the shack in a line, ten paces between each man. Twenty-five yards from the shack Shetland called for them to halt. That was as close as he wanted to get until they were sure of the point at which the dogs might emerge. Out of the ominous stillness they could hear the beasts nervously scratching around inside. The dogs were obviously aware of the men's presence and Shetland was afraid that at any moment the beasts might bolt for freedom. The last thing he wanted was for those devils to spring on them from an unexpected direction. "Where is the damn entrance," he muttered, motioning to the others to spread out to form a half-circle around the shack. His legs were turning to rubber.

How many dogs were in there, he asked himself, thinking of the monster that had come at him in the ditch. Two; he could distinguish two forms between the cracks in the wall. He thought there might be a third. "Blast anything that comes out of there," he said. Then he was hit with a sobering possibility; suppose the dogs didn't come out and the men had to go in after them. There couldn't be much light in there. Burn it down first, he reasoned; drive them out. "Do you see it yet?" he shouted. The men were twenty paces apart now and were covering three sides of the shack.

There was no reply, then someone yelled, "Lieutenant, over here!"

Ordering everyone to stay where he was, Shetland went to take a look. Threre was a hole in the side of the building near the foundation; the weeds were trampled down around it. A canine muzzle poked through the opening, sending an electrical jolt up Shetland's spine, then it quickly disappeared. Shetland told the black patrolman to keep his shotgun trained on the entrance. "But don't shoot until you're sure you've got a target; we don't want a wounded dog slipping out of here." The rest of them made a careful search for other exits; there were none.

Now it was a waiting game. The men took their positions fifteen yards in front of the dark triangular hole, watching, waiting. An ugly snout and a cold, glassy eye appeared for a split second; the sounds from the shack grew more restless. The men could hear wimpering and scratching, as if the dogs were trying to dig another way out. It was in the air; they could feel it coming, like a thunderstorm ready to break. The scratching stopped. It became quiet. The deathly silence continued, dragging on for minutes. The tension was becoming unbearable; sweat broke out on Shetland's face. He relaxed his shooting stance to wipe his eyes. In that moment of inattention one of the furred killers charged through the opening, saliva foaming around its snapping jaws. The multiple crackling report of shotguns answered the attack as the monster came apart in a whirlwind of buckshot.

"Watch it," Shetland screamed, the muzzle of his revolver zeroing in on the opening. Rotted wood whined, splintered and snapped. Shetland spun to his left as the German shepherd crashed through the boarded-up window. The huge dog hit the ground but was immediately up and rushing at him with murderous intent. Shetland looked with horror at the monster growing enormous in his gun sight. Jaws snapping like a steel trap, the beast sprang into the air. The cylinder of Shetland's revolver spun like a toy top and a half-dozen walloping thumps registered as the magnum slugs plowed into the bristling gray mass. The dog slammed into Shetland as he threw his arms up to protect his head, the impact sending them both crashing to the ground. Shetland, paralyzed with terror, waited for those gleaming white fangs to sink into his throat and take his life with a bloody wrenching jerk. It was a moment before he realized he was waiting in vain; the daggered jaws were stilled by death. Sobbing joyfully, Shetland struggled out from under the heavy bleeding carcass and was helped to his feet by the men, who had rushed forward after the first gunshot. The area was soon crowded with hunters pushing to get a look at the dead animals and to congratulate the men who had done the job. Two officers helped Shetland to a rusty oil drum nestled in the trampled weeds, where he sat down, while others broke into the shack to make sure it was empty. A few minutes later one of the police officers came out of the shack. He was very pale and was clutching his stomach. Brushing past a group that crowded around to question him, he walked toward Shetland. "Lieutenant," he said, pressing his arms to his stomach, "you wanted to know where Sergeant Tedeschevich was? We found him; his head is stuffed under a pile of garbage in the corner of the building. The rest of him is strung out in the rafters like meat in a butcher shop."

The dogs were loaded into the back of a pickup truck and taken out of the field; an ambulance was brought up to remove the sergeant's remains. Soon afterward the field started to empty. A lingering sense of uncertainty and apprehension could be detected in the hunters as they climbed into their cars, and repeatedly turned their heads to glance back toward the shack as the line of vehicles began to move down the dusty road. Too weary and strung out to move, Shetland sat and watched, knowing the questions everyone contemplated. Farrell, the virtuoso with the shotgun, stayed behind. "It's not over, is it, Lieutenant."

Shetland didn't answer.

The young officer pressed the subject as they walked back to his blue and white car. "They couldn't have done that to the sergeant—the dogs, I mean. It doesn't seem possible." Farrell wanted to drive the lieutenant straight home but Shetland insisted that he be dropped back at his car. He had never liked Tedeschevich, and no doubt would have killed him himself if he had had to. Still, the thought of anyone dying like that bothered him immensely.

As Farrell talked on Shetland kept looking back over his shoulder toward the shack. He thought he saw movement near the broken window.

"Is everyone out of there?"

His question caught his companion off guard. "Sir?" he asked.

"The shack—is everyone out of the shack?" he asked again, catching sight of movement, this time by the entrance, where the first dog had lunged through.

"Yeah, sure," Farrell said, giving him a puzzled look. "We're the only ones left. Is there something wrong? Did you see something?"

Shetland's face went ashen. The black officer stopped and glanced back. "I can go check," he said.

"No, no, it's all right," Shetland said, putting his arm around Farrell's shoulder; "you give me a hand back to the car, though—I think I've picked up a stone in the shoe of my sore foot."

When they reached Farrell's car, Shetland sat on the passenger side with the door open, pretending to rid his shoe of a stone while the black officer put in a call to dispatch. Shetland could see them plainly, if only for an instant, like the formless blotch of light and shadow that swims before eyes shut tightly against a harsh light. When he stared straight at them they seemed to slide away from the center of his field of vision, losing material form in the process. There were three of the beguiling phantom apparitions; two stood close to the building and the third was a way off in the field. One was Tedeschevich or the negative imprint of what had been Tedeschevich, the second was something alien and yet familiar, and the third was himself. A cold, hollow feeling bored through him and he gasped, "Dear God."

A hand touched his shoulder and he jumped. "Lieutenant," Farrell demanded, "what the hell is the matter with you? You're shaking like a leaf."

Shetland pulled his legs inside the car, slammed the door and abrasively ordered the officer to get them out of there. Farrell didn't ask for clarification. He floored the gas pedal. The tires spun, kicking up rooster tails of dust as the police car accelerated onto the dirt road. After putting more than a mile between themselves and the shack, Farrell, visibly shaken, stammered, "What the hell was that all about?"

"Just move it," Shetland shouted, hitting the siren switch. With siren wailing they careened along the back roads, fishtailing around corners and S-curves. Slamming on the brakes, they finally came to a bouncing halt in the Whitikers' yard. Shetland jumped out of the car into the midst of a swirling dust cloud and limped toward his own car. Farrell, bewildered and unnerved, meekly asked what the lieutenant had in mind. "Take off," Shetland answered, "and let the devil take the hindmost; that's what the lieutenant has in mind. Now get out of here and get back to your regular duties." The black patrolman took off down the road. "Turn off the damn siren," Shetland shouted after him.

Alone, Shetland leaned his elbows on the car roof, rested his head heavily in his hands and tried to think. They were all dead, all those who might have once been able to shed light on what this nightmare was about—all, that is, except Renée and that twin brother she kept in seclusion. But his two separate encounters with her had told him she was not to be gotten to easily. He had to have something to shake her up, some way to put her back against the wall. If he could just find that grave Jessica had mentioned, perhaps he could make her talk. It wasn't much of a plan: Its objectives were vague, and if he was dealing with a madwoman it was doomed to failure from the start, but it was all he had.

He drove to a stretch of road along the edge of the bluff a mile west of the Sebastian manor, and parked his car. He got out, crossed the road, and ducked into the woods on the other side. The stand of giant oak trees crowned the top of the hill on Sebastian Point, just as Jessica had described them. The open meadow surrounding the grove, Shetland guessed, lay somewhere through the woods ahead of him. He knew that with Jessica's testimony he could have obtained a warrant to search the grounds for the Savien girl's grave. But he also knew that if he found the body that way matters would be taken out of his hands. The evidence that would convict Renée Sebastian of murder was no longer important to Shetland except as a threat against her. There was something more horrifying than murder going on here and he could feel it eating his sanity from the inside out, like a worm. To find out what was really going on, Shetland was prepared to make a tradeoff with Renée. His logic was desperate but if Renée thought the truth could buy her freedom, perhaps she would reveal it.

He spotted a party on horseback galloping through the woods in the moonlight; one of the riders was Renée Sebastian. They rode past without seeing him. The trail he was using turned away at this point and he had to go the rest of the way through thick brush. He reached the bridle path, checked it to see if it was clear, then dashed across. On the other side he stopped to catch his breath and to let the pain in his foot subside. After that it was a short distance to the edge of the meadow. Out of sight on the opposite side lay the Sebastian manor and halfway up the hill was the edge of the oak grove. The majestic trees stood silhouetted against the cloudless evening sky, their long shadows reaching out into the large expanse of meadow which was bathed in the luminous white glow of the moon. Shetland started out into the open in a half-run but stopped when he thought he spotted someone looking down at him from just inside the tree line. He didn't take his eyes from the spot but the form seemed to melt before his eyes. A trick of the shadows, he thought; but, taking no chances, he broke into a full run. Reaching the first stand of oaks, he crouched low and waited and listened, suspecting that Rudy might be keeping an eye on the grove. Breathing more easily and convinced now that he was not being observed, he started his search, cutting back and forth over the mossy earth. On the carpetlike floor of the grove any irregularity indicating a gravesite should have been easy to spot, but by the time he had covered half the grove he had found nothing, and it was too dark to see without the aid of a flashlight.

He asked himself if perhaps Jessica had been correct in her theory that Renée was completely deranged. Maybe the girl wasn't buried here at all. Then he remembered, with a self-castigating groan, that Jessica told him that the girl's grave was near Azareal Sebastian's. All this time wasted, he muttered, and took the flashlight from his jacket pocket. Waving its narrow beam from side to side and in front of him he continued the search, heading deeper into the interior of the grove. Amid the largest of the oaks he came across the square slab of marble laid into the ground. He examined it carefully. There was no inscription on the stone itself, but at its foot was a bronze plaque that read: AZAREAL SEBASTIAN, PRAY THE WEIGHT OF THIS STONE HOLDS HIM IN PEACE.

Again Jessica's words about the Sebastian inheritance came to mind. In his preoccupation with the plaque, Rudy's approach went unnoticed. The closed fist landed at the base of Shetland's skull with a numbing thud and sent him slipping into unconsciousness. Trying to wheel about to face his assailant, he caught another punch in the face that snapped his head back and sent him hard to the ground. When Shetland came to he found himself staring into the muzzle of his own gun. Rudy was standing astride him, pleased and cocky with the speech he was rehearsing aloud for Shetland's benefit.

"No, he showed no search warrant. I didn't know that the prowler that I was forced to kill after a struggle, in which he pulled a gun—which I managed to wrest from his possession—was a cop. And a snooty cop at that. Of course," Rudy added, smiling, "I'll leave that last part out when I tell the story. You can get up, halfway," he said, pressing the muzzle of the gun into the blood oozing from Shetland's nose.

Shetland sat up, bracing himself on one arm.

"That's far enough," Rudy warned, backing away.

Shetland's head felt like a lump of lead and his vision was clouded by a thin film over his eyes. "You must get some bonus for killing a cop." His sarcasm sputtered in the taste of his own blood.

Rudy laughed with amusement. "People shoot cops for free in this world. Don't you read the newspapers or watch the news on TV? It's becoming a national pastime, like jogging."

Shetland knew there was no chance of reasoning with Rudy; he was a true psychotic. His one chance was to keep him talking. As long as Rudy was amused with the situation perhaps he wouldn't pull the trigger. "Oh yeah?" he said. "I never did like jogging."

"Hey, I like that, a dead cop with a sense of humor," Rudy laughed.

"Anyway, from jogging you get healthy; for killing a cop in this state you get dead."

"Well, that's my hassle, isn't it."

"Why not get paid for it, and I don't mean a go-for's salary either. I'm talking about big money, the kind that Miss Sebastian would be willing to pay to have somebody who knows what I know shut up permanently."

Rudy laughed. "How do I know what you know? And besides, blackmailing Miss Sebastian wouldn't be ethical."

"You're not thinking of your future, Rudy."

"Forget it, cop. I never mix business with pleasure. And remember, this is purely personal." Rudy was sitting on the gravestone, maybe a yard out of his reach. Shetland knew he'd never reach him before he caught a bullet, but he shifted slowly in Rudy's direction on the off chance that he might get careless.

"That's right," Rudy chuckled; "whenever you're tired of talking and living, you just do what you have in mind."

Shetland backed off. "There are things happening," Shetland said, playing for time, but he never finished his sentence. His jaw went slack then clenched tight as his gaze fixed on the freshly turned patch of earth along the base of the gravestone. Something black and viscous seemed to ooze out of the ground into the air; like oil in water it rose above and behind Rudy's left shoulder, then thinned and dissipated until it became a black mist illuminated from within. For an instant a face seemed to take form in the mist, a young girl's face, then it dissolved into swirling loops of silvery light, which spun itself about the enigma like a spider's web. Amused at what he thought was an attempt to distract him Rudy laughed scoffingly. The thing darted down and seemed to pass through Rudy's body. His mouth opened as if to cry out, but instead omitted a breathless sigh that sounded like he was sucking in air. His eyes widened, then dimmed into lifeless glass spheres. The hand holding the gun sprang open, and rigidly splayed fingers dropped the revolver onto the ground. It was as if Rudy's essence had been snatched from him, leaving behind a convulsing shell doubled over like an ant burned with magnifying glass in the sun. What happened next Shetland couldn't remember, but somehow he had the presence of mind to grab the gun and run. Blindly, directionlessly, he ran away from that place. He ran until his legs gave out and he fell. He found himself just inside the gate to the formal gardens. Panting for breath, he rolled onto his back and immediately became aware of a strange stillness. The stars seemed frozen in their courses. The moon, bright and full, refused to set behind the trees. The few scattered clouds hung like silver islands anchored in a calm sea. Getting to his feet, Shetland made his way along the slate path through the garden toward the house. The still air seemed to transmit no sound of rustling leaves, no insect chirps or clicks. Quickening his pace, Shetland rushed through the wrought-iron gate at the end of the garden and ran along a lilac-bordered path, coming to a halt before it opened onto the lawn below the terrace.

The deafening silence was broken by voices coming from above. Along the terrace wall aglow with torch light, Jessica appeared wearing an evening dress. She held a glass of champagne demurely to her lips. The Mediterranean, Markos, joined her and Shetland watched as they conversed in a very familiar manner. While they talked Jessica's eyes swept the darkness as if she were anticipating an imminent arrival. Several times her gaze settled on the place where Shetland stood hidden in the shadows and stared as if she could see him in the darkness. It didn't seem possible, yet the feeling that they were in direct eye contact was over-powering. A moment later the Mediterranean put his arm around her waist and led her away from the terrace wall.

Markos's incessant chatter almost gave the late supper on the terrace a party atmosphere. Renée delighted in it; she was youthful and radiant as always but tonight Jessica noted a gaiety that had long been absent. Markos helped Jesssica into her chair and then, at his mistress's bidding, went to her side like an obedient puppy. The table was positioned to make Aaron barely visible to the others, but even in the shadows Jessica could see the thin pale face, the surgically grafted skin drawn taut like wax, and the deep brooding eyes filled with unending pain. But Jessica was bereft of pity. She could barely control her revulsion watching his grotesque jerking movements as he made a forced show of animation for Renée's benefit. When he responded to some comment it was in a voice horribly youthful and strong, a hideous mockery of his physical appearance. It was by the sheer power of the will that Aaron kept the smashed shell of his body alive; the burned lungs breathing, the weakening heart throbbing, each pulsating beat another monumental victory for the power of the mind. But even now, as they sat confronting each other, wills warring relentlessly, Jessica detected a rapid failing, and knew he was dying. Renée didn't seem to be aware of the fact, or if she was, she concealed it very well.

"You're so quiet," Renée said, turning to Jessica and breaking off her conversation with Markos. "You're like those candle flames, motionless, when there isn't the slightest breeze to stir them to life."

"He's down in the garden," Jessica said softly.

"Who, my darling?" Renée asked with a puzzled frown.

"My lieutenant. And he will have his answers tonight. He's crossing the lawn and climbing the steps."

"And what will he do when he has them," Aaron said coldly.

Renée sprang to her feet, her lovely face flushed with anger. "Markos, stop him. He mustn't come up here," she commanded, but in complete, bewildered ignorance the man apologized: "The man is a police officer; I can do nothing."

Renée did not hear Markos, for all her attention was focused on the terrace steps, and the sound of shoes scraping up the stone stairs. Suddenly the panic that seemed ready to consume her at any moment vanished. "Lieutenant Shetland, it seems you've been expected. Where's Rudy?" she asked.

"He was detained," Shetland answered coldly. He stood hollow-eyed, bracing himself with one arm against the terrace wall.

"Did you kill him?"

"He should have been so lucky." There was fear mixed with the sarcasm in his voice. He started toward them looking like a drunken brawler, clothes disheveled, blood smeared over his upper lip. Leveling his gaze at Jessica, he asked, "Why did you come back here when I asked you not to? Because of her?"

Jessica shook her head. "No, because of you. I knew it would end here."

"Leave us alone," Renée hissed, "or I promise you'll pray for deliverance into hell."

"I've already been there, thank you," Shetland said, grabbing an open bottle of champagne from the ice bucket and belting it down greedily. He swirled some of the wine around in his mouth and then spat it out. "Fear puts an awful taste in your mouth. But don't mind me; please call your tea party to order. Of course, if you think we should wait I'm sure the other guests will be along shortly. Rudy and I just ran into one on my way here."

"You're insane," Renée said.

Shetland glared at her. "Take a walk with me in the grove and I'll show you a little bit of lunacy that'll make me sound as reasonable as a dictionary." He swallowed a thick lump in his throat that the champagne couldn't dislodge.

"I think you'd better go," Markos said, finally mustering his courage.

Shetland gave him a look that said, butt out. "I don't

know what your part in this is, pal, but you'd better take a look around."

Markos shot a puzzled look at the others. "What is he talking about?" he asked, then backed away.

Shetland turned on the silent figure in the wheelchair. "Are my nerves showing?" he asked, "Can you smell the fear on me? Get a good whiff because I want you to believe me like you believe a religion when I say, like you, that I've thrown away the rule book. I want to know what happened on that bizarre night Stephen Peel wrote about in his journal. I want to know what you arrogant bastards unleashed. I want to know how it crawls into your brain and splits you in two, but most of all I want to know how to turn it off, how to stop it." Shetland suddenly stood straight. "You're a sick, crippled man," he said, "but I'll pull you out of that chair and kick your guts out if that's what it takes to find out."

"He's insane." Renée moved defensively to her brother's side.

"No, the darkness," Markos said, his voice shaken with alarm. "It's so dark, but there's a full moon and stars." The man cringed like a small animal suddenly aware of a deadly peril close at hand. "Why don't they give light?" he demanded.

"Because," Shetland said, "they've turned them out." He turned back to Renée and Aaron. "You've been sitting up here, immune, while this nightmare slaughter has been going on," Shetland pointed his arm into the darkness, "but it's changed, hasn't it? Whatever you did to keep it at bay isn't working anymore, is it?"

Renée looked questioningly at her brother, who kept his serpentine gaze fixed on Shetland; when she saw the truth of the lieutenant's words in Aaron's eyes a stony silence came over her. Through all Shetland's threats and accusations Aaron maintained his poise like a carved statue. "In a wilderness you need a guide if you are not to become lost," Aaron began in his grotesquely youthful voice, which feebly struggled to rise above a whisper. "We wandered in a bewildering landscape, the ultimate truth always visible on the distant horizon—tantalizing, beckoning. And yet we were always turned around. Lost and floundering, we could not find our way.

Life does not approach death willingly; it must be driven and led. Arrogance, obsession, hunger, need, all of those emotions were at play on that night. You see, Lieutenant, we needed a guide, a soul, a spirit free from life to follow. The girl's unwitting sacrifice allowed us to cross over the wilderness and stand astride the eternal horizon, and the truth was made known to us—a mocking truth." Suddenly Aaron went limp, his head falling to his chest, his arms into his lap.

"You must stop this," Renée insisted, her face ashen; "he's too weak to take this; he might die."

Shetland lunged forward. "Not before I kill him." He felt Aaron's pulse; it was strong but erratic. Renée shouted to leave him alone. Shetland shoved her away. "Does he have medicine?"

She got hold of herself and said, "Tablets. In his jacket pocket."

Shetland fumbled for them. "Inside pocket," Renée said. He found the small silver pill box. "They're nitroglycerine. Put one under his tongue." The pill worked quickly. In a moment Aaron revived though he was much weakened. When he had collapsed Shetland had felt a strange sensation in his head: tingling, like blood rushing to a hand falling asleep; it was like awareness entering through an open door. When Aaron awakened the door shut and the feeling was locked out. He didn't care if Aaron lived or died but he realized it was the power of Aaron's intellect that kept the beast at bay. There was no time; he had to have the answers. "Peel," he said. "Why did he kill himself?"

Aaron gasped breathlessly, "He was the first to realize the truth and he was the only one of us with courage."

"What truth?" Shetland pressed.

Renée stepped between them. "That's enough. The truth, the truth," she repeated, "is that what you think you want? The truth that you think will set you free?" She smiled knowingly. "You've seen your other self, haven't you? Shocking, isn't it, to look upon the twin of your soul. There is nothing beyond this life but what is born in this life, created, if you will, by our own warped imagination, that is heaven and that is hell; a fantasy, real, projected and as berserk and irrational as the disjointed nightmares we dream. Do you understand; we've played a monumental hoax upon ourselves and the truth is, the hoax has come home to roost. We've opened a floodgate and there is no way to close it. You know what they say if you hit bottom before waking up from a dream?"

"The monstrosities I saw were real, they were tangible, they could tear and rend flesh. Fantasies don't murder."

"You fool, you're burying yourself deeper and you don't even know it," Renée said, glaring at him. "Isn't a thought as real as the action it produces? You want some more 'scientific' explanation; lightning is energy and when it strikes the results are devastatingly real. Thought is energy, its power enveloped in an aura."

Shetland's face flushed with rage. "You're telling me somebody thought up those creatures that butchered Mrs. Peel."

"What is the face of fear and hate?"

It was all terrifyingly mind-boggling. Shetland stood with a vacant look like the class dunce staring at an equation that contained within its mysterious factors the answer to itself.

Renée attended to her brother. "Help me get him to his room," she said to Markos, who had taken root near the liquor cart and was getting juiced as quickly as he could. His head bobbing slightly, he stared vacantly at Renée. "I don't want to know these things," he mumbled, slurring his words. "I shouldn't have listened." He lurched a few steps toward them. "You put it into my head but it comes like an invader. Can't you feel it?" he stuttered incoherently to Jessica.

"Yes," she said, gazing peacefully out into the darkness as if she were privileged to insight that had escaped the others.

Renée pleaded with Jessica to help her. "Of course," Jessica responded.

"Help him," Markos huffed; "only an evil megalomaniac would tamper with such things. I don't believe it." He shook his head, bringing his drink to his mouth. "No, no, no, I deny it. You hear, all of you; I don't accept it." He was sweating.

"Markos," Renée urged, "you must stop being afraid."

Markos was shaking. "Craziness," he muttered, sipping his drink, "lurid craziness." Suddenly the glass exploded in his hand as if it had been shattered by a bullet from a high-powered rifle. He glared, bewildered, at his empty hand, his lips bloody from the broken glass, mouth agape and moving as if to speak or scream.

For a moment they all stared immobilized at Markos's predicament. Then the torches began to sputter and crackle. Puffs of white smoke rose as the flames were extinguished. The champagne bottle on the table made a clinking sound, wobbled, then toppled over, shattering like the glass. In the spilled foam Shetland picked up a locust, its body broken like an old, soggy cigarette butt. "What the hell's going on?"

"Look at the stars." Jessica's voice was shrill with excitement. The night sky was ablaze with a snowy mist of burning white embers, which then began to fade as if they were hurtling away into space. Shetland heard the Mediterranean cry out, "Dear God," then from afar came a thrashing sound like leaves and rain being driven by the wind. The noise grew louder, changing in pitch and intensity until it became like fingernails raked across a blackboard and grated on the nerves. The night moved like some living shadow, and then the sound changed into a whirr of wings that swept over the terrace like some biblical visitation. Those on the terrace were inundated by a living storm of pelting insects that blinded, confused and pushed Shetland to the point of hysterical revulsion. His immediate impulse was to run, to get away; it was a maddeningly irresistible urge, but he fought it. He wiped the broken insects from his eyes then put his hands over his face, fingers splayed so he could see; that helped to quell the panic. But the revulsion caused him almost to lose control again. Shetland turned to help the others. Renée and Jessica managed to get Aaron inside, but Markos had gone completely out of his mind. He was screaming and staggering around, flailing his arms wildly. His eyes were encrusted with green slime and broken bits of wings and chitinous shells.

Like some kind of wild beast he charged this way and that, stumbling, then getting up again, finally running toward the terrace steps. Shetland tried to head him off and help him back to the house but Markos turned on him, clawing and throwing punches until finally he wrested himself free of Shetland's grasp and plunged into the whirring blizzard. Shetland called after him but in a moment Markos was swallowed up in the deluge. Throwing his jacket over his head, Shetland started back to the house. When he reached the double French doors, he discovered they had been locked from the inside.

"Let me in," he shouted. The door opened just as he was preparing to break through. "I couldn't get to him," he panted, stepping inside. But before the words were out of his mouth a searing pain rocketed through his shoulder, clenching his jaw shut. Instinctively he jumped back outside through the doorway, stumbling over his own feet. The fact that he had just been stabbed didn't immediately register. He saw the figure, a vague blur, rushing at him out of the darkness, the glint of the metal blade coming down. His blind attempt to block the knife missed and he felt the cold steel being planted in his chest. Just as it was being pushed to mortal depth Shetland fell backward over the porch table, momentarily putting him out of reach of his would-be murderer. He landed with a solid crack on the back of his head which knocked him senseless. He didn't know how long he lay there dazed and helpless, but it seemed an eternity. His assassin had apparently thought the job done and left him for dead. Looking around him, he could see no trace of the storm of insects that had engulfed him a few moments before. Soon Jessica would come looking for him, he thought. And when she didn't he became frightened that Renée had done something to her too. He had to get himself up or the loss of blood would put him under as the bump on his head had failed to do. He struggled first to his hands and knees and then to his feet, bracing himself on the overturned table until the world stopped spinning. Renée had tried to kill him because she had revealed something she hadn't meant to; either that or she was completely mad. But what exactly had she revealed? He tried to clear his thoughts, then remembered the look on her face at what Aaron had said just before he fainted. Of course. He cursed himself under his breath. He should have recognized the look of the betrayed then.

His shoulder was on fire with pain; that was good, he thought, it would keep him on his feet. His shirt was torn and covered with blood. The stab wounds couldn't be deep because he had already stopped bleeding. It was his head he was worried about; it had taken an awful pounding. He had been knocked unconscious three times in four days. Spots of light were swirling before his eyes, accompanied by a feeling of light-headedness; he knew he had some kind of concussion and he was afraid he might pass out—a definite minus in the survival column. He didn't know how long he would last in an upright position. He took his revolver from his belt. Thirty-three ounces felt like ten pounds in his right hand but he was no good with the left so he let it dangle by his side and prayed he could bring the gun into action in time if Renée decided to play mumbly peg on him again. The French doors were shut tight. He picked up a chair with his left hand and, spinning it like a hammer thrower, released it. The chair burst through the door, showering broken glass and splintered wood everywhere. Shetland spun for another half-dozen steps and nearly blacked out.

He entered the house, which was a black as the bottom of a well. The atmosphere was charged with static electricity. His flesh crawled and his hair stood up on his arms and bristled at the back of his neck. The house was alive with the presence that had touched him in Peel's study and stolen into his apartment; it was that same vague apprehension of birth and death and rebirth that flooded his brain. He could sense movement, a suggestion of things, like dark clouds traveling across a dark sky. He reached the broad stairway. On the landing above there was the vaguest hint of light coming from one of the rooms; it spilled partway down the stairs. He started up, pausing at the top and looking carefully along the hall; there were no other lighted rooms. He stepped softly to the door at the end of the hall and listened. He could hear no voices but there was a strange humming sound, which slowly grew louder and then faded. It sounded like an electric motor. He tried the door and it opened slightly; all the lights were on but the room appeared empty. He followed the muzzle of his revolver inside and stood with his back against the wall. A quick look around told him where the humming was coming from: the elevator that allowed Aaron to travel between stories in his wheelchair. Shetland guessed that the ground-floor entrance lay somewhere below the staircase. The elevator was running; somebody was coming up. He crossed the room and stood waiting in front of the elevator door. In a moment the lift car appeared from below, carrying Aaron Sebastian seated in his wheelchair, unaccompanied. Shetland stepped forward, then froze in his tracks as the lift car slowly rose to the door and stopped. Aaron was facing out into the room. His eyes, the eyes of a mystic seer, were transfixed on that distant horizon he had longed to stand upon and had now crossed over: he was dead. The lift started down again. Shetland found the control panel on the wall; the buttons had been jammed. He managed to free them, stop the lift and bring it back up again. Stepping inside, he wheeled Aaron's body into the bedroom. He supposed the strain on his heart had been too much until his hand brushed the back of Aaron's head and came up with a tiny drop of blood. Closer examination revealed a minuscule puncture wound at the base of the skull near the hairline; to Shetland's eyes it was nothing more than a red spot.

Jessica entered the room unnoticed. "Dear God, I thought she murdered you too," her voice trembled with emotion. Shetland was startled by Jessica's appearance. She was pale with shock and wild-eyed, her clothes were torn and disheveled and her lower lip quivered as if she were ready to burst into tears. "She's gone crazy," she sobbed.

Taking her in his arms, Shetland helped her to the bed. She sat down but wouldn't let go of his arm. He was relieved that she was safe and stroked her hair to calm her. "Where is she?" he asked gently.

"I don't know. When we got inside I wanted to go back for you, but she wouldn't hear of it until we got Aaron to his room. I didn't know what to do. Aaron was gasping for air and clutching at his chest as if he were in excruciating pain. Then the lights went out and it was so confusing; we got into the lift and went upstairs. When we got to the second floor Renée suddenly went crazy. I mean really berserk, like she was possessed. I was terrified. She attacked me but I managed to push her away. She fell back into the elevator and I jumped out and hit the button to send the lift down." Jessica sighed, putting her head in her hands. "After that I tried to get back to you. I reached the stairs," her voice caught in her throat and she swallowed, "but—but I couldn't get down; there was something there—it was too hideous to describe. It was there and it wasn't there. This feeling came over me, an empty cold feeling. I ran and hid."

Shetland knelt down before her and put his hand on her shoulder. "Take it easy," he said.

She looked up, her face livid with fear. "I can't believe what I'm about to say," she said. "I love her but you must kill her. She's mad. Aaron had managed to retain some control over this, but it was slowly killing him. For some reason she fought him, trying to call up powers of the mind like a witch summons the powers of darkness. She imagined in some lunatic fashion that she could bend these terrible forces to her will."

"In God's name why would she want to do that?"

"I don't know," Jessica said, shaking her head. "Her madness made her hate her brother, eventually to hate me too; it didn't have any direction. You see, she is the link between the two universes; she's the only one left who has crossed over the barrier and still lives."

"Of course," Shetland groaned, "that's why Peel killed himself. He realized they had formed a bridge. To his horror, it turned out to carry two-way traffic. He killed himself to destroy the bridge. You're damned if you do and damned if you don't."

"I know it's a dreadful decision to make but you must do it," Jessica said. "It's taken root in her mind like a cancer; she's helpless to do anything about it." Jessica straightened, her eyes wild with alarm. "She's standing at the foot of the stairs," she whispered.

Shetland walked out of the room, his head thudding excitedly. Renée was there as Jessica had said she would be. Renée stared up at him with a disconcerting smile.

"I have to," he said, timidly raising his revolver. She made no attempt to run; instead she started up the stairs toward him. "I have to," he cried in a voice choked with emotion. His hands sweated, tears mixed with the sweat on his face, and he knew he couldn't kill her, not like this. She sensed it too.

Jessica came out of the room and stood behind him. "What are you waiting for?" she shouted, then began to plead, "I know it goes against what you believe in but can't you see, it must be done."

"Dark witch," Renée hissed. "What has she been telling you, Lieutenant; what lies has my murderous daughter been telling you?" Her words were like fire thrown in his face. He froze there on the steps. She kept coming. "Isn't that proof enough that she's mad," Jessica screamed, both love and hate in her voice.

"Child of my incestuous love, black of heart and dark of mind as the abominable sin that bore her into this world; mine and my brother's sin; but has there ever been such a gifted child to see death before she came forth from the womb into life, to know the end before the beginning, a child blessed and cursed, a child so loved that in my atonement I gave her all, my love and the sex of my flesh. I tried to protect her from the wickedness that was within her but the blood of two Sebastians runs in her veins and that is an evil brew that no one could overcome."

"Can't you see," Jessica shrieked, "only a monster could think such things. Listen to me: it's a lie, a trick; look into the darkness behind her. Can't you see, she's summoning them and they will destroy you because you won't destroy her, their link."

It was there as Jessica said, that dark twin spilling out of the blackness, spilling out of his brain, a grotesque mirror image in which fragments of nightmares and thought were buried in the beastly private core of the mind, a kaleidoscopic enigma of good and evil. It was made up of angels and maggots. He tried to block it out, deny it, but his mind recoiled. "It's not true," he shrieked; "you made me see." His first shot tore into the wall next to Renée's head; the second struck her in the face and blotted it out in a veil of blood. She stood rigid for a moment and Shetland tried to fire again, but his hands trembled so that he couldn't aim the gun, and then she fell back. He stared at the faceless corpse lying head down on the stairs.

Jessica's voice came from above. "It's gone, you see, it's gone. For a moment I thought she tricked you into believing her."

Shetland tried to speak but his mouth was too dry. When he finally had enough saliva, his words came in abbreviated panting gasps. "I'm afraid," he said.

"But there's nothing more to be afraid of," Jessica said reassuringly, "it's done and finished. My mother is dead and now so are you." Jessica drove the long, thin, steel needle deep between his shoulder blades into his lungs and heart—he was dying as he fell. He rolled down the stairs, thereby thrusting the needle clear through his chest cavity until its point emerged on the other side. His twisted body lay with Renée's at the bottom of the steps in a macabre embrace, his mouth open in surprise, his eyes staring up at Jessica, the last twinkle of life slowly dimming beneath the gray film of death. "I liked you," she said, "but you were already beginning to realize that one of us must die. I killed you out of simple self-preservation. You do understand. But we can still be together."

Shetland's head flinched like an insect's legs in a death spasm; the blood filling his lungs made a rasping, gurgling sound bubbling up into his throat as he tried to speak. "If there's a God in heaven give me the strength," he cried. Shetland emptied his revolver, the last shot squeezed off by the constricting grip of death.

CHAPTER TWELVE

The morning was hot and still; the patchy mist covering the lawns crept up through the open front door and into the foyer of the stone mansion. The ghostly vapor curled around the stretcher-bearers' legs as they carried the last tarpaulin-draped body out of the house and placed it with the others in the ambulance. Following right behind, a police officer pushed an empty wheelchair. He rolled it out to a squad car, folded it and slipped it into the back seat. "They're just removing the lieutenant's body now," Scalley said into the radio mike; his voice, emotionless throughout the morning, now quivered. He released the mike button and the radio crackled.

"Have you been able to figure out what the hell happened, Scalley?"

It was a while before he answered. He depressed the button; his words caught in his throat: "No, Captain, we haven't. We got one possible witness, the guy we found standing by the gate, but I wouldn't count on it. The medical examiner took a look at him. He said there's nobody home and he doubts if there ever will be again. I believe it, Captain.

You almost feel like you could look into his eyes right to the back to his head; it's spooky. It's a bloody mess inside the house. They're all dead."

"Any reporters?"

"Not yet; they must be sleeping on this one."

There was a pause. "I'm coming out as soon as I can get free here. No statements, absolutely no statements," the captain said excitedly and signed off.

Scalley put the mike back in its cradle, pulled his legs inside the car and slammed the door. "We wait for the captain," he said to Casey, seated to his right and immersed in the red book they had found in Lieutenant Shetland's pocket. "It's all so crazy. What was the lieutenant doing here?" Scalley mused aloud. "You can never piece together all the facts with a massacre like that." He shook his head. "I liked him . . . though he wasn't particularly likable."

Casey suddenly looked up from the book as if he hadn't been listening to a word Scalley had said. "The lieutenant must have been sitting on this for weeks. It's evidence; why didn't he turn it in?"

"Just make sure you do," Scalley said, annoyed.

"I will, I will," Casey nodded. "But listen to this . . ."

**IN HOLLYWOOD, WHERE DREAMS DIE QUICKLY,
ONE LOVE LASTS FOREVER...**

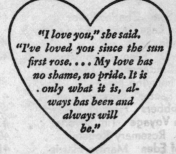

*"I love you," she said.
"I've loved you since the sun
first rose. . . . My love has
no shame, no pride. It is
only what it is, al-
ways has been and
always will
be."*

The words are spoken by Brooke Ashley, a beautiful
forties film star, in the last movie she ever made. She
died in a tragic fire in 1947.

A young screenwriter in a theater in Los Angeles
today hears those words, sees her face, and is moved to
tears. Later he discovers that he wrote those words,
long ago; that he has been born again—as she has.

What will she look like? Who could she be? He
begins to look for her in every woman he sees...

A Romantic Thriller
by
TREVOR MELDAL-JOHNSEN

AVON

41897
$2.50

THE BIG BESTSELLERS
ARE AVON BOOKS

"A MIXTURE OF HORROR AND OCCULTISM
TOLD WITH DRIVING FORCE ... A STORY
THAT TAKES YOU WITH IT ALL THE WAY."
The New York Times

WILLIAM H. HALLAHAN

KEEPER OF THE CHILDREN

AVON   45203 $2.50

Novels have been written about children possessed. Novels
have been written about unnatural evil—in most of its dis-
guises. But nothing can prepare you for the unspeakable frenzy
of this ...

Dolls move. Scarecrows animate and kill. Toys wield axes
against parents. Cats band together and attack humans in a
fury of fur, claws, and teeth. And in a terrifying dimension beyond anything ever before explored in fiction, a lone father
battles a demonic force—a new kind of evil—for his daughter's
life ... and his own.

"EERIE, SCARY ... UTTERLY FASCINATING ...
THIS IS NOT GOING TO BE WHAT YOU THINK."
Publishers Weekly

Also by William H. Hallahan:
The Edgar Award Winning Novel,
CATCH ME: KILL ME (Avon/37986/$1.95),
THE SEARCH FOR JOSEPH TULLY (Avon/33712/$1.95),
THE DEAD OF WINTER (Avon/24216/$1.75).

KPR 11-79